ROSE BY ANY OTHER NAME

The Sisters, Texas Mystery Series
Book Ten

BECKI WILLIS

CONTENTS

1

"Chief! I just saw a dead body!"

It was the fourth such call in the last five minutes.

So far, when pressed for details, not a single caller could provide specifics. With little hope this call would prove different, Chief of Police Brash deCordova struggled to hold in a sigh.

It came with the territory when living in a small town. For some people—without a mall in which to shop or a theater in which to watch—neighbors' windows and neighbors' lives filled the gaping void. Anything out of the ordinary became suspicious. Anything new became suspect. Most telling of all, to those who craved excitement and who had little else to entertain them, the mundane became interesting.

As an officer of the law, Brash gave due diligence to every report that crossed his desk. Even when it proved a waste of time and precious resources, he was duty bound to investigate, particularly a claim as serious as this.

He gave today's source of excitement the same diligence. "Slow down, Henry," he told the man on the other end of the line. "Take a deep breath and start from the beginning."

Brash heard a noisy slurp of air rattle through

Henry Bealls' lungs as he heeded the advice. "Now, let's see. About four or five weeks ago, I noticed some stirrings over at Nelda's old house. It's been vacant for—"

"Not that beginning, Henry," Brash broke in. "Tell me what happened today."

"Well, now, today, two moving vans pulled in at ten o'clock sharp. I know because I was just coming home after dropping Sadie off at work. It's her day at the library, you see. She usually drives herself, but her car's been acting up lately. It—"

Brash cleared his throat. "You mentioned a dead body?"

"Oh, right. After a good dozen or so trips inside from both trucks, the movers brought something back out. It was one of those big, long rugs, you see. It was so heavy, it took two of them to move it. That's how I knew a body was inside," Henry reasoned.

After taking the first call, Brash made it as far as the hat rack beside the door before the next report came in. Still having made it no further, Brash was tempted to return his cowboy hat to the rack and sit back down. This latest eyewitness was clearly no more dependable than the others.

"You're sure it was a dead body inside the rug?" He kept his tone conversational, tampering the skepticism he felt.

"Just as sure as you're sitting at your desk!"

"Here's the thing, Henry. I'm not at my desk. I'm trying to get out the door to head that way. That's why I need to know what you actually saw. Why do you think there was a body inside?"

"Both of those men were huffin' and puffin'," Henry explained, "like they carried something mighty heavy. That rug didn't bend in the least, so I know it had something wrapped up inside."

The lawman bit back a groan. "And you naturally assumed it was a body."

His sarcasm was lost upon the older gentleman. "I've seen it happen more than once. On television, you see. Just last week, Sadie was watchin' a rerun of Matlock, and this very thing happened. John Paul Nobles was the guest star, and his character was killed and wrapped up in a rug, just like that man today."

"And what man was that? Who was he?"

"I reckon the one from the car."

Brash snapped to attention. Three other reports, and this was the first he had heard of a car. It was the closest thing he had to a solid lead.

"Can you see the license number of the car from your house?" He dug into his shirt pocket for the notepad and pen he habitually carried for just this reason. "What's the make and model?"

"Afraid I can't tell you that," Henry Bealls said. "It drove off about five minutes ago, you see."

Allowing the notepad to fall back into his pocket, Brash's hopes fell along with it. "Henry," he said carefully, trying to keep the censure from his voice, "if the man from the car was the man in the rug, how did it drive away?"

"I reckon it must have been one of the delivery men."

From previous reports, he knew the moving vans were already gone. "Do you happen to know how many men arrived? Were they one short when they left?"

"Didn't count how many came originally, but four left," the older man supplied.

His answer came as no surprise. Two men per van was customary. Brash tried a different angle. "Did the car leave at the same time as the vans?"

"Don't know. One of the vans blocked my view. By

the time they both moved along, so had the car."

Frustration mounted within the lawman. "And you have no idea what kind of car it was?"

"It was a dark color. One of those newer sedans, you see, the kind with only two doors."

Reports of the vans had been just as vague. No one could remember the name of the moving company emblazoned on the side. No one agreed on the color or the size of the vehicles. Without specifics, Brash couldn't call in a BOLO, not without sounding like an idiot.

For a moment, he imagined how the call might sound.

Be advised. Be on the lookout for two vans of undetermined color, leaving the Juliet/Naomi area and going in an unspecified direction. The vehicles are described as either ordinary panel vans or medium-sized haulers. According to witnesses, they could be either blue or white. Or possibly orange. They may or may not have identifying graphics on the side. There may or may not be a late-model, two-door sedan traveling with them, unknown dark color.

Brash shook his head to clear the ridiculous chatter from his brain. "Thanks for calling, Henry. I'm on my way."

Vina Jones caught his eye as he barreled from his office. His expression told her everything she needed to know.

The older woman of undetermined age went by many titles. Dispatcher. Desk clerk. Moral compass. Brash simply referred to her as the glue that held the department together. He dreaded the day she finally made good on her threats to retire.

She offered a woeful expression as he barged across the room. "Sorry, Chief. I thought this one could be solid."

"If you learn anything useful, take the information and push it through."

"I should have known it was bogus when Arlene Kopetsky claimed she witnessed a murder," Vina muttered with a smirk. "All she saw was a man in a suit go in, and a couple of hours later, a rolled-up rug come out. To her, that equated murder."

"Did she happen to mention a car?"

"No. Only the moving vans."

With a nod of parting, Brash hurried out the door before another call detained him.

Four minutes later, Brash pulled up in front of Nelda Goldberg's formerly vacant house. The small foursquare on Sycamore had sat empty for well over three years, ever since the owner moved into an assisted living center in Conroe.

Having not driven past the house in a while, the police chief was surprised at the changes greeting him. The dormant grasses had been tamed and groomed. Overgrown hedges were trimmed. Potted rose bushes bloomed along the porch. Even the faded clapboard siding wore a fresh coat of pink paint.

Someone new had moved in.

Brash took a moment to survey the scene before him. To the outward eye, it looked calm and relaxing. Pristine came to mind. Yet according to eyewitness reports, a heinous crime took place here less than fifteen minutes ago. Now, it was up to him to reconcile the two vastly different tales and make sense of the deficit.

He paid careful attention to the ground as he made his way up the walkway to the front door. There were obvious signs of heavy traffic, consistent with movers scurrying back and forth with furniture and boxes. His trained eye looked for traces of blood. As he took the steps up and across the porch, he saw the telltale trace left by two or more pairs of rubber-soled work boots, the slightly muddy heel print of a single cowboy boot, and a scattered pattern left by the pointy heels of a woman's pump.

Eyes cast downward to study the tracks crisscrossing the porch, Brash was aware of the front door opening before he knocked. As his gaze fell upon the aforementioned pair of pumps, his analytical mind processed the scene as he observed it.

Leather pumps in butter yellow. Two-inch heel. Trim ankles, shapely calves. Nice tan, most likely fake. Slight smudges around kneecaps and ankles, suggesting a hasty application. Hemline shorter than Maddy wears, but still modest. Flared skirt over flared hips. Dress is predominantly pink roses on a muted background; just enough yellow to justify the shoes and matching belt cinched around a slim waist. Toned arms, generous bust. Squared neckline just a skosh above too low. Heart-shaped locket on a slightly tarnished chain. Rose-tinted lips puckered just like a rosebud. Slightly flared nostrils, straight nose, wide-spaced gray eyes. Hair too black and shiny to be natural.

Dressed as she was, Brash suspected the woman was the real estate agent.

"Hello, Officer." The woman's voice was soft and delicate, bringing to mind the petals of a rose.

Come to think of it, she even smells like a rose. Brash's nose twitched ever so slightly; the scent of roses always made him want to sneeze.

"Hello, ma'am. I'm Chief of Police Brash deCordova." He tipped the brim of his hat as he introduced himself. "Mind if I come in?"

The smirk melted into a brilliant smile. The woman stood back from the door and opened it wide, welcoming him inside.

Brash swept the room with his dark gaze, taking in the scene. His brown eyes darted around the room, pinging from one area to the next.

Fourteen-by-sixteen room, typical of the era. Large picture window on front wall, offering maximum visiting for nosy neighbors. No curtains yet. Traditional placement of furniture, all stylishly neutral; could be straight from any discount warehouse showroom floor. No signs of struggle or disturbance. Surprisingly neat and orderly for move-in day.

No rug.

"To what do I owe the honor, Officer?"

That petal-soft voice spoke from close behind him. Brash turned with caution, not surprised to find the woman standing a tad closer than considered appropriate.

Instead of answering, the chief of police presented her with his signature expression: half frown, half-arched eyebrow, nostrils slightly flared. He had perfected the look years ago, during his days as a college football coach. One crooked brow could silence the most vehement outburst. The imperial gesture had served him even better as an officer of the law.

In spite of herself, the woman took a step backward.

"I didn't catch your name," he said. The words were polite enough, but his tone asserted the fact he was in charge of the conversation.

To her credit, the woman didn't cower. She thrust her hand forward, the corners of her rosebud-shaped mouth lifting into a smile. "Rose Belvedere."

"You're the real estate agent?" he guessed.

"Oh, goodness, no!" With her one hand still curled around his, she placed the other against the too-low neckline. "I'll be living here. I'm the newest member of your charming little town."

His brown gaze never wavered from her face. His peripheral vision confirmed what he suspected. No ring.

Forget being a skosh too low, he grumbled to himself. I know this old trick. Not gonna look.

Instead, Brash offered a polite smile that didn't quite reach his eyes. "In that case," he said stiffly, "welcome to The Sisters."

"The Sisters? But isn't this darling little town called Juliet?"

"Yes," he confirmed. "But collectively, we refer to the community as The Sisters. Naomi is just across the railroad tracks." He suspected she knew as much.

"Well, they're both just darling."

Ignoring his none-too-subtle social clues, Rose Belvedere reclaimed her spot in his personal space. "And I'll feel so much safer now," she purred, "knowing you'll be here to watch over me. Living all alone in a big ole' house can be frightening at times."

Brash refused to back away, allowing his scowl to put the proper distance between them. "My officers and I do our best to protect all citizens, ma'am," he assured her. He tugged his hand free of hers and hooked his thumb into his duty belt.

The audacious woman trailed her eyes over the breadth of his chest, openly appreciating the way the movement pulled the khaki cloth taut. Brash thought of those damnable pictures of him on the internet, shown shirtless and taken completely out of context.

Inwardly, he grimaced. Outwardly, he was unaffected by her ogling. "I came by," he told her, "to make certain everything was all right. Any troubles here today?"

"Now, why ever would you ask that?" Rose Belvedere asked, cocking her head at an extreme angle. Her hand fell to her waist, where she propped it upon a shapely hip.

Again, a pose he was familiar with.

Again, his eyes remained on her face. He hadn't missed her brief look of surprise at the question.

"The neighbors mentioned a bit of unusual traffic today."

"Well, of course," she said. She waved her ringless hand around the living room. "This was move-in day. There were two moving vans on my lawn. Of course there was unusual traffic."

Brash followed her hand movement with his body, using it as an excuse to shift away from her. He stole a glance into the adjoining rooms but saw nothing unusual in the brief perusal.

"You'll find that we have a very engaged community," he told her, choosing to spin it in a positive manner. Engaged sounded so much nicer than nosy. "There's an active neighborhood watch program, so not much escapes notice."

The rosebud lips appeared again, pinched into a tiny bud of disapproval. "Good to know." She looked anything but pleased.

"Part of the charm of small-town living," Brash assured her. He reasserted his reason for stopping by. "So. Everything went smoothly with move-in? No unexpected problems?"

Her shrug was noncommittal. "The normal ups and downs. A dropped box here, a scuffed wall there." A cunning light moved into her eyes, making Brash inexplicably nervous. The tight bud of her lips flowered into a sudden and unexpected smile.

"As a matter of fact," she said, "I did have one

problem I could use your help with. If it's not asking too much."

Sensing a trap, his answer was evasive. "I'll help if I can."

She didn't bother to step to one side and go around him. Instead, Rose pushed entirely too close as she leaned across him, flooding his senses with her rose-scented aura. "I need to hang this picture," she purred, "but I can't quite reach that high. You're so strong and tall, I'm sure it won't be any trouble at all."

She used her best provocative pose to reach behind him, but it was lost upon the police officer. He was busy fighting off a sneeze.

She produced a framed print and motioned vaguely to a spot behind the couch. "If you would be so kind..."

Brash practically snatched the print from her hands, wielding it between them like an armor. "Do you have something to hang it with?" he asked, giving the back brackets more attention than they deserved.

"I have some of those sticky strips in the kitchen," she said.

"If you'll point me in the right direction..." he offered, hoping to get a better look in another room.

"No bother. I'll get it."

If she put extra swing into her hips as she left the room, Brash missed it. He was already peeking beneath the couch, looking for signs of blood or possible scuff marks. He saw neither. He snapped back to attention as her heels tapped out her approach.

"Here we go," she said brightly, holding the plastic strips up for view.

Brash easily reached across the sofa and held the picture in place. He was hardly surprised to see it was a rendition of a single rose. "About here?" he asked.

"Oh, I'll show you," she insisted.

Rose hurried to the sofa and proceeded to climb atop the cushions on her knees. She inserted herself between Brash and the picture, managing to crawl her way between his outstretched arms.

"More like… here," she insisted, moving the frame a mere smidgen of an inch. When she turned around with a bright smile, her glossy black hair tickled his cheek.

"Great," he grunted. "I'll have this up in a jiffy."

Her gray eyes widened in feigned surprise. "Oh, am I in the way? I'm so sorry!" she gushed.

Framing her chin with the tips of her fingers was overkill, especially with her lips puckered so precisely. Brash was hardly taken unawares when her knees wobbled on the soft cushions, and she pitched forward into the solid wall of his body.

He was tempted to step aside and allow her to fall on her face. It was no less than she deserved, but he was too much of a gentleman to live out the fantasy. Instead, he grunted loudly as she fell against him, subtly hinting to the discomfort of added weight.

"Oh! Clumsy me!" she cried in fake abashment. Her arms wrapped around him like clinging vines, belying her words. "I don't know what I would have done if you hadn't been here to catch me."

Brash lost no time detangling himself from her arms. With no curtains to hinder the view, he knew the neighbors were getting an eyeful of juicy fodder.

"Obviously," he told her flatly as he pried her fingers away from his waist, "you would have fallen."

"But you didn't let that happen, now did you?" she asked with a brilliant smile, still leaning into him. She stretched her shining face upward. "My hero!"

Again, he fantasized about jerking the cushion out from beneath her. It would force her to fall against the back of the couch, but he didn't trust her not to drag him down with her.

Brash chose to use his knee to nudge her away, grateful, for once, when it popped with the movement. He hoped she took it as another subtle hint. Not only was he too old for her—he guessed her to be in her late twenties, some fifteen years his junior—but he was literally pushing her away with his knee.

Rose Belvedere was not the sort of woman who understood subtle. Her smile was smug, as if she knew a secret. She took her time arching away from him but was disappointed when he refused to hold her gaze.

She huffed when he immediately went back to hanging the picture.

"All done," he announced.

"It looks lovely," she proclaimed, smiling once again as she stood behind him and studied the result. "However can I thank you?"

It was the opening he had hoped for. "You could give me a tour."

The impromptu suggestion took her by surprise. When her expression changed to one of delight, Brash regretted his hasty outburst, but the damage had been done.

"Certainly, Officer," she purred. "Right this way." She tucked her hand into the crook of his arm and pulled him along to the hallway. "This first room is the spare bedroom, but I'll be using it as a home office."

"Oh? What is it that you do?"

"I work in collections. With the internet, I can do most of my work from home." She waved the door opened and closed, allowing him little more than a glimpse of the room beyond. Two computer screens were already set up on the oversized desk. Between printers, bookcases, and an assortment of boxes, there was little room for a body to be rolled within a rug.

Nor was the narrow hallway wide enough. Brash felt the confines of the space as Rose pressed against him, insisting on staying by his side.

"Bathroom," she said, waving inward toward the small room with all the necessary ingredients. He saw nary a drop of blood on the sparkling tiles. True to the style of the house, they were tiny octagons in varying shades of pink, requiring an extensive network of grout to piece them together. If blood had spilled here recently, there would still be traces of it within the grout lines.

"Cute house," he commented. "If I had known it was available, I would have told my in-laws about it. They may be moving here soon," he lied. When she didn't stiffen at his mention of being married, Brash suspected she already knew.

In truth, after last year's remodeling show on HOME TV made their hometown famous, Brash had no illusions of anonymity; his new bride had been the reluctant star of the reality show. Sadly enough, much of their early romance had played out on television screens nationwide. Coupled with his own small claim to fame as a former pro football player and successful college coach—not to mention the fiasco this spring when a guest dropped dead at their wedding reception, and the nonsense that followed—Brash suspected only someone living under a rock could escape all the hoopla that had surrounded them lately.

Rose Belvedere didn't strike him as someone who lived under a rock. He suspected that a very keen, intelligent woman hid behind the exaggerated come-ons and the pouty lips. He had to wonder what her agenda was, flirting so outrageously with a man who showed zero interest in her.

Ignoring the reference to his in-laws, Rose went on

with the tour. "This is the master," she announced, stopping at the next doorway. She wore a cunning smile, almost daring him to step inside.

Brash took the dare. He needed to see if this room held clues the others didn't.

"Nice size," he remarked, stepping inside and visually measuring the floor space. If the supposed victim was short, his body might have fit, but it was doubtful. It took adequate room to roll a body into a rug.

Besides, this room still had a rug, solidly anchored beneath the queen-sized bed.

"It will look better, once I hang the artwork."

He hadn't realized the woman was so close behind him until she spoke. He refused to turn around and put himself in her play zone.

"To be honest, ma'am," he said, pretending fascination with the entire house, "you have everything in surprising order. It usually takes me weeks to move in and get things in shape." He turned in the opposite direction, deftly side-stepping around her and toward the hall.

"I like things neat and tidy," she replied. She had little choice but to follow him.

True to its design, the house was a perfect square. They moved into the dining room and the kitchen beyond.

Brash's eyes darted around the kitchen, noting the neat order of things. No missing knives in the knife block. No blood smears or heel marks on the white tiles of the floor. No boxes sitting around, awaiting unpacking. Nothing was amiss.

For this to be move-in day, and for the vans to have only been gone less than a half hour, everything was perfect.

Too perfect, in his opinion. A towel already hung

from the handle of the oven by one of those crochet-topped fasteners his mother liked to make, for crying out loud. Nobody was that organized an hour after moving in!

"When the in-laws do move," Brash continued in a conversational tone, "they'll need a reputable moving company. Who did you use? I'm impressed."

"I must confess," Rose purred. "I didn't hire a moving company. My friends and family pitched in and helped."

"They own moving vans?"

"My brother-in-law does. Actually, he just drives for a moving company, but he gets to keep the truck at home." Her face puckered into a pretty frown. "But please don't tell on him. I don't want him getting into trouble on my account."

"Of course not." Brash looked around again, still uneasy with the perfection he saw. He couldn't put his finger on it, but something about the scene was off. "I suppose that explains how you were able to put things to order so quickly," he murmured.

"Oh, yes. The b-i-l and the nephews were a huge help!" she beamed.

Brash crooked his eyebrow. "B-i-l?"

"Brother-in-law," she supplied.

"Ah." Brash rested a lean hip against the edge of the counter and pretended to relax. "Yeah, it's nice having an older sister and b-i-l, as you put it."

Relieved to see the man was finally thawing, her eyes sparkled. "I never said my sister was older," she said with a coy smile. She twirled a lock of shiny black hair around her finger. "In fact, I never said I had a sister."

"True. But you said you were living alone, so I assumed it wasn't your husband's brother. Am I wrong?"

"No," she confirmed. "No husband." She held up her bare ring finger as she made the gleeful announcement. Then she moved in closer, once again threatening his personal space.

"If your nephews are old enough to help move furniture," Brash deduced, "they must be in their teens, at the very least. You're obviously too young to have children that age, so it stands to reason your sister is older."

"Very impressive. And correct, by the way."

"Simple observation. Plus, neighbors reported two trucks, so one of the nephews must also be old enough to drive."

"That was a friend."

"He has his own panel van?"

The light in her eyes dimmed as she realized this was more interrogation than flirtation. Her mouth tightened, along with her voice. "Yes."

"And who was driving the car?"

She hesitated before answering. The smile lingering on her face was clearly forced. "My sister, obviously."

Brash nodded as if he believed her. "Obviously."

Her foot tapped out an impatient melody as Rose crossed her arms in a defiant gesture. "My. That neighborhood watch program is really something. You must be so proud."

"They are," Brash agreed with an earnest expression. "I am. But I gotta tell you. You really stumped them today."

"How is that?" She was curious enough to ask.

"All those boxes and furniture moving in. It's all anyone could talk about."

"Was I over the neighborhood limit?" she scoffed.

"It wasn't that. They expected to see things going in. What they didn't expect was to see something coming out."

Rose dropped her arms, along with any pretense at nicety. Her voice chilled by several degrees.

"As you pointed out, Chief deCordova, this is move-in day. I'm rather busy and don't have time for riddles."

Brash pushed away from the counter, his manner still amiable. "I understand, and I hate to be a bother. But you can't imagine how many calls we took down at the station. People are wondering why your movers brought a rug out today, when everything else was going in."

She laughed, but the sound was brittle. "Is that all? You mean to tell me you came all this way over here— even helped hang a picture on my wall! —simply to ask why movers took a rug from the house?"

"That's about the size of it," Brash admitted, noting she still hadn't answered his question.

Rose Belvedere sucked in a deep breath of air, presumably gathering her patience. Brash wondered if she weren't scrambling for a plausible excuse.

"Well," she finally said, making the word a complete sentence. "You may tell your callers to stop calling. The simple fact of the matter is that the movers made a mistake."

"You mean your b-i-l and your nephews?"

"Those, too," she snapped. She drew in another deep breath before offering an explanation. "Apparently, a rug was left in the van the last time it was used. It was inadvertently brought in with my things, but the moment I saw it, I realized there was a huge mistake. Believe me, I would never pair earth tones with this neutral pallet. It even had traces of autumn orange." Simply saying the word made her cringe. "It was truly horrendous, particularly when I'm accenting with the Miss All-American Beauty and its luminous, vibrant pink color."

She motioned around the room, indicating the subtle touches of what Brash called hot pink. Throw pillows. A lampshade. The print he just hung. The pop of color repeated itself in several places throughout the room.

To Brash, it all looked very professional and polished, just like a furniture showroom. It also looked fake and nothing like the home he shared with Maddy and their three teenagers.

"So, you see, Chief," Rose concluded, her smile regaining some of its former brilliance, "it was much ado about nothing. There's really nothing to see here."

2

When Rose informed him he could see his own way out, Brash took it as an invitation to snoop. Stopping on the bottom step, he squatted down to study the trampled footsteps in the grass.

He compared the tracks leading into the house against those coming out. The soft soil carried the imprint of multiple feet, but he could make out the distinctive cowboy heel with ease. The impressions offered one of two tales.

In the first scenario, two or more men wore cowboy boots (a likely possibility), but the heavier of the men remained on the sidewalk going into the house, leaving no indentations.

In the second scenario, only one man wore boots with a cowboy heel, and he carried a heavier load coming out than he did going in.

From the prints alone, it was impossible to know which scenario was truth. Brash snapped off a few photos with his phone before he stood and studied the remainder of the prints alongside the walkway.

"Yoo-hoo! Chief D! Over here!"

Brash looked up to see Wanda Shanks waving furiously from across the street. She had been the second caller to report 'suspicious activity' from the formerly vacant house.

The elderly woman waddled out to meet him halfway, fanning her flushed face with her hand. "I'm so glad you came. I'm not sure what's going on in that house, but *something* is!" she insisted, jabbing her finger in the general direction of the pink foursquare.

He kept his reply noncommittal. "Moving day tends to be busy."

"That place is more than busy. It's downright suspicious."

"Why don't we move into the shade, and you can tell me about it," he suggested.

"Come into the house, and I'll fix you a nice glass of iced tea."

As they moved toward the house, Brash asked, "When did the new occupant start moving in? The place certainly has been transformed."

"Four weeks ago. I know the exact date, because Bertha and I had just come back from the coast, and I noticed a light that first evening back."

Less than two years ago, Bertha Cessna—better known to most people simply as Granny Bert—gave up her title as mayor of Juliet, saying it interfered with her travels. She had since purchased a new RV, eager to roam the roads without a job tying her down. She often took friends Wanda and Sybille with her on her exploits.

In retrospect, Brash wondered what his grandmother-in-law knew about the day's events. Granny Bert had a way of knowing everyone and everything that happened in the community, and she somehow knew it first. It was uncanny, the things the octogenarian knew. Perhaps he should have called her before coming out.

"Over the next week or so," Granny Bert's friend continued, "it was one truck after another coming in.

Someone came to paint. Someone came to do the yard. Someone came to hook up the utilities. Then, last week, a black car pulled up, and that woman got out."

"You mean Rose Belvedere, the new occupant?"

Miss Wanda nodded her head, making jet-black curls swish around her pudgy jowls. The color looked even less natural on her than it did on her new neighbor.

"I went over to introduce myself last week when I saw she was there working. I knew right then; she was an odd one. And not very friendly, at that."

A cool blast of air greeted them as Miss Wanda opened the door off the carport and invited Brash inside. "Have a seat, and I'll fetch that tea." She motioned to the kitchen table as she moved past him. Grabbing two glasses from the draining board, she moved to the refrigerator, where she noisily filled them with ice cubes and the strong, sweet brew.

"Here you go," she said. Brash stood to pull the chair out for her, before settling into the adjacent seat.

"Tell me what you found so suspicious."

"First off, why would a young woman such as herself move *here*, of all places?" Wanda Shanks wanted to know. She tapped the table as she spoke. "She's not married. Not working anywhere local. Why move to The Sisters?"

"Why not?"

"Because there's little to no night life here," the octogenarian disparaged. "Bertha, Sybille, and I have to go elsewhere when we want to mingle a bit. We were thrilled when they opened *The Armadillo Hole* in Snook, but some of their music is hard to dance to. They have our sort of dancing every other week over in Riverton at the SPJST Hall, but unless there's a bingo game or something happening at the VFW, we have to go into Bryan-College Station or Navasota to stir up some action."

Brash shuddered to think what kind of 'action' she referenced.

"It has to be even worse for someone her age," the elderly woman continued. "Young folks these days just don't appreciate a spirited game of bingo." She peered over her glasses at the police chief. "You and Madison should join us for a game sometime. With an experienced caller, it can be a fun and rewarding Saturday night."

"I'll keep that in mind, if we ever find ourselves with a free evening," he murmured. "But with three teenagers and all..."

"I know you two are still newlyweds," she chuckled with a knowing smile. "When the honeymoon's over, you remember us down at the hall."

Knowing his face colored, Brash took a gulp of iced tea and quickly changed the subject. "What else did you find odd?"

"Who is this woman? Where'd she come from? Nelda never mentioned any relations, other than the one nephew down in Conroe. When her eyesight started to go, she moved down there to be near her only kin."

"Maybe Mrs. Goldberg, or most likely her nephew, listed the house with a rental company. Maybe that's how Miss Belvedere heard about it."

"Maybe. But, again, why here in Juliet?"

"She says she works from home. I suppose Juliet is as good as anywhere to have a home office," Brash reasoned.

"The cable man came a few days ago, I suppose to hook up her television and internet services."

It dawned upon him then, one of the things he found so odd about Rose Belvedere's new home.

There hadn't been any television sets.

"There's been a steady stream of people in and out, bringing and doing one thing or another, but when I knocked on her door, she couldn't be bothered. She barely cracked the door an inch. Claimed the place was a mess, and she didn't want to make a poor first impression." Miss Wanda gave a judgmental sniff. "Well, I have news for her. She made a poor impression, anyway."

The place had hardly been a mess today. The uncanny neatness still bothered him, for some reason.

"She certainly likes roses," Miss Wanda went on, as if that in itself were suspect.

"You don't know the half of it," Brash murmured, recalling that practically everything inside the house revolved around the flower.

"Other than a few herbs in her kitchen windowsill, all she has planted is roses! A bit of variety is always nice."

At this, Brash narrowed his eyes. "If she didn't invite you in, how do you know what she has on her kitchen windowsill?"

The older woman had the grace to flush. "I may have peeked in the windows a time or two," she admitted. "The day before that, I saw that car parked in the driveway, but no one answered when I knocked. I went around to the side, to see if there was any activity inside." She frowned with lingering disappointment. "There wasn't."

"Did you see the car there today?"

"Yes and no. I could tell there was a vehicle parked on the other side of the white panel van, but I could only see the tires. I guess in all the excitement, I didn't see it leave."

"Excitement?"

"What with the rug and all. When the movers

almost dropped it, I thought the man in the jumpsuit was going to have a conniption!"

"Jumpsuit?"

"One of those paper throw-away kind you put on over your clothes. It was yellow and didn't fit very well over his big belly." She suppressed a giggle behind her own chubby fingers. "I saw a little tear on the side, it was under such a strain!"

"Had you ever seen this man before?" Brash wanted to know.

"Nope, never. I didn't know any of the others, either."

"How many men did you see in all?"

She thought about it for a moment before answering. "Two men did most of the work. The man in the jumpsuit mostly barked out orders. The man in the fancy clothes about ran himself to death, moving back and forth inside the house. I think he must have been the decorator."

"Fancy clothes?"

"You know. Like Derron." She lowered her voice, as if her absent tenant could hear. "I love that boy to death, and I'm pleased as punch that he rents a room from me, but he dresses *odd*." She shook her dyed hair in wonder. "He likes those little skinny pants and tight shirts, often in pastel. That man today was dressed the same way, and he scurried about the house, putting everything in place. I figured he must be the interior decorator."

That would explain why the house was in immaculate condition, an hour after the moving vans left. And why it looked so perfect, with everything color coordinated and in its proper place.

Everything but a television set. For some reason, that still nagged at him.

He wondered why Rose Belvedere hadn't

mentioned the decorator and, if she employed one, why he hadn't hung the artwork.

"Miss Belvedere mentioned help from her sister and nephews. Did you see anyone fitting that description today?"

"I have no idea if any of the men were her nephews," Miss Wanda said with a frown. "But I only saw one woman, and that was my new neighbor."

After a few more questions, Brash thanked her for her time and for the tea, and excused himself.

His next stop was at Arlene Kopetsky's, which sat directly across from the pink house.

"You'll have to let yourself in," a voice called from within when he knocked.

With a bit of a frown at the lax security, Brash did as instructed. He saw Miss Arlene sitting in front of her big bay window, her casted leg propped up in a second chair. A pair of binoculars rested in her lap.

"It's about time you got here," she chastised. "I called a good thirty minutes ago."

"Yes, ma'am. I've started my investigation and already spoken to one of your neighbors."

"Is that what it's called these days?" she asked with a curled lip. "An investigation? It looked more like shenanigans to me, and you a newly married man!"

Brash released a long-suffering sigh. He knew someone would see it. More than likely, Rose Belvedere had known it, too, 'falling' against him and making a spectacle of them both.

He wouldn't dignify the churlish remark with a response.

"You reported witnessing what you believed was a murder?" he asked instead.

"A fat lot of good it did me," she groused. "The suspects are long gone by now."

"Miss Arlene, are you feeling all right?" It wasn't

like the older woman to be so cantankerous. Up until now, he thought the church organist liked him well enough, but she sounded downright antagonistic today. "Maddy told me you broke your leg. Is it bothering you? Do I need to get you something for the pain?"

The older woman passed a hand over her face. It was as if she wiped away her animosity with the single act. Her shoulders slumped, and her countenance softened.

"Please excuse me. I don't know what's gotten into me today," she said, shaking her head. She twisted her hands in a nervous gesture and immediately contradicted herself. "Yes, I do. It's all the goings-on at that house across the street. First, witnessing a killing, and then seeing that woman throw herself at you!" With renewed ire, she demanded, "How dare you disgrace Madison Cessna that way!"

"Madison deCordova now," he reminded her. "And I did nothing to disgrace my wife, or my marriage vows." His voice was firm and unapologetic. He straightened himself to his full six feet, one inch and placed his hands upon his belt with an air of formality.

"I'm here to investigate the 'killing' you claimed to have witnessed. But I must say, if it's no more accurate than the scene you construed as a disgrace to my wife, then we may have a problem."

This time, the woman dropped her face into both hands. When she spoke again, her voice broke. "Please, Brash. Don't pay me any attention. I'm—I'm overwrought. Ignore my foolishness. I... just need a minute." She drew in a shaky breath and slowly released it.

"It started when I fell and broke my leg," she confessed. "It's been one thing after another since then. I can't play the organ at church. I can't drive my car. I can't work in my yard. That foolish daughter of mine can't tend to her own life, much less help manage mine. My only entertainment lately has been to watch Nelda Goldberg's old house come back to life. It's been a joy to see, until… until this morning."

Brash's voice was much gentler when he spoke this time. "What was it you saw this morning, Miss Arlene?"

"About eight a.m., I saw the car pull up. Not hers. The other one."

Ah! Someone who saw the car! Brash reached into his front pocket for his trusty notepad. "Did you notice what kind of car it was? The color? Anything special about it?"

"Dark blue, I think. Or black. A coupe of some sort."

"And the man?"

"Dark pants, white shirt, and a tie. I figured he was the real estate agent or attorney or some such. He carried a briefcase."

"Could you see his face? Was he young? Old? Anyone you recognized?"

She shook her head. "Just got a brief glimpse of his face when he unlocked the front door. That's how I knew he wore a tie."

"Do you know Derron Mullins, the tenant who lives next door? The one who works for Maddy at *In a Pinch*?"

"Sure. He stops by a few times a week to check in on me. Carries my trash out to the curb on trash day and brings my mail. A fine young man."

"Was this man dressed in clothes similar to what Derron wears?"

"No, no. That man didn't come until later," Arlene said, making a motion with her hands. "*That* man got out of the panel van. No, this man was dressed all proper-like, in business attire. Only thing missing was his suit jacket, but in this heat, who could blame him?"

"And after he went inside, what happened?"

"Not much. I watched him walk past the window, and I reckon into the kitchen. I never saw him again."

"And when did Miss Belvedere arrive?"

"Is that the new owner?"

"She's the new occupant, at any rate," Brash confirmed.

"About an hour and a half later. I saw her walk past the windows a time or two. Then in a bit, the vans arrived, and she was busy directing traffic. She and the other man, the one you mentioned who dresses like Derron, put the house in order."

"Did you see another woman there this morning?"

"No, just the men. They carried in a whole truck load of furniture, and another full of boxes. And then..." She drew an unsteady breath before she spoke again. "And then they brought out the rug. It was so heavy, one man staggered a bit, and I thought he might fall. They heaved it up into the truck, the rest of them got inside, and they drove away."

"And the car? When did it leave?"

"Just before the trucks. The lady came out on the porch and watered her plants, of all things. On move-in day, with the vans still in front of the house. Doesn't that strike you as odd?"

"A bit," Brash agreed. It seemed to him there would be more pressing matters at a time like that, other than tending to plants. "But that hardly equates to murder," he reminded her.

"No, but I'm telling you. That man did not come out of the house! The only way he came out was rolled up in that rug. I had my eyes on the woman, wondering what on earth she was doing with a watering can, and almost missed the man who got in the car and drove away."

"And you're certain it wasn't the man who arrived first?"

"Positive. This man was much bigger, and he wore one of those tear-away suits, the kind they wear when they paint, or work in the meat market, or such. He left in the car."

"How many men left in the vans?"

"Two in the bigger truck, one in the blue panel van."

Brash jotted down the information, knowing fully well it contradicted some of the other eyewitness information. Miss Arlene said the panel van was blue; Miss Wanda called it white. Miss Arlene said three men drove away in the vans; Henry Bealls said it was four. Brash only hoped their other information was more reliable.

"And you never saw the first man come out of the house?"

"No. So when I saw the rug come out, and how heavy it was, I knew he must be rolled up inside."

"You don't by chance watch *Matlock* reruns, do you?" Brash ventured to guess.

"Why, yes, it's one of my favorites. And just a week or so ago, our own John Paul Nobles was a guest star on the program! Lana came over and watched it with me. She's always had a crush on him. She even had her picture taken with him last year, and he kissed her on the cheek."

Calling the movie star one of their own was a bit of a stretch. He had been a close friend and rumored love-interest for Caress Ellingsworth, a one-time soap opera queen who resided in The Sisters after her retirement. When she was killed last year by a jealous lover, John Paul came for the funeral and to settle her estate. Brash wouldn't be the one to tell Miss Arlene that her daughter was hardly the movie star's type. He knew for a fact that Derron filled those shoes much better. Plus, Lana Kopetsky had a crush on just about any man. Himself included.

"I think I have everything I need for now, Miss Arlene." He stuffed his notepad back into his pocket. "Before I go, is there anything I can do for you?"

"I hate to be a bother, but there is one thing..."

One thing morphed into three. She insisted she repay the favor with a glass of tea.

Another half hour elapsed before Brash made his way to Henry Bealls' house to hear yet another version of what truly happened, and to have another glass of sweet tea.

3

"Brash? Is that you?" Madison deCordova asked as she heard the chime, alerting her to an opened door in the house.

She could easily hear the disgust in her husband's weary reply. "Finally," he grunted.

Madison hurried across the kitchen to brush a kiss upon his lips. "Hard day?"

"To say the least." He caught her by the waist and pulled her in for a hug. "But it's getting better."

"This wouldn't have anything to do with the town's newest resident, would it?" she guessed. "The one who brazenly murdered a man in her front window, rolled him up in a carpet, and shipped him off in a moving van?"

His snort of laughter lacked humor. "You've heard."

"Oh, yes." Her amused smile held just a trace of genuine horror. "I was having coffee at *New Beginnings* when the calls started coming in. Genny threatened to take the phone off the hook. Why everyone thinks they have to call the café and share every little tidbit of news is beyond her. Meanwhile, Granny started working things on her end, trying to find out more about the new tenant. She has a call in to the assisted living center in Conroe, but the nurses say Miss Nelda's mind isn't what it used to be. They'll try having her call back after her physical therapy session."

Brash shook his head, a dazed look of wonder upon his handsome face. "I don't know why I didn't just turn this investigation over to you three in the first place," he muttered. "You have a better network of information than any of my official sources."

"I'll loan you my secret weapon," his wife promised, giving him another kiss before moving away.

Brash unbuckled his duty belt with a frown. "Your grandmother should have been with the FBI."

"I'm not sure all her methods are strictly in line with government standards," Madison admitted.

"I'm not sure all her methods are *loosely* in line with government standards!"

Madison laughed at her husband's expression as she grabbed two glasses from the cupboard and moved to the refrigerator.

"Just water for me," he cautioned. "I've had enough sweet tea this afternoon to float a battleship. Not to mention launch myself into the early stages of diabetes."

His knee popped as he lowered himself into a kitchen chair and stretched his long legs out before him. Madison side-stepped his legs moments later when she placed their glasses on the table. She moved behind him to massage his tense shoulders. "Want to talk about it?"

"Not much to say. Four callers, four versions of what happened. All swear they saw a dead body rolled up in a rug. But when I press for details, there are none. No one actually saw a body."

Maddy worked on a particularly tight area,

working the knots out with firm pressure from her thumbs. "And the new homeowner? You met her, right?"

His grunt could have been in reference to the massage, could have been in reference to the homeowner. "Oh, yes. I met her." He drew out her name, the enunciation saying more than the simple words. "Rose Belvedere."

Madison paused in her ministrations to lean down and get right in his face. Her hazel eyes danced with amusement. Her tone was conspiratorial. "Did she really try to make out with you in the front room?"

This groan was long and frustrated. "I'm going to issue a public safety mandate," he decided. "All windows will be ordered covered to avoid the spread of rampant gossip."

In reply, Madison laughed. "Ah, sweetheart. Women just can't keep their hands off you. I know I can't."

"Then what happened to the massage?" he grumbled.

As she worked on his shoulders and the tight spot at the base of his neck, Madison said, "Don't think you're off the hook, mister. I want to know more about this Rose woman."

"I'm sure the gossip mill has filled you in already."

Madison spewed out the details as she knew them. "Late twenties, black hair, good figure, pink lips all puckered like a rose. Well dressed, especially for move-in day. Oh, and quite beautiful. Does that sound right?"

"Close," he agreed. "I'd lean more toward *pretty* than beautiful—"

"Good answer, Mr. D," she murmured.

"—but you're right about the well-dressed part. Tell me something. When you're moving into a new house, what do you usually wear?"

"You saw me last fall. Jeans and a t-shirt. The older, the better. It's a messy job."

"That's what I thought. But this woman wore a dress and heels, all color coordinated and perfect. Doesn't that strike you as odd?"

"Not just odd. It's also impractical and definitely uncomfortable."

"And you should see the house. Everything is already in its place. I was there not thirty minutes after the moving vans left, and it looked like a model home."

"Wow. She must have a fantastic moving service."

"She said it was her b-i-l."

"B-i-l? Oh! You mean her brother-in-law."

"She says her sister helped, too, but no one remembers seeing another woman over there."

"That's weird."

"It gets weirder. Arlene Kopetsky considers that big front window her personal movie screen. She watches with binoculars."

"Sort of weird, but typical. At least around here."

"That's not the part I was talking about. Miss Arlene says there was one man whom she assumed was the interior decorator. He ran around like the Energizer bunny, putting furniture in place and getting everything in order. But if you hire a decorator, even if he's family, wouldn't he hang the artwork, too? That's the weird part. When Kiki decorated here, she attended to every last detail."

"True. But don't forget. Kiki was hired by the network, and they were airing everything on national television. They didn't dare leave out a single detail." Just for a moment, Madison was lost in the memory of those maddening, rewarding, whirlwind months. For the price of her privacy and what little pride she had left—and often her very sanity, it seemed—HOME TV paid for all the renovations to the stately old mansion known as the Big House. She now had a beautiful, fully restored, television-worthy, forever home for herself and her twins, but getting here had been a difficult process.

Madison shook the haunting memories away. The melancholy was replaced by a much happier thought: she now shared the home with Brash and his sixteen-year-old daughter Megan, when she wasn't at her mother's. The rambling old house was now filled with love, laughter, and family, and Madison had never been happier in her life.

"But you're right," Madison said, forcing her mind back to the conversation. "Most decorators finish down to the last detail. Many consider that the most important part."

"In case your spy network didn't mention this fact, that's what I was doing today. I hung a piece of artwork for her."

"I think I may have heard mention of something like that."

"I wasn't about to fall for that trick when we viewed the bedroom."

Her hands stilled. "Wait. Even after she threw herself at you in the living room, you willingly walked into her bedroom?" Her tone wasn't as playful as it had been.

"I had to see the rest of the house," he reasoned. "I didn't have a warrant. I didn't even have probable cause."

"In other words, all you had were your good looks, your muscles, and your charm."

"Those wouldn't be *my* words," he pointed out. "But, yes, I was there only because she allowed it. When she caught on to what I was doing and asked me to leave, I had no other choice than to do so. At least by then, we had made it back into the kitchen."

"Did you see anything suspicious?"

"Other than her home office, everything was in immaculate order. In my opinion, *that* was suspicious. She even had one of those dish towels with the little crocheted doohickey on top, the kind my mom makes. She gave you one for Mother's Day."

"I know the one you mean. It's hanging right over there."

"Who already has that in place, an hour after moving in?" he demanded, still bothered by the minute detail.

"Maybe it has sentimental value. Maybe it doesn't feel like home until she has that one item hanging in her kitchen."

Brash was unconvinced. "Nothing in there felt homey. It felt staged."

"Maybe that's it. Maybe she's planning to sell the house and had it professionally staged for buyers."

Considering the possibility, he murmured, "Maybe."

"I suppose we'll know more when Miss Nelda returns Granny's call." Madison took the chair beside her husband and reached for her water. "No other clues?"

He told her about the boot indentations and the lack of a rug in the living room.

"Most of the rooms are rather small," he continued. "There wouldn't be much room to lay a body out and roll it up in a rug. But Miss Arlene insists she saw a man in a dark car enter the house first, go into the kitchen, and never come out again. She claims a different man got in the car a few hours later and drove it away."

"That is odd," Madison agreed. "By the way, how's

she managing with a broken leg?"

"Not very well. I did a few chores for her before I left."

"Ah, you're such a good man." Her playful smile shone through again. "And just think. If that first date with Lana had gone differently, she might be your mother-in-law right now."

His horrified grimace was comical. "That date was a mistake. I had no idea of her reputation, or I would have never gone out with her. It only took that one time to form my own opinion. Let's just say, it wasn't favorable."

"Granny says it's because Miss Arlene had her late in life and spoiled her rotten."

"She's rotten, all right," he muttered. "Did I tell you Rose Belvedere didn't even have a television set?"

"Should I be worried?" Madison asked in a point-blank tone.

Her question threw him. "Because she doesn't have a TV? Why would that worry you?"

"No, silly. Because you seem to be preoccupied with this woman. One minute we were talking about Lana, the next you changed the subject back to Rose Belvedere."

"The reason is two-fold. One, I have nothing more to say about Lana Kopetsky. And two, I can't put my finger on it, but something about Rose Belvedere bothers me."

"Besides the fact that she openly flirted with a married man?"

"Besides that." If he noticed her snippy tone, he chose to ignore it. His thoughts moved on. "Did I mention everything in her house revolves around roses? It's a bit of overkill if you ask me. She even smells like a rose."

"Roses make you sneeze."

"Exactly. And something about this whole day just makes my nose itch."

Granny Bert called as Madison was cooking dinner.

"Well, that was a bust," her grandmother reported in disgust. "Poor Nelda is worse off than I thought. She barely remembered who I was!"

If anyone was memorable, it was Bertha Hamilton Cessna. Joe Cessna had died nine years ago, but not before the two of them built a legacy of love and community service. Together, they had four sons, six grandchildren, and numerous great-grandchildren. As an elected county official and mayor of Juliet for many years, Granny Bert's feisty exploits were known far and wide. At eighty-one, she still enjoyed skydiving, motorcycles, and trips in her RV. Musical superstar Willie Nelson had even written a song about her.

Bertha Cessna had her finger on the pulse of The Sisters. When something happened in the community, she knew about it. And when nothing happened in the community, she *made* it happen. Always quick to offer a helping hand or to dish out unsolicited advice and sage bits of wisdom, Granny Bert was not a woman easily forgotten.

"I'm sorry to hear that," Madison said. "Her mind must be really bad."

"She kept talking about a great-niece, but she doesn't have a niece. Her sister Carla just had the one son, and he never had kids. He was working at that power plant when it exploded several years back. They say the radiation drowned all his little swimmers."

"More information than I needed, but okay."

Without warning, her grandmother changed

topics. "Wanda tells me this Rose woman has been coming to the house several times over the last few days and spends most of her time in the front bedroom, where she's setting up some type of office. She supposedly will be working from home."

"A lot of people do that, Granny. You make it sound suspect."

Her grandmother rattled on as if she hadn't spoken. "I suppose that's better than her expecting to get a job here. Unless she plans on working at the school or commuting every day to a bigger town, there's not many opportunities here. Although, Jubal did tell me he's thinking of hiring a new clerk for the *Five and Dime*."

There was absolutely nothing at her great-uncle's *Five and Dime* that sold for under a dime. Even penny candy was packaged to sell for more.

"Unless Uncle Jubal is offering a very generous salary, I doubt it pays enough to live on."

"You know my brother. It won't be too generous." Granny Bert's voice was frank. "I swear, that man plans to line his casket with hundred-dollar bills. I keep telling him. He can't take it with him, but he still squeezes a dollar till it rains nickels."

"At any rate, Brash says that Rose Belvedere works for a debt collector."

"Sounds about par," her grandmother scoffed. "A job at the school sounds much more pleasant. I hear she also has a fondness for flowers, particularly roses. Maybe she could get a job with Myrna Lewis in her horticultural venture."

A note of suspicion slipped into Madison's voice. "Why are you so concerned with getting this woman a job? You don't even know her."

"Because it sounds to me like she needs something to keep her hands busy," Granny Bert snorted, "so they won't be reaching for your man!"

"I appreciate your concern, but I'm sure Brash has everything under control."

"You mark my words. When a young, pretty thing makes a move on a married man the very first day she arrives, she's going to stir up plenty more trouble in the days to come!"

4

"I want these old shrubs dug up," the homeowner instructed. "We'll replace them with rose bushes."

Sixteen-year-old Blake Reynolds followed the man's sweeping arm gesture. "All of these?"

"Yes," Israel Ballard confirmed. "Keeping them trimmed has gotten to be too much for me." His face wrinkled into a rueful expression. "I'm afraid I'm not as young as I was when I planted them."

"No problem," the youth assured him. "I'll have these done in no time."

"When you're done, I'll have you some sweet tea ready," Mr. Ballard promised as he retreated into the cool interior of the house.

Before tackling the project, Blake fished a jerky stick from his pocket for an energy boost. He wolfed it down in two bites, stuffing the wrappings into his pocket so he didn't leave any trash. The last thing he wanted was for Mr. Ballard to complain to his boss.

It was his first job, and the boy was eager to please. There weren't many job opportunities in a small town, and stocking shelves and sweeping floors didn't appeal to him. He felt fortunate to have snagged this job with the landscaping and lawn service. Not only did the job allow him to be outdoors, there was the added bonus of seeing Danni Jo Combs each day. Marvin Combs was her grandfather, and she was working in the office this summer.

A summer job at *Marvin Gardens* meant he could save up to buy his first truck. Blake wasn't sure how it worked now that his mom had remarried, but prior to that, he knew there was absolutely no extra money for a second vehicle. When his dad died in a car accident, he had left them broke. They had to leave their house in Dallas and move here to The Sisters, the town his mom had grown up in.

For the better part of a year, they had lived with Granny Bert. She was cool enough, but he knew it was hard on the older woman, having her house full again after years of peace and quiet. Blake had adjusted easily enough, but it had been harder for Bethani. His twin sister had worshiped their father, and she hadn't wanted to leave her friends behind. He didn't think she understood how hard all this had been on their mom. Late at night, he would hear their mom crying, trying to muffle her sobs.

Their mom opened her own temporary service *In a Pinch* to make ends meet. Moving into the Big House strained their finances even worse. The renovations on the house may have been free, but the utilities weren't. His mother never complained, other than to caution them to close doors and keep the thermostat at a modest number, but he knew it was hard for her. He knew she took some of the worst jobs possible, just so he and Beth could have and do the things they wanted, while she did without. There were uniforms to buy, practices and games to go to, cheer camps to attend. And there was food to buy. Lots and lots of food. Blake knew he ate a lot, but he couldn't help it. He was *always* hungry.

He didn't know if Daddy D would offer to buy him

a truck now that he had married his mom. He doubted the police department paid very well, but Brash deCordova had once been a pro football player, and then a college coach. Plus, his family owned a huge ranch. Surely, he had squirreled away some of that money for later years.

Not that Blake would ever ask for any of it. He didn't know what financial arrangements the newlyweds had, but he wasn't expecting any handouts. Even if Daddy D had plenty of money, he was the sort of dad who believed in strong work ethics and learning the value of a dollar. Megan didn't even have a car yet.

That was fine with Blake. He *wanted* to earn his own way. He wanted to know he had put his time and energy into something and came out the victor. The landscaping and lawn service might not pay much over minimum wage, but he knew he could feel pride in cashing those checks.

Over time, he would have enough for the down payment. And when he did, he would ask Daddy D to go with him to choose a truck. Just like when he asked him about getting a job before he discussed it with his mom, it seemed like a father-son kind of moment.

Blake's thoughts stayed occupied as he dug up the old shrubs. He was strong and had plenty of stamina. Digging the shovel into the earth and pulling out a blade full of dirt was easy enough, even in the blistering heat. Once he freed the roots from the soil, he put the discarded shrubbery into the wheelbarrow and carried it to the back of the pickup for later disposal. It was a process to be repeated over and over, until only one shrub remained.

He took a quick break, cooling off under the shade of a large mimosa tree. He ate a granola bar and washed it down with a full bottle of water. The day was hot, and he had worked up quite a sweat, but there was still one more shrub to go.

Going back to work, Blake plunged the shovel with gusto, determined to make quick work of this last bush. Once he was done here, he could head home to a shower and a hot meal.

To his dismay, Blake heard the dull, metallic plunk of metal against his blade.

"Crap!" he muttered aloud. "Don't tell me I hit a water main."

He dropped to his knees and pulled the fresh earth away with his hands. A glimpse of something silver shone through the soil. *Hitting a gas pipe would be even worse!* Blake ran his fingers under the dirt, making certain the tarnished metal didn't curve into a pipe.

Relief washed through him. Whatever it was, it was flat and smooth.

Using the shovel, Blake carefully dug out more earth, until he had a clear view of the piece of flat metal. A bit more excavation, and he realized it was the top to a box. He scooped dirt away until the entire box came into view.

His heart thumping with excitement, Blake pulled the box from the ground. It looked like a strongbox of some sort, like the one Granny Bert kept in the hall closet.

He hadn't meant to be snooping when he discovered the box. Not exactly. He knew his mother sometimes hid snack food in random places around the house, hoping he wouldn't graze through a week's worth of groceries in a single day. He had been searching for chips when he found the strongbox with the Army insignia.

He knew not to open it without permission. He waited until Granny Bert came home and asked her about it. She proudly showed him the medals Grandpa Joe was awarded in the service, and the cool old pistol he carried. There were a few old letters and other memorabilia inside, too, but she hadn't offered to share, and he hadn't asked.

This box was similar in size and appearance, minus the Army logo. Time and damp earth had darkened the patina to a dull gray. There were marks where his shovel scraped against it, but otherwise, it was in perfect condition. It was securely latched with a heavy old-time combination lock.

Blake sat back on his haunches, studying the box. He idly fiddled with the lock, knowing he would never come up with the random combination. Even if he did, he wouldn't look inside. The curiosity might kill him, but he knew not to pry. This box didn't belong to him.

After several minutes of studying the locked box, wondering what lay inside, Blake moved to set the buried treasure aside so he could finish his work. The box was heavy, and he misjudged the weight, balancing it as he was with just one hand. It fell to the ground, its timeworn hinges giving way. The lid loosened enough for a yellowed sheet of paper to escape.

Blake caught the paper before a breeze stole it away. He didn't mean to pry, but the fanciful script caught his eye. The words were written in cursive, with graceful curls and flowing precision. He studied the style more than the content, fascinated with the art of handwriting. Schools were phasing the craft out, favoring block printing over this beautiful art form.

His mind churned in slow motion. Almost as an afterthought, the intricate letters formed into words, and words into conscious thought. He had read the first page before it dawned on him what he held.

...will never allow us to be together. My heart breaks at the thought of letting you go, but I know it's the only decent thing to do. You have a bright future ahead of you. Waiting for me will only hold you back. My heart is heavy—with love, and with despair—at having to say goodbye, but I feel I must. In time, you will realize the truth of these words. I will forever...

The page ended, and Blake realized it was part of a very personal letter. He felt guilty having read the intimate thoughts. He had no idea whom they were intended for or who wrote them, but he felt like an intruder on a private conversation. He tried slipping the paper back through the lid's narrow opening, but all he did was crinkle it.

In the end, he placed the letter on the grass, anchoring it with the box. He went back to work, digging up the final shrub. When he was finished, he gathered his tools, carted the bush and the tools to the truck, and cleaned up the backyard work area.

Satisfied with the job he had done, Blake brushed the dirt from his hands and clothes. Retrieving the letter and the box, he knocked on the back door.

"All done?" Israel Ballard asked when he came to the door.

"With digging them up, yes, sir. I'll be back tomorrow to plant the rose bushes. Would you like to make sure what I did was okay?"

"I trust you, but maybe we should take a peek. And then I owe you a big ol' glass of iced tea."

"Sounds good," the boy confessed.

The older man's steps were slower than his, so Blake tempered his long-legged gait to match Mr. Ballard's. He wasn't good at judging people's age, but he thought seventy-five sounded about right. His hair was completely gray, and there was a road map of wrinkles upon his face, etching the journey of his life.

"That looks fine, young man. You did a good job. Better—and far faster—than I could have done."

Pleased to have exceeded his expectations, Blake thanked his client with a proud smile. He then motioned to the box in his hands. "Crazy thing is, I found this, buried beneath the last shrub."

The older man's brow drew together in a perplexed frown. The oddest thing happened after that. The color leaked from his face.

"Wh—What?" he croaked in a hoarse cry.

"I, uh, found this box." Blake tried to hand it over, but the man pulled back, visibly shaken.

Because he didn't know what else to do, Blake blabbered on. "It's heavy, but it could be the steel construction. They don't make lock boxes like this anymore. My great-grandfather had one of these in the Army. It's still solid."

Mr. Ballard stared at the box, his color still pale.

"The hinges on this one," Blake went on, nervously pointing to the loosened pin, "are weak. I, uh, accidentally dropped it. This... This fell out." He held up the single page. Sunlight turned the aged paper translucent, making the flowing letters appear to float on the air.

Instead of taking what the boy offered, Mr. Ballard ducked around him. "I—I'll go get that tea," he mumbled. His retreat into the house was twice as fast as when he came out. He was practically running by the time he reached the door.

Puzzled by the strange behavior, Blake took the box and the rejected letter to the patio table, where he settled in one of the wrought-iron chairs to await his client's return. *Did that make this a rejected rejection letter?*

A smile tickled his lips, but it seemed wrong to laugh at a time like this. Mr. Ballard was clearly upset. *Distressed* was a more apt word for his reaction.

When the older gentleman took longer than expected to make tea, Blake began to worry. He didn't know what kind of health Mr. Ballard was in. He had been so pale outside. What if he had gone inside and had a heart attack or something? Should he go in and check?

Before he had to decide, the back door opened, and Mr. Ballard banged his way through, balancing a tray in his hands.

"I thought you might be hungry, too." His voice sounded strained as he set the tray on the table and handed Blake a small plate with chunks of apple and cheese, and a few green grapes. His hands shook so badly that when he handed over the iced tea, some of the liquid dribbled down the side.

Blake pretended not to notice. "Thanks! Truth is, I'm starved," he admitted, diving into the fresh fruit.

"I remember being your age."

Blake noticed how his eyes strayed toward the box. His color was better, but he was still visibly shaken.

"Not to be nosy," the boy ventured, "but is that yours?" He nodded to the box.

Israel Ballard took so long to answer, Blake thought he wouldn't. When he finally spoke, his voice sounded choked. "It was. A long, long time ago."

Because he didn't know what else to say, Blake said, "Cool," and took a long gulp of tea.

Eyes still riveted on the box, the old man seemed lost in thought. After a long while, his thoughts spilled out. "It's been so many years, I had forgotten all about it. Seeing it again..." He pulled in a shaky breath as he spoke his thoughts aloud.

"I buried it so long ago... Another lifetime, another

life. But there was a time..." His voice lingered over the memory before he continued in a soft voice, "A time when she was my whole life. I thought..." He pulled a hand over his face, as if to pull a curtain down over his rambling memories. "Well, it doesn't matter what I thought. It wasn't to be."

"I tried to stuff the letter back in," Blake murmured. "But it wouldn't go. I'm not sure how it even slipped out." He wiped his hand on his grimy pants leg and then inspected it to make certain it wouldn't leave a smudge. Satisfied his fingers were marginally clean, he reached for the paper. "If you remember the combination, you may want to put it back in."

Again, Israel Ballard refused to touch the aged paper. "My—My eyes," he mumbled. It was clearly an excuse. He swallowed hard before asking, "Do you know how to work one of those?"

"If I have the combination."

He readily supplied the numbers. "08-17-68." The next words were whispered, but Blake heard them all the same. "The day she broke my heart."

Blake spun the combination, using the numbers the older man supplied. The lock magically opened, but he was slow to pull it from the clasp. He wasn't sure it was his place.

Seeing the boy's hesitation, Mr. Ballard's voice came out hoarse. "Go on."

Blake did as instructed. A stack of yellowed letters sprang out, as if straining for a first glimpse of sunlight after decades underground.

Israel Ballard pulled in a ragged breath, but he made no move to collect the spilled papers.

"I'll, uh, just put this on top then," Blake muttered, dropping the partial letter atop the collection before riffling them into a semblance of order. As he stuffed the papers back inside, he caught a glimpse of old rose petals, a frayed, faded ribbon, and a small velvet box.

It was one of the saddest sights he had ever seen. The older man had buried the box in the earth decades ago, hoping to bury the heartache alongside it. The ploy may have even worked, but one glimpse of the box was all it took to bring it all rushing back. Seeing the pain in the man's watery blue eyes now, Blake regretted his part in digging up the old memories.

"Thank you, son," Mr. Ballard said. His voice was still unsteady. "I can't bear to touch it, myself."

"What should I do with it?"

"Leave it here. It won't blow away."

He's right, Blake thought. *As much heartache as that thing holds, it's way too heavy to ever blow away.*

The buried box of memories haunted Blake's mind that evening and into the night. He was surprised to arrive at Israel Ballard's the next day and find the box still sitting on the patio table, exactly where he had left it.

As predicted, it was too heavy to budge.

Blake worked hard all morning, planting a variety of rose bushes in the newly tilled soil and lining the bed with landscape stones. Mr. Ballard gave instructions, offering suggestions and minimal help. The two worked comfortably together, but the box was never mentioned.

As lunchtime neared, Mr. Ballard disappeared inside the house, only to surface again with a tray in his hands.

"Lunchtime!" he called.

"Thank you, sir," Blake said, wiping sweat from his brow, "but I'm not sure that's allowed."

"Nonsense. I've already called Marvin and cleared it with him." Israel looked through shaggy white brows to pin the boy with his gaze. "And don't tell me you're not hungry. I heard your stomach grumbling from the kitchen."

"I'm never not hungry," Blake admitted.

"Wash up there by the potting shed. I'll have this laid out in no time."

Blake washed the soil and grit from his hands, arms, and face. His blond hair stood in spiked peaks when he was done, but his host made no comment as he returned to the table. Mr. Ballard's eyes were glued to the box.

"I normally say grace before eating," the older gentleman told him.

Blake dutifully bowed his head, hoping his stomach didn't add the punctuation.

After the amens, Mr. Ballard passed a plate of sandwiches to Blake. "I didn't know if you preferred ham or turkey, so there's both. Help yourself."

Never shy around food, the teen took one of each. He heaped his plate with potato salad and sliced cucumbers, but passed on the radishes. Before he took the first bite, he had drained a glass of iced tea.

"You worked up quite a thirst," chuckled Mr. Ballard.

"Appetite, too." Two bites, and the ham sandwich was half gone.

His host nodded with understanding. "I remember that age. My father claimed I had a hollow leg."

"Did you live around here then?"

"We moved here to Juliet when I was fifteen. My dad liked to say that was his first mistake, moving away from the farm. At least there, he claimed, he could grow enough food to keep me from starving."

"Hey," Blake said, struck by the similarity. "I was fifteen when we moved here last year."

"You remind me of myself at that age. Like you, I was a hard worker."

Starting on the turkey sandwich, Blake asked, "Where did you work?"

"Jolly Dewberry's gas station." Pride still lingered in his voice. "'Course, back then, it was owned by his father, Mr. Luther Dewberry. Jolly was drafted into the Army, so they needed someone to pick up the slack. In those days, all pumps were full-service. Checking the air in tires and washing the windshield were all part of a fill-up. I did plenty of both, I can tell you that."

"Mr. Jolly still does that," Blake put in. "Granny Bert won't go anywhere else to fill the Buick."

"It's good to support local businesses, especially ones like Dewberry's. They've been in business for almost seventy years and are a cornerstone of our town."

"My best friend dates Mr. Jolly's granddaughter Latricia."

"And you? I imagine a good-looking, strapping boy such as yourself has at least one girlfriend on the string, if not more."

"Not really." Blake shrugged. "I stay busy with baseball and football, and fishing, when I get a chance. Now I have this job. Girls take up too much time."

"An admirable outlook. But that will change when you meet the right girl," Mr. Ballard predicted. A knowing light touched his eyes. "When you meet her, you'll decide fishing and playing ball aren't quite as important as they once were." His gaze slid to the box, shoved now to the far edge of the table.

Blake followed his eyes. "When did you meet her?" There was no need to elaborate. They both knew he meant the girl who had written the letters.

"The next summer. She had been away at finishing school but came home for summer break to visit her grandparents."

Blake scrunched his face in confusion. "What's a finishing school?"

"A girl's academy, I suppose you would call it."

The distinction didn't offer much information. "Like a private school?" he guessed.

"Yes. A very elite private school. Along with their course studies, the girls learned the proper way to walk and talk, and how to host a dinner party."

Blake's blue eyes bugged out. "They actually *teach* those things? In a school?"

"Yes, indeed," Mr. Ballard assured him. A bit of scorn leaked into his voice. "There's a whole host of rules and etiquette for society's upper crust. A finishing school is the perfect place for that last bit of polish and shine."

"Is that where they learn which fork is used for the salad, and which one for the appetizer?" the teenager asked.

"I would imagine so."

"Then my Grandmother Annette probably went to one," he surmised. "She knows all about those forks, and how to stuff an envelope with those little pieces of thin tissue inside, and how to plan a fancy dinner party. She says there's a certain time of year when you can wear white, and that different colors of flowers mean different things. When we stayed there last summer, I heard her gripe out the maid because she used the wrong color for the centerpiece. Said it sent the wrong message, whatever that meant." Blake rolled his eyes as he stuffed another cucumber into his mouth.

"Your grandmother sounds like the perfect hostess." Even though the words could be construed as a compliment, the older man's tone didn't sound that way.

"She likes to throw parties, that's for sure," the teen muttered. "I have to wear a jacket and tie, and my sister has to wear dresses. Her parties are kind of boring, to tell the truth."

"But you don't tell her that." This time, there was a touch of reproach in his voice.

"Nah. I don't want to hurt her feelings. She goes to a lot of trouble, making everything just so."

"Some people set great store in social standings and social gatherings." By now, Israel Ballard's voice sounded sad.

Blake recalled the words from the letter *...will never allow us to be together.* Had the girl been a snob? Had she (or maybe her family) been more concerned with social standings than with true love? Because one thing was for sure. If seeing that box again after so many years could still cause that look in Mr. Ballard's eyes, he had definitely been in love with her, no matter how young they may have been.

"Did she go back?" Blake wanted to know.

The question jolted the older man out of his melancholy. "Back?"

"To the finishing school."

"Yes. But the next summer, she came home again."

"What happened to her?" He didn't mean to sound nosy. He was simply curious.

"That," Israel Ballard said softly, "is a good question. After the summer of '68, I never saw or heard from her again. I have no idea what became of her."

"You mean... she like, *vanished*?"

"Not exactly." His shaggy white brows puckered together, and he slowly turned his head toward the strongbox. After a long moment of staring at it in silence, the older man spoke again. "I haven't thought about Rosa in a very long time. And I think I've given her more than enough thought for today, so how about we get back to work?"

There was nothing more Blake could say. He gathered his plate and utensils, but Mr. Ballard shooed him away. "I'll get these. You finish up with the rose bushes, eh?"

Blake returned to his work, taking extra care to do the job right. He liked Mr. Ballard and didn't want to give him any reason to be unhappy with his performance. He knew it was little in comparison to a broken heart, but the elderly gentleman had seen enough unhappiness in his life; there was no need to cause him additional distress over his rose garden.

Before leaving for the day, Blake knocked at the back door and asked him to inspect the day's efforts.

"Well done, young man," Mr. Ballard approved. "Well done."

"Thank you, sir."

His gaze swept the lush yard. "You know," he said. "These rose bushes look so nice up here, perhaps I should add some at the back for balance. I'll talk to Marvin tomorrow and see about getting you back out here in a few days."

"Yes, sir. That sounds good."

"Very well, then. Thank you for a job well done."

"Thanks for feeding me. Oh. And one other thing." Blake shot a glance at the strongbox, still resting on the table. "I didn't mean to pry earlier, Mr. Ballard. I know it's none of my business. But you seemed so sad about the box, and you were talking about the girl... I didn't mean to stir up bad memories."

A ghost of a smile moved past his lips. "They weren't bad memories, son. Just old ones."

"Still, I shouldn't have asked so many questions."

"You did nothing wrong. The truth is, I've often wondered what happened to her. I was drafted into the Army that fall, and we went our separate ways. When I returned, there was no trace of her, or her family."

"No one around town knew what happened to her? Not even Granny Bert?" From what Blake could tell, his great-grandmother knew *everything* that happened.

"To be honest, I didn't try to find her. She made her position clear before I left for Vietnam."

There was little else to say, other than a murmured, "I'm sorry."

"I met my first wife soon after that. It was time to move on and forget about my first love."

Blake wondered if he had done either. In his opinion, burying the box in his backyard wasn't exactly 'moving on.' To him, it reeked of holding on. And while the older man may not have thought of this Rosa in a long while, he had hardly forgotten her, not in his heart. Nor had he forgotten his feelings for her.

Knowing better than to speak his thoughts aloud, Blake hoped his silent nod would be taken as agreement.

"Do me a favor, son."

"Sure."

Israel Ballard spun on his heels and marched over to the patio table, where he took the old box in his hands. His trek back was more halting, slowed by the weight of memories.

"You take this for a few days, will you?"

Blake's voice came out in a squeak. "Me?"

"I can't bear to see it just yet," Mr. Ballard

admitted. His hands shook as he handed over the old relics. "But I'm not quite ready to destroy it, either. If you could just keep it for a while…"

"Absolutely, sir. I'll take good care of it."

"I know you will, son. That's why I entrust this to you." He settled a hand onto the teen's shoulder and lightly squeezed. "I never had children," he said unexpectedly, "so I don't have a grandson. But if I did, I'd want him to be just like you."

Blake felt a lump invade his throat. "Thank you, Mr. Ballard," he managed to say.

"I'll call Marvin and see about getting you back out here. Until then, hang on to that."

"I won't let you down, sir."

5

When Brash arrived home that evening, instead of his bride, he found their two daughters in the kitchen. Best friends before they became stepsisters, Megan and Bethani were deep in conversation as they banged their way through cabinets and rummaged through drawers.

"I hope this works," Bethani said in a wistful tone.

"Why wouldn't it? It's one of his favorite meals. We'll ply him with food, and then we'll ask for his blessings."

Brash cleared his throat, making his presence known to the teenagers. He wondered what the teens were up to this time, particularly if it required his blessings.

Megan whirled around, her dark auburn hair flying like ribbons through the air. It was the same shade as her father's, minus the few strands of silver. "Oh. Hi, Daddy," she said, offering her cheek for a kiss.

Bethani repeated the gesture. "Hi, Daddy D."

"How are my beauties this evening?" he asked, draping an arm around each of their shoulders.

"Good."

"We're cooking dinner tonight," Megan

volunteered.

"King Ranch chicken?" he asked with a hopeful expression. Aside from steaks, it was his favorite.

"No. Chicken Basghetti," Bethani offered. "Happy's recipe."

According to Maddy, it was one of the few dishes her mother knew how to make. Like its name suggested—and like the woman who created it—it came with a few quirky ingredients. Brash liked it well enough, but it was far from being his favorite.

"It's Blake's favorite," Megan added.

"Oh," Brash said with realization. "You're wanting to get on your *brother's* good side." He almost felt guilty when the knowledge brought with it an odd rush of relief.

"And we all know that the best way to reach Mr. Always Starving is through food," Bethani continued.

Brash popped an olive into his mouth. "You're trying to butter up your brother *why*?"

"So he'll let us help him with his new job."

"I think that's a matter for his boss to decide, don't you?"

"Not that job," his daughter explained. "The one he doesn't know about yet. The one Beth and I are going to convince him we need."

Not for the first time, Brash had no idea what the girls were talking about. He gave his head a good solid shake, hoping the words would rearrange themselves into a sensible order, but they sounded as confusing on replay as they had the first time.

"Maybe you should start from the beginning," he told them, only to hold them off with a hand gesture. "Sounds like Maddy is coming down. She may need to hear this, too." A telltale creak from the back stairwell alerted him to her approach.

The home's original owner, Juliet Randolph

Blakely, didn't approve of servants using the grand staircase. She relegated their transit between floors to this more modest version at the back of the house. Granny Bert speculated that could also explain why the old mansion had so many secret passages; Heaven forbid Miss Juliet's dirty laundry be carried openly. The townsfolk did a fine enough job of airing that publicly.

"Something smells good in here!" Madison sang out as she stepped from the last stile. Her face brightened when she saw her husband. "Hi, sweetheart. I didn't know you were home."

"Just came in."

Megan turned to her stepmother with a bright smile. "How was your nap?"

"Nap? Are you sick?" A worried look puckered Brash's face as he bent to kiss his wife. His lips lingered as she snuggled into his embrace.

"Not at all." He read the slight smirk upon her lips. Her tone told him so much more than her words. "The girls insisted I rest while they cooked dinner."

Yep. The girls were definitely up to something.

With a sigh, Brash braced himself. "You may as well spill it."

"Well," Bethani began, twirling a long lock of blonde hair around her finger, "Blake has that new job with *Marvin Gardens*, helping to landscape people's yards and all."

Brash simply nodded, encouraging her to continue. He had secretly been delighted when the teen came to him first, before discussing the matter with his mother. Blake reasoned it was because a job was 'the sort of thing a guy discusses with his dad,' making Brash's heart swell with pride and appreciation. He couldn't love the boy—or his twin sister—more, even if he were their biological father.

"So, yesterday," she continued, "when he went to plant new shrubs at Mr. Ballard's place, he found a box buried in the ground. And not just any box. An old tin lockbox!" Her blue eyes glittered with excitement.

"Guess what was inside?" Megan was clearly as excited as her stepsister.

"Money?" Brash guessed.

"Nope."

"Jewels?"

"It wasn't a chair, Dad," Megan admonished him.

To an outsider, the comment wouldn't have made sense. Madison's recent discovery—gold nuggets and a jeweled necklace, hidden inside a chair she had reupholstered for Brash's birthday—wasn't common knowledge. But for the family, it was great fodder for an inside joke.

"Then what was it?" he asked.

The girls looked at each other, squealed with excitement, exchanged high fives, and spoke at once. "Love letters!"

"Really?" Madison asked, the same hint of a wondrous smile reflecting on her face.

Brash rolled his eyes. "Women and their romantic notions," he mumbled, only half-grudgingly.

"It is *very* romantic," his daughter informed him. "Someone poured their heart and soul into those letters, and someone else, most likely Mr. Ballard, kept them safe and sound all these years. That's true love."

"Or he buried them thirty years ago and forgot all about them."

His wife gave him a playful slap on the chest. "Stop it! Can't you see how excited the girls are about this?" Nudging him aside, she turned to the girls with a suitable expression of interest. "Ignore him. He's just being a man. Who were the letters from?"

Bethani's smile fell. "We don't know."

"Well, who were they to? Mr. Ballard?"

It was Megan's turn to look dejected. "We don't know that, either."

"What *do* you know?"

"Not much. That's why we're making Blake's favorite dinner tonight. We're going to ask him if we can take the case."

"Whoa, whoa, whoa," Brash said, suddenly back in the conversation. "What case? Who said anything about a case?"

"The case of the buried letters, of course!"

"Stop staring at me like I have two heads," he told the girls. To Bethani, he said, "You sound just like your mother. You get one whiff of a mystery, and you're ready to jump in, feet first."

"What other way is there?" she asked. He couldn't determine if her innocent look was real or manufactured.

"You need to think about your actions *before* you decide to jump. You need to give it proper consideration, think about the pros and the cons, decide a possible course of action, and think about the consequences your actions might cause."

"We have thought about it." Megan defended them both with the statement. She propped her hands on her hips, eyes blazing behind her fashionable glasses. "And you sound just like a dad!" she accused.

"Maybe because I am?"

"Yeah, but you're usually a cool dad, not such a... such a..." Bethani broke off, unable to find the right word.

Brash was touched. *Beth thinks I'm cool. Not so long ago, she thought I was disrespecting her father's memory.* Knowing their relationship was still rocky at times—she was sixteen; her emotions were always in turmoil—he didn't call attention to the casual compliment.

Instead, he gave her the arched brow look and supplied, "Lawman?"

"Yeah. That!"

"I happen to be that, as well. As both a father and an officer of the law, I have to think about things like safety and privacy and what kind of trouble you girls could stir up."

"Trouble? Why would there be trouble?" Megan wanted to know.

"There had to be a reason those letters were buried in the first place," Brash pointed out.

"To keep them safe," Bethani reasoned.

"Maybe. But there are safer places than in someone's backyard."

Megan looked at her stepmother and pulled a face. "I hate it when he gets all rational and stuff," she sulked.

Madison laughed as she hugged the auburn-haired teen. She reached out her other arm to encompass the blonde. "Let's ask Blake a few more questions over dinner. It could be that the mystery is already solved."

"And if it's not? Will you help us solve it?" Bethani asked eagerly.

Madison looked over her shoulder at Brash. She saw through his gruff exterior and recognized a twinkle of amusement in his brown eyes.

"That's up to your father," she told the girls. "If there's truly a mystery to be solved, and if your dad doesn't object, and *if* I have time, I'll try to help you girls." When they would have cheered with excitement, Maddy held up a staying hand. "But!" she warned. "Those are a lot of ifs."

"Please, Daddy?" Megan begged.

Bethani added her own puppy-dog eyes. "Please,

please, please?"

"You know I leave for camp next week. I won't be here if you girls run into any trouble."

"We won't!" Bethani was quick to say.

"And if we do—which we won't, but still—Momma Maddy will be here." Megan's voice held equal confidence.

"Like Maddy said," Brash reiterated. "Let's see what Blake has to say about it."

"Cool! Chicken Basghetti." Blake gave his approval as they seated themselves around the kitchen table.

"How was work today?" Brash asked.

"Hot." He reached for his mother's hand on one side, his sister's on the other, as per their tradition for the blessing. "Find any more dead bodies today?" he asked his mom.

There was a hint of indignation in her voice. "I did not."

"Making progress." He bent his blond head while Brash said grace, but it popped up before the 'amen' cleared his lips. Blake was already reaching for the spaghetti.

"Your sisters made supper tonight."

"I'm so hungry, I'll eat anything."

"You brat!" Bethani said, punching him in the arm.

She grunted as Megan's foot issued a none-too-gentle reminder to be nice.

"We know how hard you've been working. We thought we'd surprise you with your favorite meal." Megan's thousand-watt smile gave him pause, but he swallowed the first bite of spaghetti without comment.

Three mouthfuls later, he gave them the thumb's up sign.

"Did you open the box today?" Bethani asked, unable to wait any longer. The suspense was killing her. "What else was inside?"

"I dunno," he said around another mouthful. "He didn't want to open it. In fact," he added, swallowing down the food with a healthy swig of tea, "he didn't even want to see it. He gave it to me for safe keeping."

"Really? You mean it's here?"

"Can we see it?" Megan asked.

"You can look at it. But we're not going to open it."

"Why not?"

"Because it's not mine. I'm just keeping it for him, until he decides what to do with it."

"Who are the letters from?" Bethani asked.

"I don't know. Some girl he used to know named Rosa. I think she broke his heart." He looked at his mother and asked, "How does first love work, anyway? Is it ever real? Does it really last?"

Madison wasn't sure how to answer. She had been half in love with Brash since she was a freshman in high school. That didn't mean she hadn't loved Gray, at least not in the beginning. If he had remained faithful, that love may never have faded. A part of it never would, because he had given her two amazing children, but there was no denying the fact she was happier now than she had ever been in her life. It seemed a part of her heart had always belonged to Brash.

"It can be real," she said slowly. "And yes, it can last." She glanced up at her husband and was rewarded with a warm smile.

"But if it's for the wrong person, that's gotta suck," the teen observed. With that revelation, he shoveled in another forkful of spaghetti.

"Why did he bury the box? What happened to the girl?" Megan quizzed him.

"Did he never get over her?" his twin asked.

"He's been married at least twice, so I guess he fell in love with other women. But I think he never got over his first love. Not really. He buried the box before he went away to Viet Nam. The house belonged to his parents then, but I guess at some point, it became his. I don't know if he forgot he buried the box, or if he was hiding it from his wives. But the look in his eyes when I asked him about it... He still has it bad for her. I know it. He can't stand seeing it again, but he can't stand to get rid of it, either."

"Whatever is in the box," his mother said, "it obviously holds painful memories for him."

"So, you think it's possible? To fall in love when you're only seventeen, and still be in love with that person when you're like seventy-something?"

She was slow to answer. "I think it's possible to be in love with the memory of someone. The *idea* of someone. But people change. Years and circumstances change who we are and how we view the world. Sometimes, the people from our past simply no longer exist."

"But what if they do? What if this woman is still out there, and she's as lonely and miserable as he is?"

"Are you thinking what we've been thinking?" Bethani asked, her blue eyes twinkling. "Because Megan and I have been talking about it. We think we should find out who wrote these letters, and find her!"

"Yeah. I was kind of thinking the same thing," Blake admitted. The light was slower to build in his eyes, but it was there, just the same. "I thought about offering to help him find her."

His sisters squealed in delight.

Concern crinkled his parents' foreheads.

"I'm not sure about this, Blake," Maddy said with caution.

"Your mother's right. You need to give this careful consideration, son."

"Why's that?" he asked his stepfather. "I think not knowing has eaten into him all these years. At least it would give him closure."

"That's true, but that has to be his decision to make. What if you locate this woman, only to find out she died, long ago? Or that she's sick and dying now? He would lose her all over again."

"I hadn't thought about that."

"I think it's very kind and considerate of you, sweetie, wanting to bring this man closure," Madison said, laying her hand on her son's. "But this is something you really need to think through. If whatever happened in the past was terribly painful for him, he may not want to go through it again. What if you do find her, and she doesn't want to see him? What if she's moved on and is perfectly happy?"

"We could do it without him knowing," Bethani broke in. "We could locate her first, find out if she wanted to see him, and if she does, then we could tell him. That way, he'd never know if she didn't want to see him."

"Hey! That might work!" Blake said. Both sisters chimed in at once, excited to pitch their ideas.

"Hold it!" Brash said, his chief's voice calling them all to attention. The table fell silent.

In a much more controlled volume, he said, "Until you have this man's permission, you cannot and will not open that box. It's still his private property."

"Geez, I know that. I respect Mr. Ballard too much to snoop like that."

"Girls? You understand you can't open the box. Right?"

"We don't even know the combination," Megan reminded her father.

"We won't open it," Bethani assured him.

No one promised not to ask questions about the elusive Rosa from Mr. Ballard's past.

68

6

Like most small towns, The Sisters had the essential businesses required to function, plus a handful of specialty shops. It fell short, however, when it came to big box stores and malls. The nearest national chain and discount warehouse were less than an hour away, but Madison liked to stack her errands for better efficiency. It made for a long day in the summer heat, but why go to Bryan-College Station three times in one week, when she could spend a full day there and get everything done?

It helped that Genny had gone with her today; even the drudgeries of grocery shopping were more fun with her best friend along. Plus, the drive gave them ample time to visit. Between two husbands, three teenagers, Genny's busy restaurant, and Madison's steadily growing temporary services, the long-time friends found it increasingly difficult to find quality girl time.

Cutter and Genny had married on Valentine's Day, just six weeks before Madison and Brash. It was a first marriage for both Montgomerys, so Madison often found herself the voice of experience.

"I swear, the man isn't happy unless he's tracking mud or worse across my kitchen floor," Genny deplored.

"Learn to choose your battles," Madison advised. "Brash is bad about leaving the cap off the toothpaste, but I'm learning to just smile and put it back on myself. Believe me, there are worse things than leaving a cap off."

"Yes. Like tracking cow crap and soot across my floor," Genny said, crossing her arms over her chest for emphasis. Her blonde hair danced as she bobbed her head in a vigorous nod.

"You live on a ranch, Gen. Your husband is a volunteer firefighter. On top of that, he's a good man. Keep that in mind when he leaves footprints on your floor."

"Whose side are you on, anyway?" Genny grumbled, trying hard to maintain her frown.

"Just remember, he designed that kitchen with you in mind, long before you two were even dating. He revived his grandparents' old farmhouse for a woman he had yet to kiss. That took a lot of faith on his part. I think a love like that deserves a stray track or two, don't you?"

Genny was determined not to give up so easily. "Two, yes. Two dozen, no."

"I just have one thing to say about that." Madison kept her eyes straight ahead, but her mouth curled in a smirk. "Warming drawers."

Beside her, Genny stuck her tongue out.

"I saw that, Genesis Baker Montgomery. And you should be ashamed of yourself. The man put in your coveted warming drawers and a soapstone counter— pre-kiss, mind you—just because you liked them."

"And window seats," Genny mumbled grudgingly. "But!" she added, too stubborn to admit defeat just yet. Her finger wagged to make her point. "He had an ulterior motive with the warming drawers. He hoped I would keep them filled with apple turnovers."

"Again," Madison said in a sing-song voice. "Missing the point. He did it in hopes of sharing the home with you, Genny. Weeks, maybe even months, before you were an item."

With a cute pout that showcased her dimples, Genny grumbled playfully, "Shut up and drive."

"You know that you and I hit the jackpot with our men. They just don't come much better than Brash deCordova and Cutter Montgomery."

Genny clung to her stubborn streak. "You've made your point. Can we change the subject?"

"You're not usually so grumpy," Madison pointed out, but her voice softened. She knew the other couple was eager to start a family and had been trying, almost from day one of their marriage. "Still no luck with the little blue line?"

"Not yet. But we aren't giving up. It's only been a few months."

"You'll be a fantastic mother, Genny, but don't rush it. It will happen when it happens."

"I know." Her answer was lackluster as she stared out the window, watching scenery pass as Madison took the back way into town.

"Remember," Madison said, explaining the route, "I've got to swing by Granny Bert's and pick up a bag of fresh squash Uncle Jubal left for me."

The change of subject was appreciated. "Your uncle must have a huge garden this year. He brought three crates of squash and one of cucumbers to the restaurant the other day. He wouldn't let me pay for them. Said they'd go to waste if I didn't take them off his hands."

Madison nodded in agreement. "He sells what he can down at the *Five and Dime*, and the rest he gives away. Last week, he gave me tomatoes and zucchini."

"My customers are loving all the new recipes I've come up with," Genny commented.

The trek to Granny Bert's took them past Sycamore street, bringing to mind the town's newest resident. "Has the infamous Rose Belvedere been in the café yet?" Madison asked.

"Not yet. Have you met her?"

"Not yet."

"I hear she's a real looker. And that she always dresses up, even when she's home all day. Apparently, she doesn't go for the sweats and t-shirt ensemble like normal people. I know when *I'm* home, I sometimes stay in my jammies all day."

"Yes, but you have some of the cutest pajama sets in the universe," Madison responded.

Genny was known for her cute lounge sets, particularly those with witty sayings emblazoned on them. Before marrying Cutter, she said it was consolation for spending her nights alone. Her new husband continued to humor her, buying her sleep shirts that said, 'I'm so hot, I come with my own firefighter' and 'Zzz night is ours.' He bought himself one that said 'Moove over, heifer. That's my side of the bed.'

"Maybe she believes if she looks professional, she'll come across as a professional on the telephone," Madison mused.

"Unless you're on Zoom or FaceTime, no one can see what you're wearing." With a flick of her wrist, Genny said breezily, "I just fake it. One time, a bride-to-be called just as I was getting dressed, and I ended up negotiating the whole reception while wearing nothing but my bra and panties."

"Remind me not to FaceTime you without forewarning!" Maddy laughed, turning onto Live Oak. Her grandmother's large, rambling craftsman reigned at the end of the street. "Looks like Granny Bert's not home. She and Miss Sybille must still be at their Bunco game."

"Need help?"

"Nah. He leaves it in the Avocado, so I don't even have to go in. I'll just be a jiffy." She put the gearshift in park and closed the door behind her so the air conditioning wouldn't escape.

The Avocado Wonder was the nickname for the seventies-era, avocado-green refrigerator still in her grandmother's possession. Despite its outdated color, the machine worked as well as it ever had. It now resided in the garage as second-in-command for Granny Bert's refrigeration needs.

The detached garage angled away from the house, its entrance obscured from street view. Madison skirted around Sassy, her grandmother's over-sized motor home, to enter through the opened garage doors. She was already thinking of what would accompany the squash for dinner tonight.

Well before she reached the large green appliance, she noticed the interior shelves leaning against it. The Tupperware bowls, excess dry goods, and wheel of red rind cheese that usually occupied the second shelf were now scattered on the ground, along with a stray squash or two.

"Good grief!" she murmured aloud. "I hope Uncle Jubal didn't leave me *that* much squash! What on earth will I do with an entire refrigerator full of squash?"

She eased the door open with trepidation, envisioning yellow crookneck squash in every shape and size possible. She could feel the weight pressing against the door, straining to be set free.

"Great. Now I'll have squash rolling all around the garage floor. Why in the world did he leave—" The sentence died in her throat, replaced, instead, by a startled gasp. That immediately gave way to a scream.

It wasn't squash that tumbled from the interior of the refrigerator and fell in a heap at her feet.

It was a body.

And from the looks of his colorless skin, the man was decidedly dead.

"Slow down, Mrs. deCordova. Tell me again what happened."

Of all times for Brash to be at the county courthouse. I need him here with me, instead of Berry Perry, of all people!

Madison kept the thoughts to herself as she drew in a deep breath and started over. Again.

To her dismay, Officer Perry had answered her 911 call. As the oldest officer on the force, the man had years of experience and took a no-nonsense approach to the law, but he was sorely lacking in the personality department. It didn't help that he had been on the force long enough to remember Maddy and Genny's grand adventure to paint Seniors '95 on the water tower in giant, hot-pink letters back in the day. The nickname came from an incident that hadn't ended well for one berry-stained police uniform. As wife of his current boss, Madison was careful to never use the name aloud, but it sometimes crept into her thoughts.

"My uncle, Jubal Hamilton, left fresh squash for me in—"

"And when, exactly, did he leave the squash?" the officer interrupted. The same way he had the first three times she told the story.

"Like I told you, I can't remember if it was yesterday or the day before. You'll need to call him to confirm the exact day."

"Believe me, I will." He tugged and straightened his service belt, the way some men straightened their ties. It was a sure sign he was agitated. Or perhaps it was his way of relieving an itchy trigger finger.

"Anyway," she continued, trying hard to hide her impatience, "I stopped by to pick it up, and when I opened the door, his body tumbled out." She knew he was only doing his job, but the man's attitude put her on edge. His tone made it sound as if he suspected her of lying.

"*His* body? Do you know this man?" He pierced her with his sharp gaze.

Madison forgot all about her attempts to stay unflappable. "For the umpteenth time, no. I've never seen him before. But I can clearly see he's a male, so, yes, *his* body."

"It's just a strange way of putting it, ma'am. It makes it sound like you have a personal connection to the deceased."

"Well, he did fall on my foot," she pointed out, her voice dry. Despite her flippant reply, she couldn't help but shake said foot. If only she could shake the memory of that cold, lifeless body as it plopped onto her sandaled instep.

She darted another glance at the body, still awaiting pick-up by the county coroner. There was no splatter of blood. No visible wound of any kind. Nothing eluding to cause of death. Except for the unnatural absence of color to his skin and the fact that he had been stuffed inside a refrigerator, the man could have been sleeping.

Two things were for certain. One, Madison had never seen the sandy-haired man before. Two, whoever he was, the man was well dressed. He wore navy slacks, a white dress shirt, shiny loafers, and a plain red tie. It was difficult to tell in death, but she suspected he was a nice-looking man while alive.

Madison also noticed tan lines where a watch and ring should have been, but neither were there now. Her guess was that his wallet was missing, as well, leaving no means of identification.

The portly officer stated the obvious. "You seem to have a knack for finding dead bodies, Mrs. deCordova. Why do you suppose that is?"

Determined not to cringe, Madison's reply was stiff. "Unlucky, I suppose. In the wrong place, at the wrong time."

"And this time, that place happens to be in your grandmother's garage."

Fire flashed in Madison's hazel eyes. "Surely, you aren't suggesting Granny Bert had anything to do with this. My grandmother is a pillar of society. I can assure you, she had nothing to do with a dead body being stuffed inside her refrigerator. A refrigerator that is freely accessible from the street, I might add. The garage doors are wide open. Anyone could have walked in here."

"What?" he taunted. "And crawled inside the fridge for a little nap? It may be hot outside, but it's not that hot."

A door slammed nearby, and there was the sound of hurried feet. Even before she reached the police tape, Granny Bert's voice rang loud and clear. "What in tarnation is the meaning of this? Why are there cop cars and fire engines all around my house? What is going on?"

"You can stop right there, Mrs. Cessna," Officer Perry said, motioning for her not to cross the barrier.

"I'll do no such thing, Otis Perry!" she snapped. With the ease of someone decades younger, the elderly woman dipped under the tape and stomped forward. "I'll remind you that this is my property. Tell me what you're doing on it."

"I'm investigating a suspicious death. *That's* what I'm doing."

Granny Bert turned her perplexed gaze to her granddaughter. "Madison? What is he talking about?"

"I came by to pick up the squash Uncle Jubal left for me. Instead, I found *that*." She stepped aside as she pointed, allowing her grandmother a full view of the body slumped in front of the refrigerator door.

"Is that a dead man?" The older woman didn't sound as horrified as she did confused.

"Unfortunately."

"Do you recognize this man, Bertha?" Officer Perry demanded.

"Well, being as all I can see from here is his backside, no, I can't say that I do."

When she stepped forward for a better look, the officer cautioned her not to contaminate the scene. She gave him a withering look before getting close enough to peer down at the dead man's face.

"He does look vaguely familiar," Granny Bert murmured, trying to place where she had seen him before.

"Who is he? Where's he from? How do you know him?" Otis Perry pelted her with his sharp inquiry.

"I didn't say I knew who he was," the old woman snapped. "But I do think I've seen him before."

"Why was he stuffed in your refrigerator?"

"In my—" The surprise on her face gave way to irritation. She spotted the refrigerator's previous contents scattered out on the floor with narrowing eyes. "Is that why my cheese is out here on the concrete? Do you have any idea how much a wheel of that stuff costs these days?"

"There's a dead man not two feet in front of you,

and that's all you have to say? You're more hysterical about your cheese ruining than you are at seeing a dead body." There was accusation in the officer's words.

"I don't get hysterical, Otis Perry," she informed him, her tone indignant. "And you seem to forget I served three terms as Justice of the Peace. I've seen more than one dead body in my time. Ones a far sight worse than this one."

"Step away from the body, Bertha." His voice was stern as he readjusted his belt.

With a hauteur expression on her wrinkled face, she did as told. It was more for her own comfort than per his command; she found no pleasure looking at death, no matter how many times she had seen it.

"Who is this man, Bertha?"

"Is your hearing going, along with your hair? I told you. I don't know."

"But you say you've seen him."

"I can't be for certain, but he looks familiar. Why is he here in my garage? And who threw my cheese and cornmeal down on the floor?"

The officer wasn't pleased when she turned the questions around on him. "*I'm* the one asking questions here."

"Then ask someone who knows more about it than I do. I just got home." She indicated the purse dangling from her arm as if it were all the proof she needed.

"Where have you been?"

"Playing Bunco. Our Tuesday afternoon game was postponed to Thursday because Lavonne Wynn was still recovering from cataract surgery. Not that it helped her any," the older woman said with a disgruntled sniff. "She cost us the win at the head table when she rolled a Bunco and didn't even know it. Thought one of the sixes was a five. Verna Bishop swooped in and grabbed the dice, and just like that, we lost." Granny Bert was a fierce competitor and hated losing.

"And your brother? Have you spoken to him lately?"

"I spoke to him on the phone yesterday. The day before, he brought a big mess of squash over and put some of it in the Avocado Wonder here. I suspect that's what my granddaughter is here for, to pick up her share." She nodded toward Madison, before moving her gaze on to Genny. "Genny, did you get some? He brought plenty."

"We're not here to distribute squash, Bertha," the officer cautioned.

The women all but ignored him. Madison confirmed her grandmother's statement. "That's how I found the body."

"Again?" Granny Bert shook her head in amazement. "Girl, what is it with you and dead bodies? You're like a dead body magnet."

The police officer took a step forward, his expression grim. "My point, exactly," he ground out.

Bertha Cessna was taller than most women. Otis Perry was shorter than most men. She peered down at him with a condescending glare. "Are you plumb out of your mind, man?" she demanded. "You aren't suggesting my granddaughter had something to do with this man's death, are you? Because if you are…"

"Actually, Granny Bert," Madison broke in, sending the officer a cool look, "we were having this very conversation when you walked up. Except, then, *I* was defending *you*."

Her gaze turned acrid. "You think *I* had something to do with this?"

"It is your refrigerator," the officer pointed out.

"In an open garage. Where anyone could wander in off the street."

The words, almost the very same as those that fell from Madison's lips, made the officer suspicious. He squinted his eyes, his gaze bouncing between the two of them. "Did you two rehearse your story?"

For the first time, Genny spoke up. Her face was still pale from the gruesome discovery, but her blue eyes blazed with fury as she propped her hands upon curvy hips and stared him down. "Oh, for heaven's sake, Berry Perry!" She had no qualms about using the nickname aloud. "Even a rookie officer could spot the obvious. There's absolutely nothing to stop someone—anyone!—from walking in here off the street. If opportunity is your only lead, then the entire town is suspect. Including you."

He zeroed in on only one part of her tirade. "What name did you just call me?"

Before Genny was forced to answer, she was saved by her husband's appearance. His rubber bunker boots made an odd squeak as he sauntered across the concrete. Despite the easy way he carried himself, she recognized the stubborn set of Cutter's jaw. He obviously overheard the exchange, or enough of it to know Perry was giving the women trouble.

"I've got traffic control in place," Cutter Montgomery reported. "The street is blocked off except for residents and first responders."

Cutter was chief of the volunteer fire department, which often worked hand in hand with law enforcement. With only three squad cars plus Brash's new SUV, the police department was short of vehicles—and officers—when it came to traffic control. The big red firetrucks served the purpose well.

"Fine, Montgomery. That's all for now."

Unaccustomed to taking orders from the man,

Cutter ignored the dismissal. He knew better than to antagonize him, so he made no direct attempt to interfere with the investigation. He stood quietly in the background, allowing the man to continue his line of questioning. If he dared.

Officer Perry wisely chose another course, but the tops of his eyes glowed red with suppressed anger.

"Have any of you seen any strangers around here lately?"

"No more than usual," Granny Bert said.

"That's not exactly right," Madison spoke up, contradicting her grandmother's statement. "Remember? A few weeks ago, right around the time I was recovering the chair for Brash's birthday, that black car kept circling the block."

"It drove up and down your street, too, as I recall." Her grandmother shrugged with no apparent concern. "Kids, most likely."

"What about the woman?" Genny asked. "Didn't you have to get the water hose after some nosy woman who was looking in your window?"

The memory cracked a smile across the older woman's face. "You should have seen her run! I don't know who she was or what she wanted, but one swipe of the sprinkler and she was soaked through."

"Who was this woman?" the officer wanted to know.

"No idea. Hadn't seen her before, or after. Of course, she had on big sunglasses and a scarf around her head, so I really couldn't tell much about her. She took off down the street, headed toward the woods there."

The Cessna house sat on three city lots, allowing for a large yard, a flourishing flower garden, and a wooded area lining the end of the block. Madison nodded toward the woods now.

"Those woods would make nice cover for someone waiting on the opportunity to sneak into the garage," she pointed out.

"You may consider yourself some sort of amateur sleuth," Officer Perry said, his voice condescending, "but *amateur* is the key word. Leave this to the professionals. A man is dead. That's nothing to play around with."

His words reminded them of the seriousness of the situation. He was right. A man was dead, his body still crumbled on the floor just feet away. In silent accord, all three women took a step backward, their eyes drawn to the corpse.

"Maddy?"

She heard Brash's voice calling from beyond the garage. "Maddy, are you okay?" She heard him speak to someone out of sight. "Where's my wife?" he demanded. There was a low murmur of a reply, and Brash burst into the garage, dodging the caution tape.

Seeing her husband weakened Madison's stoic veneer. She wanted nothing more than to hurl herself against his broad chest and take comfort in his embrace. The tears she had held at bay pricked her eyelids, but she refused to give Berry Perry the satisfaction of seeing her turn into a hysterical mess.

Out of respect for her pride, Brash read the warning in her eyes and held back.

Her chin lifted ever so slightly as she said, "Officer Perry was inquiring about how a body came to be in Granny Bert's refrigerator."

Doing an about-face, Brash walked to the yawning cavity of the garage's entrance. He noted the heavy network of cobwebs stretched across the overhead door. The silky, dust-covered threads wove around the side and encompassed hinges and tracks, knitting a trail onto the ceiling. That, alone, was evidence that the doors had been open for an extended period. He made a point of staring at the street out front to the spot where he stood, mentally judging the distance. He made a similar survey of the trees in the distance.

Marching back to the group gathered inside, he issued his findings. "It seems to me that virtually anyone could have accessed the garage from the street, the backyard, or even those woods there."

They all pretended not to notice the way Officer Perry bristled, his face flushing with anger, as his boss continued, "I hate to say this, but, Granny Bert, you have zero security measures in place. You don't even close your garage doors, much less keep them locked."

"Until today, I had no reason," she pointed out.

"Until today," Brash murmured. He walked over to the prone body, studying it from all angles. His knee popped as he squatted down for a better look. He took out his cell phone and took a dozen photos from every angle. He called over his shoulder for his officer to join him.

Cutter came forward to engulf his wife in his arms and to offer all three women a human shield from the unpleasant sight behind him. After a moment, Brash murmured something to his co-worker, and Perry reluctantly returned to the group.

"You ladies are free to go. I think I have enough for now. Mrs. Cessna, I'll have to ask you to stay out of the garage until further notice."

Granny Bert pinned him with her sharp gaze. "You let me know when you've scoured the inside of that refrigerator and disinfected the entire area."

"Now, see here..." the officer objected, tugging at his service belt again.

"Officer Perry," Brash broke in calmly, "I need you to look at something."

With a sniff of importance, the officer rushed to

his boss' side, eager to prove his worth.

Over Perry's shoulder, Brash winked at his wife and gave them the all-clear to go.

7

Madison and Genny stayed with Granny Bert until the elderly woman shooed them away, saying they made her nervous with all their well-intended chatter. The silent looks passing between them added to her discomfort. The older woman insisted she was fine, even though someone had invaded her garage and stuffed her refrigerator with a corpse. She refused the offer to go home with Madison or to let one of the kids spend the night with her.

Her son Joe Bert had arrived by then, as well as Jubal and Lerlene Hamilton. Officer Perry gave the older man the fifth degree, only to discover questioning him was as maddening as questioning his sister. Both had as many questions for him as he had for them. Jubal wanted to know what had become of the squash he had delivered, suggesting the man wasn't competent enough to notice it missing.

Madison and Genny slipped out as Granny Bert lamented the loss of her prized red rind cheese.

It was late when Brash came home that evening. Madison saved him a plate but encouraged the kids to go ahead with dinner. She had already gone upstairs when she heard him come in.

"What a week," he groaned, finally making it up to

their bedroom. He plopped into the chair Madison had given him for his birthday, his shirt already half off.

"It has been full of surprises," Madison murmured in sympathy. "Any clues on who the body belonged to?"

He confirmed her suspicions. "No ID. Too young for hearing aids or dentures, so can't trace those. No signs of blunt force trauma or defense wounds. No skin under his nails. No obvious stress factors that would induce death. For all we know, he died of natural causes. We won't know for sure until the coroner does an autopsy. That could take weeks."

"Even if he died of natural causes, someone went to a lot of trouble to hide his body. Do you think he's the man from the rug? I know the eyewitness reports were sketchy, but now that there's a body..."

"I went back to Miss Belvedere's house this evening and spoke with her. She adamantly denied anyone else being at the house other than the movers, or of anyone being there before she arrived."

"Not even the real estate agent?"

"She freely offered the name of the agent and agency. I have a call in to them, but it's after hours. I don't expect to hear from them until tomorrow morning."

Madison was quiet as Brash tugged off his boots and set them aside. When she spoke, her tone was pensive. "Wonder why Granny Bert's?"

"Opportunity. As I said, literally anyone can access her garage."

"Plus, it's only two blocks from Sycamore. They could have easily hidden the body in the woods and moved it to the Avocado at the first opportunity," Madison surmised.

"Keeping the body cold will make determining the

time of death harder. A fact I'm sure the killer knew."

"I guess you could talk to the people who live between Sycamore and Live Oak and see if anyone remembers seeing the van."

Brash smiled proudly at his wife, holding his arm out in invitation. "You're pretty amazing, you know that?

"How's that?" She settled gingerly on his knee, but he pulled her in close.

"I know it had to have been quite a shock today, opening the refrigerator and having a dead body fall out."

"On my foot," she told him. Remembering the terrible sensation, she pulled away. Her face scrunched in horror. "It touched my foot, Brash!"

He made a sympathetic sound in his throat as he pulled her back in place. "I know, sweetheart. And I'm sorry you were the one to find it."

"*Again*," she wailed. "Do you know how many dead bodies I had seen in my lifetime, before moving back here to The Sisters? Not a single one. None that weren't already in a casket and made to look decent. Then I move back here, and all that changes."

"At least this one was in good condition." He offered the small consolation as he rubbed his hand along her arm, covering the goosebumps that danced beneath his calloused palm. These weren't the kind that stirred with quickened breath and anticipation. These were the kind derived of clenched breath and dread.

"True. But you should have heard Blake when I broke the news to the kids. He already calls me a dead body magnet. He's says I've attracted another one now."

"That's one of the reasons I think you're so amazing. A lot of people would be hysterical at the sight of a dead body. You just take it in stride. You're already thinking of ways to identify it and find out how it got in Granny Bert's refrigerator."

Her voice was low, but it held a decided note of steel. "Perry insinuated we had something to do with it. That *we* may have killed the man and stuffed him there."

"Perry is a good officer. He's thorough, which means questioning everyone and everything. He's only doing his job."

"I know," she admitted grudgingly, resenting her husband's calm reply. He had an annoying habit of keeping his cool, even in an emotionally charged argument. "But if I killed the man, would I have put him in my grandmother's garage and then called the police? How stupid does he think I am?"

His low chuckle rumbled within his chest, reverberating onto hers. "He knows neither one of you had anything to do with it. He had to ask, and he had to put it in his report. You both are already cleared."

A begrudged grunt lingered in her voice. "That's good to know."

Brash leaned his head back, a few silver threads revealed among the dark auburn of his hair. He heaved out a weary breath. "Of all times for me to be leaving. I'm debating whether or not to cancel."

Madison sat up in protest. "You can't cancel! It's *your* camp!"

"I know. And I don't want to. I look forward to it, almost as much as those kids do." The disappointment was evident in his handsome face.

For the past six years, Brash had sponsored a summer football camp for underprivileged youth. The ten-day camp was held successionally, five days each in Waco and College Station, honoring his ties to Baylor and Texas A&M. Between a brief stint in the

NFL and his career now in law enforcement, he had coached at both universities. His youth program offered sportsmanship, camaraderie, skills (both athletic and social), life-long friendships, and one-on-one mentoring to kids who often didn't get the encouragement needed for a successful life. Brash personally made certain the children were well-fed during their stay, knowing, that, too, wasn't a luxury they always had at home. He went the extra mile in keeping up with the kids after the camp, and, for those who truly excelled, there was a scholarship awaiting them when they graduated.

"You have no choice, Brash. You *are* the camp. You're the reason those kids go there. You can't let them down."

"But after today..."

"You said it yourself. Officer Perry, despite his non-existent people skills, is a good, thorough officer. He can handle the investigation."

"And like you said, he lacks people skills. Sometimes, people have pertinent information to share, but they refuse to share it with him."

"You have two other officers. They can collect the information."

"*Or,*" Brash said, allowing the word to linger into a sentence of its own.

Maddy saw the gleam in his brown eyes. "Or?" she questioned.

"Or, I could do what I should have done in the first place. Let you and your little network tackle the case from a different angle."

Eyes wide, her tone was slightly less than flabbergasted. "You'd do that?"

A shadow of doubt moved into his eyes but cleared quickly enough. "Yes," he said. The word almost sounded defeated. "Unless Perry digs something up, we have nothing to tie Rose Belvedere's appearance in town to this dead body. We can question her again, but we have no grounds for a search warrant. My gut tells me she's connected, but I won't be here for almost two weeks. The best I can do is turn you ladies loose on her so you can find out who she is, where she comes from." His sigh was heavy. "We both know Granny Bert has connections that go far beyond our meager departmental resources. Between you, Granny Bert, and Genny, you can make some innocent inquiries."

"In other words, we can collect the gossip, and your department can collect the legal details."

Brash arched his brow in his trademark expression. "Isn't that how it usually goes? Even when I expressly ask you not to?"

In reply, Maddy wrinkled her nose. "Do I have to answer that?"

"I'll settle for a kiss."

"In that case..."

One kiss led to two. As the third kiss heated, she pulled away just enough to ask, "What if Perry gives us trouble?"

His look was a mix of innocence and mischief. "All I want you to do is ask a few questions. Get to know our new neighbor. Since when is a Welcome Wagon illegal?"

"Is that what we're calling ourselves now?" she smirked.

"Call it what you like, but it gives you an in."

"I like the way you think, Mr. D," she said, moving in for another kiss.

The humor fell from his voice. "I'm thinking it's going to be a very long, lonely two weeks without you."

"Both towns are close enough for me to visit. You'll

have your own room, right?"

"Yes."

"Then I can sneak over for a night." She dropped kisses between the words. "One night in Waco, one in College Station."

"Like a booty call?" She felt his smile against her mouth.

"Call it what you like," her lips curled in response as she returned his words, "but it gives me an in."

"Woo-hoo!" Genny said, pumping a fist into the air. "Soup 'n Snoop is back in business!"

It was a joke between the friends. Genny claimed it was the perfect partnership; she could provide the soup (nourishment), Maddy could provide the snooping (details). One-stop shopping, she called it, particularly since Maddy credited the back booth at *New Beginnings* as her first official, unofficial office. Until she bought the Big House from her grandmother for a paltry five thousand dollars, she met all her clients at the café.

"Brash said to call it what we liked, but I don't think he had that in mind," Maddy admitted, wrinkling her nose. "Soup and Salutations, maybe."

"Sounds like Soup and Salad," Granny Bert snorted. "And who says 'salutations' these days? Same folks who ride in a wagon, that's who! We need something snappy. Something that reflects youth and vitality."

"Says the eighty-one-year-old," Maddy drawled.

"Darn tootin'. But I'm a young eighty-one, unlike some of us at the table, forty years my junior." She pinned her granddaughter with an accusing glare, challenging her to deny the claim.

With a bright voice, Genny broke into their stare down. "So, what's the modern-day equivalent of a Welcome Wagon?"

"How should I know?" Granny Bert scoffed in good nature. "I came over on the Pina Colada."

The other two snickered at the comment. If Columbus had a ship with that name, that's the one she would have chosen.

"How about the Welcome Warriors?" Madison suggested.

"Definite possibilities." Genny bobbed her blonde head.

The name wasn't quite right. Madison drummed her fingers in thought. "Brash told her we had an active neighborhood watch program. Maybe we could work with that."

"Nosy Neighbors?" Granny Bert suggested.

"Too direct."

"You mean too honest."

"That, too."

"Neighbors Helping Neighbors?" Genny suggested.

"That's a good one," her friends agreed.

They threw out several more possibilities, some too silly to get past the giggle on their lips. The more Gennydoodle cookies they ate, the sillier the suggestions.

"I'm getting a sugar rush," Granny Bert groused.

"Sounds like a rock band," Genny shrugged, "but I guess it could be a welcome committee."

"What if we just went with that?" Maddy asked. "It's simple and direct. States the purpose. The Welcome Committee."

"It's about as boring as the Welcome Mat. *Step right on me.*" Seeing the look her granddaughter threw her, Granny Bert snapped, "Get that look off your face. It could freeze that way."

"I used to believe you when you told me that, you know. I went around practicing different smiles just in case it was the one that froze on my face."

"That was the purpose. You had such a long, unhappy face as a child. You needed to smile more."

"It was hard, being the only adult in the house."

"But at the age of eight?"

Madison shrugged. "You know my parents. You raised one of them."

"I'm just glad to see my boy finally decided to grow up. Only took sixty years."

Genny glanced at her watch. "We still haven't decided on a name to call ourselves."

"Neighbors Anonymous?" Granny Bert cracked. *"You don't have to drink here, but it helps!"* She held her coffee cup up in salute.

"Brash says she's obsessed with roses," Maddy murmured. "Maybe we could come up with something she found impossible to resist."

"Men in uniform?"

"Granny Bert!"

"Just sayin'."

"Petal Pals? Blooming Buddies?" Genny thought aloud.

"Blooming Idiots?" Granny Bert countered.

Madison gave her a huge frown. "That sugar really did go to your head."

"Maybe it was the three cups of coffee I washed it down with."

"In that case, make it the Floating Blossoms," Genny corrected.

"Good one, girl!" the older woman cackled. "But not on a full bladder."

"Okay, we need to settle this," Madison said, folding her hands in a serious pose. "What were our best suggestions?"

"We should have been writing these down," her best friend said in retrospect. She glanced down at her watch again. "I need to get back to work soon. Honestly, I'm good with whatever you two decide. Sisters stand together, right?"

"That's it!" Madison said, her face lighting up. "Sisters, Forever!"

"That's perfect!" The name was dimple-approved. She panned the imaginary slogan in the air. *"Even if you leave, the Sisters will be part of you forever."*

"Nothing like a good, old-fashioned haunting," Granny Bert said, but her smile was endorsement enough.

"Now that that's settled, do we have any new information? Granny, have you learned anything new?"

"Not really. I'm thinking about going down to visit Nelda in the old folk's home. The girls and I could take Sassy for an overnight trip." By girls, she meant Sybille and Wanda. "I hear there's a new club in Conroe called *The Joint.* Sounds like the kind of place where they have good country music and cold beer on tap. Good for dancing."

"Could be a different kind of joint," Madison pointed out.

Granny Bert shook her gray head with regret. "Then I'd better keep Wanda out of it. We don't want a repeat performance."

Madison didn't dare ask what her grandmother meant by that statement. She quickly redirected the conversation, before Granny Bert volunteered further information. "Do you think Miss Nelda will be more alert in person?"

"I'm hoping seeing us will jog her memory. We used to play Bingo together over at the hall. She was a fierce competitor. Had a knack for getting a blackout."

"Be sure and ask her what happened to her house. Find out if she's renting or selling."

"I know the ropes, girl. Some say I braided them, myself," she boasted.

"If that's another way of saying you're nosy, I agree."

"I get solid information, now don't I?"

She had her on that one. Madison had no choice but to agree. "That, you do."

"How soon do you think you can go?" Genny asked. "I'll bake the cookies this weekend, so I can deliver them on Monday."

"I'll have to call the girls. If they're free, we can go this weekend." Wrinkles pushed across her cheek as her lips puckered. A note of ridicule slipped into her voice. "That is, if Wanda can pull herself away from her new beau."

"Miss Wanda has a boyfriend?" Genny asked. It was the first she had heard of it.

Madison was surprised by the news as well. Her employee usually kept her abreast of any gossip he was privy to. "Derron hasn't mentioned it, either. Who is he?"

"Some fella she met online." Granny Bert huffed in disgust. "She stays up all hours of the night, talking to the man."

"How did they meet?"

"She signed up on one of those dating websites. Silver Partners, or some such nonsense."

Genny's brow puckered. "I thought she swore off men when her husband of fifty years did her dirty."

"You mean when she found him *doing* the dirty. With Pearl Simpson, of all people," Granny Bert snickered. She shook her head, a smile of wonder replacing the previous frown. "I sure wish I could have seen her pull that shotgun out and chase a butt-naked Pearl down the street! The gun was empty, of course, but Pearl didn't know it. Nelda saw the whole thing, mind you." She rapped her knuckles on the table with a new thought. "You know, that may just be the thing that jogs her memory."

"If Miss Wanda goes with you," Madison advised, "you may want to avoid that subject. I doubt she wants to be reminded of such a betrayal. And in her own house." The thought sent a repulsive shiver through her shoulders.

Grayson, at least, had had the decency to buy his mistress a place of her own. He had mortgaged the house he lived in with Madison and the twins to do so, but at least he hadn't brought his lover into their home.

"Oh, she tells a hilarious version of the event," her grandmother assured her. "Very descriptive, I might add."

Madison stopped her with a splayed palm. "Please. Don't."

Granny Bert sniffed at the snub, but continued, "If she's too busy sending all those little symbols and smiley faces—"

"Emojis," Genny supplied.

"Yeah, those, too." She waved away the interruption, until it reminded her of a new story. "By the way, those things need to come with an instruction manual. We went to the Dairy Queen in Riverton for ice cream last week, so of course Wanda had to share the big news with lover boy. She used that little brown swirl to say we were eating soft serve." Her frown pushed out a new wave of wrinkles. "Turns out, that's not the ice cream symbol."

Over her companion's giggles, she went on, "If the girls don't want to go, I'll just take the Buick and go by myself."

"Brash leaves tonight, so I'll have the whole weekend to work my end of it." At the thought of being separated from her husband for ten whole days, her voice turned glum. "I won't have anything better to do."

"It's not like you have teenagers in the house, or anything," her grandmother reminded her.

"Bethani is going to a family reunion with Megan and the Aikmans, so it will just be me and Blake. And he and Jamal will probably go fishing when he gets off work. *Marvin Gardens* closes at noon on Saturdays."

"Will they see that famous cousin of Matthew's?" Granny Bert wanted to know, referring to Megan's stepfather.

"Maybe. The reunion is up near Dallas. But I think he's making a surprise appearance at one of Brash's camps. Waco, I think he said."

"That reminds me," Granny Bert said. "Nelda loves football. She's a die-hard Cowboys fan. If nothing else, that may spark a memory. She threw one whopper of a bowl party in '78, the year the Cowboys broke the Broncos." She chuckled at the memory, slapping her knee in glee. "That was one heck of a party, I can tell you that!"

"Have they released your garage yet, or is the tape still up?" Genny asked.

"Still up. Jubal and I still haven't figured out what happened to all that squash. He doesn't much favor the thought of feeding a killer."

"Maybe they dumped it somewhere."

"Maybe. But that would be a darn shame. It's bad enough that I had to lose my cheese and cornmeal. I was planning on frying a big mess of squash this weekend, and that cornmeal would have come in handy."

"But if you go to Conroe, you won't be frying squash," Genny pointed out.

"True."

"Did you ever place where you'd seen that man before?" Madison asked.

"Not yet. It's been burning a hole in my memory, but I can't quite see my way through. It will come to me, though. I know it will."

"I like your optimism."

"I've always been an optimist, you know that. I choose to see the glass as half-full, not half-empty." She tipped her coffee cup over and peered into the bottom. "But this cup is bone dry for the third time, so I reckon I'd better visit the little girl's room before I go."

Madison refolded her hands, calling their informal meeting to a close. "So. We all know our parts. I'll make up some cards and labels that say Sisters, Forever to add authenticity. Genny, you'll bake the cookies. Granny, you'll reach out to Miss Nelda." Their plans were taking shape. "Phase One can officially begin."

8

With the house empty on Saturday morning, Madison settled in at her desk. She made a logo for their non-existent community welcome wagon—aka Sisters, Forever—and printed out a handful of business cards. The stickers would go on Genny's delicious baked goods.

If Rose Belvedere turned out to be innocent, at least their newest resident would be well fed while they probed into her life story. It was the only positive spin Madison could put on their intrusive inquiry, particularly when it felt more like a full-out assault.

Perhaps she was more sensitive than most. After last year's exposé on *Home Again*, she knew what it was like to have one's privacy invaded. The 'fans' were the worst. Blinded by stardust, they forgot that the Reynolds were normal, ordinary people, trying to pull their life together after a tragic loss. The very people claiming to adore them overstepped appropriate boundaries by a mile.

Banishing the thought from her mind, Madison called residents who lived between Sycamore and Live Oak. She concentrated most of her efforts on Pecan, the street between them. It backed up to the woods and gardens surrounding Granny Bert's.

It made for a busy morning.

"Hello, Mrs. Bishop. I'm not sure you remember me. I'm Madison deCordova—"

"Madison! Of course, I remember you. I taught you in the eighth grade. You were always such a bright student. Bright enough to marry the most eligible bachelor in town, I might add. Congratulations on your marriage to our chief of police. He was an excellent student, too, as I recall."

"Thank you. I appreciate that."

"We couldn't come to the wedding because Duke came down with a bad case of gout. I hear we missed quite the event!"

Inwardly, Madison cringed. Why did people always dredge up the only stain on an otherwise glorious occasion? "Yes, ma'am. It was a lovely wedding and a grand reception, right up until Mr. Barrett died."

"That was such a shame. But I'm sure you didn't call to talk about your wedding. What can I do for you, dear?"

"As you may know, I have a business here in town—"

"Oh, yes! *In a Pinch*. George Gail Burton can't say enough nice things about you. And you were sweet enough to hire Darlene Mullins' boy, even after all the mean things she did to you. You're a good girl, Madison Cessna. Just like your granddaddy."

She remembered how Granny Bert always claimed the former schoolteacher had a crush on Grandpa Joe. Hearing no mention of her grandmother now, just Grandpa Joe, she had to wonder if it were true.

"Joe Cessna was a fine man," the woman carried on. "And quite a looker, too. If I had met him before Duke..."

Unsure of how to respond, Madison stumbled

through her practiced spiel. "Uhm, yes, ma'am. Well, the—the reason I'm calling is that I have a client thinking of moving here to The Sisters. He's—"

A surprised squeal broke into her speech. "Another new resident? Why, one just moved here this week! When did we suddenly become such a mecca? Once the television cameras finally left, I thought things had settled down. You don't have another new project in the works, do you?"

"Me?" The question caught her by surprise.

"The cameras came for the Big House, and then for the wedding. They hung around to catch another glimpse of your hunk of a husband without his shirt on. I thought maybe you were bringing them back again."

"If it were up to me," Madison assured her in a firm voice, "all television cameras would be banned in The Sisters. But, back to my client. He's looking for a reputable moving company, and I wanted to know if you could recommend one."

"Why, no, dear. We haven't moved in thirty years. And when we did, we just piled everything in Duke's Chevy pickup and hauled it over. There was no need to waste money on a moving van."

"I understand that a couple of moving vans passed your house earlier this week. Do you happen to remember seeing them?"

"I recall seeing one. It looked like one of those do-it-yourself kinds you rent, but it looked a few years past its prime. It was a dinged-up white, with faded orange and blue writing on the side. I don't know much about it, but I don't think I would recommend that particular truck."

"Did you happen to see it stop along the street anywhere?"

"Only at the stop sign. A lot of folks run the one on

Third, you know. You should mention that to your husband. He may want to post an officer here to catch offenders."

"I'll try to pass that information along," Madison promised vaguely.

"What kind of work will your new client be doing here?" Mrs. Bishop inquired. "I didn't realize anyone was hiring right now. I hear the new tenant in Nelda Goldberg's house is a computer whiz of some sort, so she'll be working from home. My nephew installed her internet service. Said she needed all sorts of extra gizmos and gigahertz and what not."

"Oh?" she asked, straightening in interest. This could be a possible lead. "I may be looking for a new service," she fibbed. "Who does your nephew work for?"

"I don't remember the name of the company, but I can get it for you, if you like."

"Yes, please. That would be lovely."

One more bit of ammo for the assault. The guilty thought nibbled at her conscience. As she thanked her former schoolteacher and hung up, Madison jotted down what little information she had gleaned before placing the next call.

"Hello, Mrs. Hadley. This is Madison deCordova. This may sound like a silly question, but—"

"No, no, not at all," the woman interrupted her. "If you're calling to see about getting more squash to replace the mess you lost, I have plenty. It's a shame someone took yours. Even worse, they left another dead body for you to find!"

There was no such thing as keeping a secret in this town. No such thing as censoring tasteless comments. Madison shook her head in wonder. Had everyone forgotten that a man had died? That she had had the misfortune of finding a lifeless body? And did they really have to keep count of how many times it had happened in the past?

"It was quite the shock," she admitted in a solemn voice.

"How much squash would you like, dear? Do you need any tomatoes? Our garden has done very well this year."

"I'm not calling about vegetables, Mrs. Hadley. I'm calling to ask if you saw the moving vans in town this past Tuesday."

"You mean the ones that left from Nelda Goldberg's with a dead body inside? Are you wondering if I saw them circle around and dump the body at Bertha's?"

She could have made an objection. She could have pointed out that reports of a dead body inside were still unconfirmed. She could have pointed out that, if there *had* been a body inside, it wasn't necessarily the one she had found.

She could have done any of those things.

She did none. It was easier to sigh and murmur an agreement.

"I wish I could say yes," the woman on the phone told her. "It's the only thing that makes sense. Strangers and dead bodies are few and far between around here, so it's doubtful we would have both in one week, unless they were connected. But the truth is, I didn't see a thing."

The next three phone calls went much the same. One person remembered seeing both moving trucks but said they sailed down the street, never to be seen again. Another saw only the larger of the two trucks. She claimed it circled the block one time, before driving away in what struck her as a hurry. She assumed they had taken a wrong turn and were making up for lost time.

The third person hadn't been home on Tuesday because he had an ingrown toenail cut out. He then proceeded to tell her about the new technique the podiatrist used. He may have seen lights later that evening in the woods across the street, but he wasn't sure; his doctor warned against mixing alcohol with pain medication, but after his wife went to bed, he indulged in his usual nightcap. The bourbon hit his head faster than normal, so the lights could have been in reaction to disobeying doctor's orders.

Sighing as she hung up the phone, she heard the alarm's familiar ding, alerting her to an open door. Blake's voice soon came through the intercom, letting her know he was home. After a shower and lunch, he and Jamal were headed to the deCordova Ranch to fish.

That left Madison with the afternoon to herself, free to snoop.

Despite the heat, Madison ventured out into the sunny day. She wanted to see for herself the best vantage point for covertly accessing her grandmother's garage.

In a town as small and as nosy as Juliet, someone had to have seen something. After studying the garage from different angles, she decided the most likely possibilities to have witnessed an intruder were the neighbors behind Granny Bert, the neighbors catty-corner across from her, and Eloy Palacios. His house on Second Avenue sat across the street from the wooded corner.

She started at the house catty-corner to her grandmother's. The childless couple had moved there about five years ago, but Granny Bert claimed they were still outsiders.

An unsmiling man cracked the door only wide enough to snarl, "I ain't buying nothin'."

"That works out well," Madison replied with a hint of a smile, "because I'm not selling anything."

"Then what do you want? I ain't donating nothin', either."

"And I'm not collecting."

The door eased open a fraction of an inch. "What do you want?"

"There was a disturbance across the street this week," she began, pointing toward her grandmother's house.

"I heard about it. A body was stuffed in Bertha's freezer. The man's nose was froze plumb off." He groused as if it were old news. "What about it?"

Not bothering to correct him, she went on, "Did you happen to see any unusual comings and goings earlier in the week?"

"With that one, there's always comings and goings. Doesn't she know a woman her age ought to be at home, and not out roaming the countryside? Whatever happened to knitting as a pastime?"

Madison had to bite her tongue to keep from chastising the man's outdated notions about senior citizens, particularly *her* senior citizen. On top of that, Don Beevis was pushing sixty-five, himself.

She forced herself to exert a cheery smile. "I hear it's almost as popular as joining a neighborhood watch program."

If Madison had learned anything from her grandmother through the years, it was to 'go with the flow.' Granny Bert was a gifted storyteller (or con artist, depending on one's point of view) with a flair for drama. She could spin a believable tale from the slightest bit of yarn.

On a whim, Madison took a page from her grandmother's playbook, embellishing on the fly.

Bobbing her head enthusiastically, she rushed on, "Neighborhood watch programs are all the rage these days, you know. Insurance companies and banks love them; they make for a better investment. They sometimes give huge discounts for being a member. I take it you haven't signed up yet?"

The mention of saving money caught the man's attention. "Do we have a neighborhood watch? Because that's not a bad idea." He looked thoughtful, darting his gaze across the street toward the flapping police tape. "We don't need more trouble, that's for sure. One dead body in the neighborhood is enough. And you say there's a discount..." He rubbed a hand over his stubbly chin. "How do I sign up?"

"I think you have to pass some sort of observation test first." Madison mentioned this 'fact' with a vague wave of her hand. "You know, so your neighbors can feel confident in your ability to protect them."

"What sort of test?" he wanted to know.

"Oh, you know. Being able to identify vehicles. Noticing when people are home. Reporting suspicious activity and strangers. Knowing if lights are on or off. That sort of thing."

"That don't sound too hard."

"If you're the observant type, it shouldn't be hard at all."

"Not much gets past this guy," he bragged, tapping himself on the chest.

Madison looked suitably impressed. "Really? Like, you can remember if there was a strange car in the neighborhood?"

"Sure can. I've seen at least two this week. A shiny little black sports car, and a dark-blue two-door coupe. The black one came by just yesterday."

She smiled and nodded, as if fascinated. "Really? You notice something like that? What about the blue one?"

"It was Monday, I believe. No, it was Tuesday. Early Tuesday afternoon."

"There's no way you could have seen a license plate, or anything special about the car." Her voice sounded almost wistful. "I know those sorts of things give you extra points."

"I think I saw a bumper sticker of some sort. Driver's side rear fender. And there was something hanging from the mirror."

"Like those fuzzy dice?"

He shook his head with a frown, trying to recall exactly what he had seen. "No, I don't think so."

"Maybe a parking pass of some kind?"

"I think it was more like a ribbon, or a cord."

"A nametag lanyard?" she suggested.

"Maybe."

"Did you notice the make and model of the car? Guys are good at that sort of thing. I hardly know a Chevy from a Ford."

"It was definitely a Nissan. One of their new sports models."

"Very impressive," she murmured. She hoped the information would help Brash locate the mysterious car from Rose Belvedere's house.

"The black car is a Chevy Camaro," the man went on. "The latest model. The one with the new taillights." Getting into the spirit of things, he rambled on. "About a month ago, there was another black car up and down the street. An older model Ford Crown Victoria, but I haven't seen it in a while."

Madison remembered the car. It had circled the Big House like a bee around a hive.

"Wow. Information like that has to be worth bonus

points." In truth, she was rather impressed that he still remembered. Even Brash hadn't been able to catch up with the elusive prowler. "What was the other black car doing, do you remember?" she asked.

"Just circling the block, from what I could tell. This newer one just cruises by now and again. I suppose it's going to visit someone further down the street."

"Those are the kinds of things they're looking for," Madison nodded. This was where Granny Bert would lay it on thick, offering praise and empty admiration. Smiling broadly, she went on, "They want detail-oriented people who notice the little things. With your eye for details, I wouldn't be surprised if they didn't make you the leader!"

As long as he didn't ask who 'they' were, she was doing fine.

His smile was greedy. "Does the leader get a bigger discount on home insurance?"

From watching her grandmother, Madison had also learned the art of being agreeable without making promises. "Don't most leaders?"

"Nancy will be happy about this," he predicted.

"Of course! Especially if you have other information to share. For instance, did you see lights last Tuesday night coming from your neighbor's garage?"

"Uhm, it's hard to say..." He clearly wanted to claim he had, even though they both knew it was doubtful. The angle wasn't right. "The doors open yonder way and all."

"But you could have heard something," Madison suggested, hoping to jog his memory. "A car at midnight. A door slamming. Dogs barking. Anything out of the ordinary."

He snapped his fingers. "You know, I do remember

hearing the Campos' dogs carrying on one night. I think it was Tuesday now that you mention it."

"Late at night, that's so irritating, isn't it?" Madison's murmur was sympathetic. "Especially when you're already in bed. What time do you think that was when the dogs were barking?"

"I'd say after midnight, for certain. Say, about that discount—"

Madison made a show of checking her watch. "Would you look at the time! I'm sorry, but I have to run." She started walking backward toward the street. "Listen, I'll tell them how observant you are and that you would be a great addition to the program."

"But—"

"Don't worry, I'll give you a great recommendation!" she promised hastily. She all but ran back to her car.

Madison didn't know much about the man at her next stop, Eloy Palacios, other than he was the dual language arts and Spanish teacher at The Sisters High. After moving to town a few years ago, he lived alone in a small brick house along Second Avenue. He kept to himself and seldom attended community events, even those at school. He could have been fifty-five or seventy; most often, he wore a frown and a frumpy gray cardigan, making him appear old, even if he weren't. The sweater draped about his narrow frame now, even in this heat.

"Hello, Mr. Palacios. You remember me, don't you? Madison deCordova?"

"I do." The greeting was neither friendly nor frigid.

"I'm not sure you've heard, but there was a disturbance across the street this week." She waved toward the other side of the street and the woods facing them. The highest point of her grandmother's gabled roof was barely visible among the leaves.

"I heard."

He wasn't making this easy. Madison instinctively knew she couldn't imitate Granny Bert's shenanigans with this one. She took the straight-forward approach.

"Did you happen to notice any unusual lights among the trees this week?"

"I'll tell you the same thing I told the police. I have better things to do than monitor what's happening at someone else's home."

It occurred to Madison that he neither denied nor confirmed seeing anything. She tilted her head to one side, matching her salty, no-nonsense attitude to his. "So. That's a no?"

Something moved within his dark eyes. The unyielding lines around his mouth softened ever so slightly. "There may have been something on Tuesday night."

She tried to mimic his aloof manner, but the admission could be a possible lead. In spite of herself, a crack appeared in her cool facade. She visibly brightened. "There was?"

He lifted a thin shoulder, his voice neutral. "It seemed different."

"Could it have been a flashlight, moving through the trees?"

"I suppose."

"Were there any vehicles parked along the street that night?"

"None that I saw."

He meted out his answers in concise, stingy offerings. He volunteered nothing.

Without his help, the conversation quickly fizzled. She almost felt as if he were toying with her.

"Wait," she said, as a thought occurred to her. "You didn't see any parked vehicles that night. What about during the day?"

A light of appreciation flared in his eyes, making Madison wonder if he used this same approach with his students. Did he withhold pertinent information until they precisely asked the right question? Maybe this game of his—*I have the answer if you have the question*—taught deductive reasoning. Maybe mind reading was part of his curriculum.

"Does changing a tire constitute a parked vehicle?" he asked.

Her heart thumped with excitement. "A vehicle stopped to change a tire? Where?"

A long, slender finger indicated the spot across the street.

"A moving van?" she guessed.

"A van, at any rate," he supplied.

"Can you describe it?"

"Panel van, no windows."

"What color?"

"At one time, I imagine it was white."

"When was this?"

Like his shrug, his answer was vague. "Before dark."

Catching on to how he operated, she considered her words before she spoke. She imagined that was the point.

"Earlier in the day, there were two moving vans seen on Second Avenue. Was this one of those vans?"

"I can't be certain, but I feel that would be a reasonable conclusion."

"There was also a blue car that day. Did you see it?"

"No."

Surprised, she asked again. "Are you sure? Dark blue, two doors?"

He acknowledged the description with a slight inclination of his head. "I know the car."

This surprised her even more. "You do? You mean, you'd seen it before that day?"

"I didn't see it that day," he reminded her.

"Right. But before that, you had seen it? On this street?" She thought to make the distinction.

"That is correct."

"Do you know when you saw it? How often? Which way was it usually traveling?"

"I've seen it at least twice. It went that way." He pointed with his finger. "A half hour or so later, it came back this way."

"Both times?" she confirmed. "Toward Sycamore?"

"Correct."

Madison released her breath in a rush of excitement. "Thank you, Mr. Palacios. You've been very helpful."

"I have?" He seemed amused.

"Yes, you have."

She hurried to her car and started the motor. The air conditioning roared to life, spewing out warm air. Before the cooled air could take over, she had turned on Sycamore.

9

Just as Brash had reported, she found Arlene Kopetsky camped out in front of the big bay window. She had a small table pulled close, offering easy access to her reading glasses, a box of tissue, and her beloved romance novels. The binoculars were in her hands.

"What a nice surprise. Please excuse the mess. It's hard to keep things in order when you're on crutches."

"How are you feeling?" Madison inquired.

"My leg is doing nicely. Swells a bit, but that's to be expected. My nerves, on the other hand, are shot."

"Oh? I'm sorry to hear that. Anything I can do to help?"

She nodded vigorously. "Find out who that body belonged to, and what *that* woman had to do with it!" Using the binoculars, Arlene motioned to the house across the street. "I told your husband there was a body in that rug, and I was right, now wasn't I?"

"That's still to be determined."

"Where else would it have come from? I'm telling you, strange things have been happening over there."

Madison helped herself to a nearby chair, so she wouldn't be towering over the other woman as she pumped her for information. "What kind of strange things have you seen?"

"Cars coming and going. Lights flickering at night. A man goes in, never to come out again. A rug so heavy two grown men almost dropped it. A woman obsessed with roses. And, with other women's husbands!" She added the last with an impertinent nod.

Madison ignored the reference to Brash. "What cars?" she asked instead.

"For all the different workers. And the one the man was in."

"The man?"

"The man in the rug! The man you found in Bertha's refrigerator."

"We're not entirely certain there was a man in the rug." Madison felt compelled to make that distinction. Again.

"Of course, there was. And you found him, not two days later. Dark slacks, white shirt, red tie. Right?"

"I, uh, really wasn't focused on his clothes," she said evasively. "I hear you saw his car. What can you tell me about it?"

"Dark blue. Two doors."

"Had you seen it before?"

"Yes, I remember now. It came a few times before. Usually midday."

Madison felt a rush of excitement. It was the same car Don Beevis and Eloy Palacios had described. With Arlene's eyewitness account, a clear connection was established between the man, the car, and Rose Belvedere. Most importantly, it confirmed that the car had been to the house before Tuesday. Somehow, that fact felt significant.

"I may have forgotten to mention it to the chief," Arlene worried. "Just like I forgot to mention the lights."

"Lights?"

"I saw them sometimes at night. At first, I thought it was a reflection in the windows. They seemed to flicker and move about, like a candle. Now I think—"

Whatever she may have said was cut short by a loud crash.

Madison jerked around to see Lana Kopetsky coming from her mother's kitchen. A metal tray had clattered from her hands and landed at her feet. Two glasses of iced tea, a plate of spaghetti, and a bowl of cherries now perished on the ground in a tangle. Lana wore a stricken expression on her face.

"Lana!" Arlene wailed. "What have you done now?"

Madison jumped to her feet to help. The lanky bleached blonde stood in shock, her gaze oscillating between her mother, the tray, and their guest. She made no move to swoop down and pick up her mess. Distress had frozen her in her tracks.

"Let me help," Madison offered, raking what she could back onto the tray.

"Don't just stand there, girl! Get a broom and dustpan," her mother instructed.

Lana moved as if in a fog. While Madison set things right, she took her time finding the broom. She returned with it at last, only to hand it over to her guest. She stood by helplessly while Madison cleaned the entire mess by herself.

As she worked, Madison studied the other woman from the corner of her eye. Lana was known to have a fondness for low-cut blouses and high heels, with little else between. Today, however, her short shorts were replaced with a pair that almost brushed her knees. Instead of tight and clingy, these were baggy and wrinkled. Her shirt was an ordinary tee, its faded logo of a long-defunct band now smeared with spaghetti sauce.

Even without the stain, Lana looked terrible.

Madison had never seen the other woman without her makeup perfectly applied and her hair arranged in artful curls. Today, her face was pale, dark circles echoed beneath her eyes, and her hair fell limply against her shoulders.

If Lana was sick, Madison worried, should she be here caring for her mother? The elderly woman might come down with whatever ailed her daughter.

"Lana Elaine! How could you just stand there and let Maddy do all the work?" Arlene berated her daughter. "You should be ashamed of yourself!"

"It was nothing," Madison murmured. "Really."

"The girl has been like this all week," her mother harrumphed. "Okay," she admitted, as if someone had contradicted her. "She's been like this her whole life. But she's worse this week!"

Madison felt a stab of empathy for the younger woman, caught in her mother's tactless tirade. "Are you feeling poorly, Lana?"

Instead of answering, Lana simply stared at Madison. She batted big, tear-stained eyes that were devoid of makeup. Her mouth moved as if to say something, but no sound came out.

Without warning, the distraught woman whirled around and fled from the room.

"That girl." Arlene was clearly unhappy with her daughter's erratic behavior. "You see what I deal with. The girl has always been flighty. She can barely take care of herself, much less me. And if putting up with her mood swings isn't enough, now I have to deal with a murderer living across the street!"

"Please remember, Miss Arlene. We don't know for certain that a murder took place. Or that anyone actually died across the street."

"Did your grandmother kill that man and stuff him in her refrigerator?" Arlene demanded with a point-blank look.

"Of course not!"

"Then don't try telling me that wasn't the same body that left here in a rug the other day."

There was no sign of Lana as Madison said goodbye and let herself out. Still baffled by the woman's strange behavior, she put it out of her mind and stepped back into the afternoon heat.

Her phone rang as she did so.

"Hey, Granny. Are you back home?"

"Turning off the highway now," the older woman reported. "Where are you?"

"Just left Arlene Kopetsky's."

"How's she doing?"

"Her nerves are shot."

"I imagine so, with that daughter of hers," her grandmother sniffed.

"Do you want me to meet you at your house?"

"First, I want you to go next door and knock some sense into my friend."

"Miss Wanda?"

"Yes. She's gone plumb gaga over this new fellow of hers. I think you should check him out. See if he's on the up and up."

"I suppose I could drop by and say hello to Derron. Ask a few questions."

"You do that. I've got to stop by Dewberry's for gas, but I'll be home by the time you get here."

Derron, she soon learned, wasn't home. Wanda Shanks didn't know when her tenant would return. "With that one, it's hard to ever know," she claimed.

Madison saw a laptop computer on the kitchen table, its screen open. She wondered if Miss Wanda was talking to her online friend now.

"I hate to ask you this," she said, sounding embarrassed, "but I'm really thirsty. May I come in and have a drink?"

"Of course, dear. Would you like sweet tea? Coffee?"

"Water is fine."

"Have a seat, and I'll fetch that water," Wanda invited.

Madison took the chair next to the computer. It allowed her to see the screen through her peripheral vision. A chat box was open, but without deliberate effort, she couldn't read the conversation. It took far less scrutiny to see the litany of colorful emojis marching across the screen. Hearts, balloons, and symbols of food made up most of the icons. She didn't dare wonder if the honey pot and champagne glasses had special meaning.

"I thought we were going with Granny Bert to visit Miss Nelda," Madison commented.

"She invited me, but I had letters I needed to write."

"That's nice. Most people don't send letters through the mail anymore."

"Oh, not those sorts of letters," the older woman giggled. She nodded toward the computer as she set the water in front of her guest. "The computer sends them so much faster."

"Are you on social media? Or do you prefer email?" Madison probed.

"I'm part of a community circle," Wanda explained, taking the seat next to her. She proudly turned the laptop so Madison could see. "I can write to the group as a whole, or to just one or two. This is just one of my halos." She motioned to the screen.

"Halo?"

"Private conversation."

"What site is this?" Madison asked. Her eyes zeroed in on the ID box in the top left corner, where she saw the name Silver Fox.

"It's called *Silver Circle*. I tried to get Bertha to join, but you know how stubborn she can be when she gets an idea in her head." Wanda rolled her eyes in exasperation.

"Granny Bert doesn't spend a lot of time on the internet." Maddy tried to sound nonchalant. "I think she mentioned you met someone online?" She lifted her voice at the end, making it a question.

Wanda blushed like a schoolgirl, rather than the eighty-something-year-old she was. "Yes," she admitted. "I have."

"Is this him?" Madison casually waved at the screen, but her eyes were intense. She caught a few phrases amid the messages sent. *Sounds so exciting... high up in your company... no portfolio.*

She could only hope the portfolio referred to artwork, and not investments. Was Miss Wanda in over her head?

The older woman's look was a cross of shy pride and outright delight. "He goes by the handle Silver Fox. But his real name is Vartan Roosevelt. Doesn't that just sound scrumptious?" She wiggled her sizable body in glee. "I can hardly wait to meet him!"

Alarms went off in Madison's head. "Are you sure about that, Miss Wanda? You don't want to rush into anything you may regret."

"Who's rushing? We've been talking for several weeks now. I'm anxious to meet him."

"Where does he live? What do you know about him?"

"He works for an investment firm in New York City. Doesn't that sound exciting?" The hand she placed on her chest sank into her pillow-soft bosom as she took a deep, dreamy breath.

Exciting wasn't the word Madison would use.

Suspicious was more like it. "What sort of investing?"

"Oh, you know. Stocks and bonds. Money. He says he has a real knack for finding the next sure thing."

"How interesting."

Wanda missed the skepticism in the younger woman's voice. Thrilled to have an audience—Bertha and Sybille were both jealous and refused to share in her happiness—she rushed on. "Isn't it, though? I find it utterly fascinating. He told me all about turning a one-thousand-dollar investment into over one *million* dollars. It's simply almost too much to comprehend."

"It certainly is. What company does he work for? I'd love to get more information."

Wrinkles swam across her scrunched forehead. "I'm not sure he ever said a name."

"You should ask him."

Wanda peered at her curiously. "Why, dear? Are you interested in investing?"

"Maybe. But I would never, ever invest my hard-earned money unless I had thoroughly vetted the company *and* the stock. You know how important that is, right?"

"Oh, absolutely. I would only invest with someone I had complete faith in."

"If you're interested in investing, I'm sure my cousin Joe Glenn Cessna could give you some solid advice. He's been with the First Bank of Juliet his entire career."

Wanda nodded her jet-black hair in agreement. "Or I could ask Vartan. He seems very knowledgeable about these things."

"It's always important to get a second opinion," Madison stressed.

"I agree completely, dear. There're several investment bankers in our group. Rolex Roy is in Denver, and Lexus is in London. I wasn't supposed to be in it," she admitted, hiding a giggle behind her puffy hand, "but I was accidentally included in one of their private halos. They were discussing some huge new stock that is supposed to take the world by storm. They're all planning on getting in on the ground floor."

"Miss Wanda! You know better, don't you? You—"

She held up her hands in surrender. "I know, I know. I wasn't supposed to see it. It's almost the equivalent of insider trading. It was a private conversation among professionals."

"That's not what I meant. You don't—"

"Don't worry," Wanda interrupted again. "I don't have the kind of money to invest that they were talking about. Lexus is investing a half a million dollars of his own money! Rolex Roy is in for a quarter mil. My Vartan is getting a group together to invest a cool one million dollars. Can you imagine? Most of it is his own money, but he's sharing the opportunity with his top investors. Even at that, the buy-in is way beyond my means."

"Please, Miss Wanda," Madison begged. "Don't do anything without discussing it first with Joe Glenn. These online investment opportunities can be very tricky."

"I'm not parting with any of my money, dear. But it's fun to hear them talk about it, all the same."

The assurance made her feel marginally better. "That's good to know. I would hate to see you make an investment and lose." She would also hate to see her grandmother's friend lose her heart. After taking a sip of water, she asked, "What else do you know about your friend? He sounds interesting."

"He's led such an intriguing life. He loves to travel and has been to all kinds of exotic places. He's taking a trip out to Las Vegas next month and suggested I meet him there. That way we'd both be on neutral ground and not feel intimidated. Isn't that thoughtful of him, to think of such?" Madison would swear she saw stars dancing in Wanda's eyes.

"Next month? Isn't that rather soon?" she asked.

"At our ages, we can't afford to wait too long, dear."

"But summer is so hot in Vegas. I hear November is much nicer."

"I'll ask Vartan what he thinks. I'm just afraid by fall, he'll be too busy with this new deal he's working on. This may be his last chance to get away for a while," she fretted.

"Please, don't make any hasty decisions," Madison implored. "Have you discussed this with Derron?"

"No, but I suppose I should." She scrunched her face in contemplation, making Madison feel some better. Her hopes were dashed when Miss Wanda visibly brightened. "Derron knows exactly what to wear for every occasion. He can help me pack!"

Realizing she was getting nowhere fast, Madison let the conversation slide for now. Perhaps between Granny Bert and Derron, they could talk some sense into the infatuated senior citizen.

"I did have something else I wanted to ask." Madison changed the subject, hoping to have better luck on this score. "You saw the moving vans on Tuesday, right?"

"I certainly did. They brought in load after load of boxes and furniture, and then they brought one thing out." She paused for dramatic effect. "A long, heavy rug. The more I think about it, the more certain I am that I saw a pair of feet hanging out from one end."

Maddy almost choked on her water. She hadn't heard this account.

Wanda's chins wiggled as she nodded vigorously. "The rug was obviously heavy and had something inside. I'm positive it was that body you found."

"And you saw his shoes?"

"I think so." Another nod, and she was decided. "Yes, definitely. Peeking right out the end there."

It probably would do no good, but she asked, anyway. "Did you happen to notice if either of the vans had a low tire?"

"No, I can't say that I did."

"But you saw the car."

"I didn't have a clear view of the blue car that day, but I saw it the day before."

"You're certain?"

"Absolutely." When her computer dinged, a pleased smile broke across her face. "It's him! My Silver Fox." She giggled as she pulled the laptop in closer. Forgetting all about her guest, she laughed with delight at something she read on the screen.

Even with a computer involved, Madison decided two was company, and three was a crowd.

Miss Wanda never knew when she put her glass in the sink and let herself out.

"How was Miss Nelda?" Madison asked when she reached her grandmother's house. "Did you learn anything useful?"

"Not as much as I hoped," Granny Bert reported.

"Oh?"

"Her eyesight is terrible. She could hardly see an inch in front of her face. She's gone to using her hands to navigate around the room. But it's her mind that was most troubling. The woman has gone dingy."

"That's a shame. Did she not remember you?"

"She remembered me, all right. Worse than that, she's 'remembering' folks that don't even exist!"

"What are you talking about, Granny?"

"She insists she has a great-niece, but it's just not so. Her one nephew never had children."

"Maybe she's the nephew's stepdaughter."

"I helped hostess their wedding shower. There was no kid."

"Maybe they adopted a daughter you didn't know about," Madison suggested.

"If that's the case, they adopted her full grown within the last two years. I saw them when they packed Nelda up to leave. Yet according to her, this great-niece of hers comes by to visit and brings her presents. Showed me a little pot plant the girl left."

"Maybe there is someone who visits. Like a candy striper, or something. Maybe Nelda just has the relationship mixed up," Madison reasoned.

"She's mixed up, all right," her grandmother harrumphed. "She even talks about remembering the girl when she was young. Says she came to stay with her one summer, and they spent their days going to the park and getting ice cream."

"And you don't think that happened?"

"Where do you see a park here in The Sisters?" Granny Bert demanded. "There's not one!"

"Obviously, she's simply confused. Maybe she's remembering taking the niece to play on the swings in the school playground."

"Are you not listening to me, girl? There is no great-niece. Whoever this person is, she's got Nelda convinced they're kin, when nothing could be further from the truth."

"What about her nephew? Surely, he would know if there was someone claiming to be family."

"He's working way off somewhere, on that new pipeline. His wife went with him."

"Maybe Miss Nelda is just lonely," Madison

deduced, "and likes to pretend the candy striper is family. You know it gets lonely in there, without anyone coming to visit."

"Pretending is one thing," Granny Bert said. "Believing is another. She must have told me five or six stories about the girl, most of them about when she was young. Claims this niece loves to relive all her favorite memories of her favorite aunt."

"Could it be Miss Nelda made all this up? It may be embarrassing, if she's the only one of her friends without family that comes to visit."

"I saw a card the 'niece' wrote. She was thanking Nelda for all the great childhood memories."

Madison couldn't help but frown. "That does sound strange. How do you remember something that never happened?"

"You don't," her grandmother replied. "Those weren't memories. Those were flat-out lies."

A knowing look passed between the two women.

"Did you ask her about her house?" Madison asked. "Is she renting it out?"

"Not renting. When she found out her favorite 'niece' was moving to The Sisters, she insisted she stay in her empty house. She's pleased as punch to have somebody living there again."

"And let me guess," Madison said dryly. "This so-called niece's name is Rose Belvedere."

"She calls her little Rosie, but yes. Somehow, that woman hornswoggled Nelda into thinking she's kinfolk, and now she's living in the house, rent free!"

"And with her only legitimate relative out of state," Madison added, "no one's the wiser."

Her grandmother thumped the table, making Madison jump. "What are we going to do about it?"

"I'm not sure what we can do about it. It sounds like Miss Nelda willingly agreed to it."

"Only because she was duped," her grandmother insisted. "It gets under my skin, knowing that woman is taking advantage of poor Nelda. Especially with her being a murderer, and all."

"We don't know for a fact that she is."

Granny Bert looked at Madison as if she had lost her mind, causing her to squirm uncomfortably in her seat. "Seriously," Madison insisted, but the argument was weak. "We don't *know* it. Not for certain."

"You think that man just crawled up in my refrigerator and died?"

"Of course not."

"You'd best find out what this Rose woman is up to. Whatever it is, we need to nip it in the bud."

10

The scent of freshly baked goods wafted up from the basket as Madison and Genny waited on the porch. Two rings of the bell, and still no one answered.

At last, sounds of movement came from within. The door cracked open, revealing one side of a woman's face.

"Yes?" a tentative voice asked. "May I help you?"

Genny put on her brightest smile and announced, "We're with Sisters, Forever, and we're here to welcome you to our towns!" She stepped forward expectantly.

The woman behind the door hesitated a few seconds longer, perhaps deciding whether to open it. Madison suspected that if nothing else, curiosity won out.

The door opened wider.

"In that case, do come in," she said. Her smile was friendly enough, but it never quite reached her eyes.

Her guests introduced themselves as they stepped over the threshold.

"I'm Genny—"

"—and I'm Maddy—"

"—and we want to welcome you to The Sisters."

"Thank you. I'm Rose."

"Ah, like your artwork," Genny grinned, swinging her eyes to the living room's far wall. Her gaze skidded along the rest of the room, looking for clues. Of exactly what, she wasn't certain, but Maddy had said to keep her eyes peeled.

"Yes," Rose purred in a petal-soft voice. Ever so slyly, the raven-haired woman cut her eyes toward Madison. "A friend helped me hang that." Her voice lingered over the word *friend.*

Madison decided right then and there that she disliked Rose Belvedere.

For one thing, the woman was much too confident. She moved with a regal bearing, gliding effortlessly in her high-heeled pumps. Even though her smile was polite, a faint smirk of superiority lingered in her expression.

For another thing, she was dressed to perfection. Madison wasn't sure why that needled her so, but it did. Her own outfit—blue buttoned-down oxford shirt, khaki capris—looked dowdy and boring alongside Rose Belvedere's rose-patterned sundress. The lightweight sweater around her shoulders was a perfect match to the rose petals studding her ears and the pink shoes on her feet.

And for another thing, that 'friend' she spoke of was *her* husband! The woman had nerve.

Bristling, Madison nonetheless refused to let the cheeky woman get under her skin. She waved her hand in dismissal. "Oh, we heard all about it," she said breezily. She forced the laughter into her voice. "Don't feel bad. We're all clumsy, now and then."

It was clearly not the reaction Rose Belvedere had anticipated. Her smirk faltered. Madison knew the exact moment the niggling of doubt set in. Suggesting the handsome police chief had dubbed her clumsy was the equivalent of mentioning she had lettuce between her teeth.

Genny all but shoved the basket into Rose's hands. "This is for you," she said, defusing the awkward moment. "If you have a moment, we'd love to visit with you."

Rose was caught within the delicate web of Southern hospitality. She clearly didn't welcome the impromptu intrusion, but she couldn't very well refuse. Not without being rude. The smile on her face was forced as she invited her guests to sit.

"Would you ladies care for some refreshments? Tea, perhaps? Or coffee?" Her smooth veneer was back in place. It reminded Madison of glass.

"Tea would be lovely," Genny agreed.

"If it's not too much bother, I'd love a cup of coffee." Madison hoped it would take longer to make, giving her more time to snoop.

Nostrils flared ever so subtly, Rose hid her displeasure well. "Of course. I won't be but a moment."

"We'll come with you," Genny offered. "Can we help?"

"Don't be silly. You're my guests." If she had trouble making the last sound genuine, she covered it with a glossy smile.

"I love what you've done with the house," Madison volunteered. It gave her the excuse to move about the room, pretending to examine the tiny touches added here and there.

As Rose moved into the kitchen, Genny worked to keep a steady babble of conversation flowing between the rooms while Madison snooped.

The office opened off the hall, just steps from the living room. A peek inside the partially opened door revealed the edge of a desk, the backside of two computer monitors, and some sort of retractable screen behind the chair bearing a silver and blue emblem.

Madison was reminded what Genny said about video calls and Zoom meetings; the screen fit that theory. Perhaps Rose truly did spend part of her day in front of the camera. The thought helped ease some of the unfounded resentment Madison felt toward the woman's meticulous wardrobe, but she still resented the fact that she had referred to Brash as her 'friend.'

"Do you need help carrying that in?" Genny asked, her voice a tad louder than necessary. It was Madison's signal to hurry back to the couch.

"This is just the *cutest* house," Madison murmured, whirling around with outswept arms. She hoped the exaggerated arm movement disguised the fact she had been over the threshold.

"I know," Genny said, bobbing her head enthusiastically. Both pretended not to notice Rose had entered from the other side of the room, a tray in her hands.

"If you'd care to join us," Rose said coolly, her sharp eyes on Madison, "we can sample some of the goodies you've brought."

Madison took her place on the couch by her friend, leaving the chair for their reluctant hostess. Rose settled the tray onto the coffee table and doled out drinks, along with small plates and napkins. "Do you take anything in your coffee?"

It hadn't taken as long to brew as Madison had hoped. She probably had one of those one-cup-at-a-time makers. Hiding her disappointment, she murmured, "Black is fine."

Reaching for the basket they had given her, Rose asked, "What shall we try first?"

"Anything Genny makes is delicious," Madison

assured her. It was one of the first sincere things she had said to the woman. "We brought you a sampling of cookies and some of her mini croissants."

"But these are for you," Genny insisted. "You don't have to share."

"You brought more than I could possibly eat," Rose insisted. She poured a bag of cookies onto an extra plate and passed it around.

It was as good an opening as any. "Is it just you, or are we depriving your family of their share?" Madison asked as she selected a Gennydoodle cookie.

"Nope. Just little ole' me." Rose took her own cookie and settled back in the chair. She crossed a leg over her knee, allowing it to swing just a bit. Madison wondered if it was powered by irritation or impatience.

"Are you related to the Belvederes in Riverton?" Madison went on. She had no idea if there was anyone by that name in the nearby town. She was making it up on the fly. "I used to date Sam."

"Again, just little ole' me. My family is all down in Houston."

Blue eyes twinkling, Genny grinned at her friend. "I had forgotten about Sam. Anyway, Miss Belvedere—"

"Please. Call me Rose."

"Anyway, Rose, we're delighted to have you. What brings you to The Sisters? Are you a schoolteacher?" Genny pretended to guess. "I know they're hiring a new kindergarten teacher."

"Heaven forbid! I could never spend a full day with twenty or so little heathens. I am most certainly *not* a schoolteacher."

"Ooh," Genny continued, feigning excitement. "Are you a travel agent? My husband and I are thinking of taking a cruise. We're looking for a reputable agent.

Please tell me that's what you do."

"Nothing so glamorous," Rose assured her. "I'm in collections."

Genny played her part well. "Like, art collections?" she wanted to know. "Is that where you got this gorgeous painting of a rose?" She waved toward the print behind her. Unless she missed her guess, the piece came from an ordinary chain store and sold for no more than $39.95.

"No." Their hostess' smile was tight. "I work with a debt collector to recapture delinquent accounts."

"Oh, silly me! You must think me such a simpleton."

"Not at all." The lie fell smoothly from her lips.

"That sounds interesting," Madison said with a nod. "Do you work for several agencies, or just one?"

"I'm not sure working for more than one agency at a time would be ethical." Rose's tone was slightly reproachful. "I work for a company out of Chicago. With today's technology, I can work from literally anywhere. Even here in your delightful little town."

"So," Genny said, as if this were her cue. "Let us tell you a bit about our community." She folded her hands atop her knee and launched into her welcome speech.

Rose listened with interest. When Genny was done, interrupted only twice with input from Madison, the newcomer narrowed her eyes and leaned forward.

"You're saying this charming little community was started by two sisters who couldn't get along?"

"That's about the size of it," Madison admitted. "It was the only way their father could get any peace. He gave Naomi a town on the north side of the railroad tracks, and Juliet a town on the south side. The area in between was for communal use. Even today, we share public services."

"So, you live in Naomi," Rose concluded, pointing at Genny before directing her finger to her friend, "and you live in Juliet. And together, the towns are called The Sisters."

"Exactly."

"And the father was filthy rich, you say?"

"One of the richest men in the state," Genny confirmed.

"Interesting," Rose murmured, running a polished nail along her chin.

Something about her response set Madison on edge. She had the distinct impression Rose Belvedere was plotting something. A light had come into her eyes, a calculated gleam that turned the gray depths into polished steel. And like steel, they were cold and impersonal.

Sucking in her breath, Madison recalled with sudden clarity why they were here today. The woman could be guilty of murder.

"Tell us," Madison said, truly interested in the answer, "why did you choose The Sisters?"

"And why not?" Rose challenged softly.

"Oh, don't get me wrong. It's a lovely place. But few people move here unless they have family ties, or they get a job here. I know family played a big role in my decision to move back."

"Oh? I took you for a born and bred." Even though the words were purred, they had a bite. "But as I said, that's not an obstacle for me, as I work from home. I simply felt it was time to get out of the city. When I discovered an opportunity to move, I jumped at it."

Madison bit back a retort. *I just bet you did,* she fumed silently.

Aloud, she said, "I think you'll be happy with your choice. We're a very tight-knit community. We support one another in any way we can. In fact, if you take outside clients, I would be happy to pass your business cards around."

"I have a full load as it is, but thank you."

"I understand. But if you should change your mind—"

Rose broke in with a firm, "I won't."

Soon after that, the Sisters, Forever welcome team left. The door shut behind them with a distinct click.

As they crawled into Madison's hot car, Genny grumbled, "Well, that was awkward."

"She's not the most gracious hostess, that's for sure."

"Did we learn anything new? Or was that thirty minutes of torture for nothing?"

"We learned a couple of things," Madison decided. "For one, she's definitely not telling the truth. She told us she has no ties to the area, yet she's supposedly Miss Nelda's great niece. One way or another, she's lying."

"Did you see her face," Genny said, a giggle building in her chest, "when I asked who her decorator was?"

"I don't know how you kept a straight face, carrying on about how 'magazine-ready' her house was. Those furnishings were straight from a discount warehouse. That 'art collection' you raved about was from a chain store. All the accessories were. Cute, mind you, but hardly designer quality."

"Every time my mouth opened, I felt my IQ dropping ten points. I tried to sell it, but did she honestly think I was that gullible?"

"I'm not sure Rose Belvedere knew *what* to think about our little Sisters, Forever Welcome Wagon," Madison chuckled. "We definitely caught her off guard, which is good. And if she thinks we're just a bunch of simple-minded busybodies, so much the better."

"I love it when people from the city assume they're so much smarter than small-town folks."

"It definitely makes outsmarting them much easier," Madison agreed.

Genny's dimples deepened as she thought about their visit. "I think my favorite part of the whole thing was the look on her face when you made the comment about being clumsy. From all accounts, she did her best Jezebel imitation on Brash. To think he may have described her as clumsy had to be a blow to the old ego." With absolutely no trace of compassion, she laughed aloud at the other woman's humiliation.

"Served her right for flirting with my husband." Madison's grunt deepened when she saw the arm come down on the railroad crossing. Two cars were already stopped in front of them. "Oops. Looks like we're caught by the train."

The tracks served as the boundary line between the two towns. The daily trains were a nuisance but part of life in the small community. Madison put the gearshift in park and eased off the brake. As the first rail cars rattled past, she checked her phone for missed messages.

"Whose car is that in front of us?" Genny asked after a few minutes. "I don't recognize it."

"I think it may be Lana Kopetsky's. I saw it in her mom's driveway when I stopped by the other day."

"You're right. That looks like Lana in the rearview mirror, but I didn't recognize the hair. It looks different from normal."

"*She* looks different from normal." Madison flipped down her visor and used the mirror to apply a fresh coat of lip gloss. "This heat dries my lips out worse than a dust storm," she murmured. She rolled her lips together before continuing her line of thought. "I swear, she looked a wreck when I saw her Saturday. Her hair was stringy, her clothes were—"

"What is she doing?" Genny interrupted. "She just got out of her car and is storming this way." Her voice revealed a new level of surprise. "Wow. I see what you mean. She looks terrible. Not to mention irate."

Before Madison could fold the visor away, the angry woman had reached the car. She rapped on the driver's side window, demanding Madison open it.

Lana didn't allow Madison to utter a greeting. The moment the window was halfway down, she screamed, "What is the meaning of this? Why are you following me?"

Madison blinked in surprise, flabbergasted by the woman's angry outburst. "Uhm, because we're going in the same direction?" she offered innocently.

"Don't act all sweet and innocent with me! I know you're following me. First you show up at my mother's. Now you've followed me from my house to town. Who hired you? Who put you up to this?"

Instead of answering the unfounded accusations, Madison merely said, "I see the end. You'd better get back to your car."

"Don't you threaten me, Madison Cessna," Lana demanded, wielding her finger in a menacing gesture.

"It's deCordova now."

"You just love lording it over the rest of us, don't you? You think you're a hot shot now, married to—"

A horn honked behind them as the last car lumbered through the crossing. Lana shot the finger at the waiting car before looking down at Madison and snarling, "Leave me alone. Or. Else."

She stormed back to her own car, got inside, and jerked the transmission into drive. The car lurched forward when she forgot to put her foot on the brake.

"What was *that* about?" Genny squeaked.

"I have no idea."

"I don't think I've ever seen her like that." Genny was still dumbfounded. "She's usually dressed to a T. And even though she's a huge flirt and can come off a bit snotty, she's never like *that*. *That* was insane."

"Having to care for her mother must be more than she can handle," Madison agreed.

Genny shook her head in amazement. "If I didn't know better, I'd say she's coming unhinged."

"She thought I followed her from her house, but I don't even know where she lives."

"She lives in that little brown house on Cedar. The one with the magnolia tree in the front yard."

"I thought that's where Paulette Evans lived."

"They're roommates. The house backs up to Sycamore, so I guess we could have been behind her and didn't realize it. She assumed we were following her on purpose."

Madison pulled into the back lot of *New Beginnings* to drop off her passenger. "If nothing else, it's been an eventful morning."

"You can say that again."

Madison did as told. "If nothing else, it's been an eventful morning." The playful smirk on her face abruptly faded, replaced, instead, with a thoughtful frown.

"What?" Genny asked, glancing around in suspicion. "What do you see? Lana's not back, is she?"

"No. But I just realized something."

"What?"

"The furniture at Rose Belvedere's. It was positioned on the far side of the room."

"Right. There was nothing against the outside wall. That's why I felt so foolish asking about her 'decorator.' Who would do that?"

"Someone mimicking the showroom display," Madison answered thoughtfully. "It was almost as if they picked up the display, transferred it by flying carpet, and set it down in her living room."

"Minus the carpet," Genny pointed out.

"Exactly." Madison's hazel eyes sparkled. "Minus the carpet."

"That's it! That's what was missing!" Dimples appeared in her cheeks as Genny bobbled her head in agreement. "I kept thinking something was off. The furniture was in a tight arrangement, but something about it was wrong. That's what it was. Normally, a rug would pull the look together. It would even excuse leaving the far side of the room bare, because a rug would give the space definition."

"What do you bet there *was* a rug, but instead of using it as intended, it was used for another purpose?"

"Like wrapping a dead body inside and sneaking it out in broad daylight?"

With a satisfied smile, Madison gave her friend a high five.

"I'd say our thirty minutes of torture paid off. I can't wait to tell Brash!"

11

Blake's job was going well at *Marvin Gardens*. The hours were long and the days hot, but it felt good to earn a paycheck. He especially liked working outdoors.

By midweek, he was back at Israel Ballard's house, putting in more rose bushes. At the end of the first day, he asked his client about the box.

"I still have the box, Mr. Ballard. What should I do with it?"

After a long moment, the older man replied. "Keep it. I don't want it."

"No problem," the youth said amicably. "I don't mind hanging onto it a while longer."

"You don't understand. I'm telling you to keep it. I don't want it. It brings back too many painful memories."

Blake thought of all that beautiful handwriting. The curlicues and graceful loops. It seemed a shame to destroy them all.

"You want me to get rid of it?" he asked, the reluctance evident in his voice.

"Do what you like with it. Keep it or destroy it, it makes no difference to me."

This hardly sounded like the same man from a

week ago. Today, he sounded more hardened than he did heartbroken.

"I think there was something besides the letters in the box, sir," Blake reminded him. "Are you sure you don't want to keep some of it?"

"If you mean the ring, the answer is no. You can have it." The older man's voice was brusque.

Stunned, Blake shook his head. "You can't mean that, Mr. Ballard. You can't just give me a diamond ring."

"Believe me, it's not that impressive," he said with a short, unamused laugh. "The diamond is so small, you may need a microscope to see it. It cost me a month's salary, but it still wasn't big enough to impress her." His voice soured as he spat, "It certainly wouldn't have impressed her grandfather."

"Are you... are you sure, sir?"

Israel Ballard lifted his gray head, staring off into the distance. The stern expression on his face softened, melting into the timeline of wrinkles upon his face. "There aren't many things in life a man can be sure of," he said, his voice turning philosophical. "When I was young, there was one thing I had no doubt of, and that was Rosa's love for me. We made plans for a future together. When I bought that ring, I was sure she would wear it on her finger. I was sure she would stand up to her grandfather and choose me, a poor country boy, over his wealth and prestige. I staked my heart on it."

He cleared his throat of the emotions that gathered there. When he spoke again, his voice had hardened.

"But I was wrong. Dead wrong. She rejected me. She rejected the ring. She chose wealth and society over what little I had to offer." He pulled watery blue eyes back to meet Blake's. The pain in them was raw, inflamed by the salty sting of wounded pride. "I went off to war, not caring whether I lived or died. I came back a changed man, but a much wiser man when it came to the ways of the world. No," he said harshly. "I don't want the ring. I don't want the box. You can have them to do with as you please."

Blake nodded as if he understood, though he really didn't. He didn't understand why the man had kept the box through all the years, only to give it to a virtual stranger now. He didn't understand why the sight of the box had brought heartache last week, only to bring bitterness now. He didn't understand how someone could love someone, and yet hate them at the same time. He suspected Mr. Ballard felt both emotions for this Rosa person.

He carried the box back home with him, knowing he wouldn't tell his sisters of this latest development just yet. Tomorrow, the older man might change his mind. And if he did, Blake would have the box waiting for him.

The day, however, passed without a change of heart. The box was never mentioned, but Blake sensed an edginess in his client. Mr. Ballard spent most of the day inside. When he did come out, his answers were short and terse.

This time when Blake left, he didn't feel the same sense of satisfaction and camaraderie he felt that first time. Once again, he wished he had never found the buried box of heartache.

His sisters were both home when he got there. With their parents in Waco, it was just the three of them this evening. Orders from Mom were to stay home, stay together, and stay safe.

After showering and grabbing a snack, Blake took the staircase up to the third floor where the girls' bedrooms were.

When Nick Vilardi and the *Home Again* team remodeled the old mansion, the front turret's upper level was transformed into a fairytale bedroom for his twin. He much preferred his room on the second floor to hers, but she liked the frills and the fluff, and the ridiculously tall four-poster bed.

The other turret served as a lounge area, up until Mr. D married his mom. Even though Megan often spent the night with best friend Bethani, now that she was part of the family, his mom insisted she have her own room. The turret became Megan's room for when she wasn't at the Aikman household.

The former ballroom that stretched between the two turrets became a game room. He found his sisters there now, practicing their cheerleading routines. The wide, open space and shiny hardwood floor offered the perfect setting.

"What's up?" he asked. With the ease of youth, he sidestepped Megan's perfectly executed triple backflip.

"Our feet." His twin sister grinned, corralling her long, blonde locks into a ponytail and securing it with a band.

"Got a minute?"

"Sure. Hey, Meg. Let's take a break."

Megan grabbed three bottled waters from the mini fridge, tossing the offerings at the twins as she collapsed onto a futon in the casual seating area.

"Long day at work?" she asked Blake, noting his face was still flushed from the heat.

"Yeah. And it seemed twice as long because Mr. Ballard wasn't in a very good mood. He's still bummed about the box."

"Did he ask for it back?" Bethani wanted to know.

Blake took a long draw of water before he shook his head and admitted with a note of sorrow, "He says he no longer wants anything to do with it. He gave it to me."

His sister frowned. "I thought he did that last week."

"I mean *gave it to me* gave it to me. For keeps."

"You're kidding." Both girls were stunned.

"Nope. Basically, he said since she didn't want anything to do with him, he didn't want anything to do with her. Or her memory."

"Do you think he really meant it?"

"I don't know. I get the feeling it was his pride talking, as much as his heart. He told me this yesterday, but I thought he might change his mind. He didn't."

"What are you going to do?" Bethani asked.

"I don't know yet."

Bethani glanced at Megan for support. "We, uh, did a little checking," she admitted. "We asked Granny Bert if she knew a girl named Rosa from back in the day."

"And if she remembered Israel Ballard when he was young," Megan added. "I also asked my Grandma Lydia. She knows almost as many people as Granny Bert does."

"What did they say?"

Megan went first. "Both said that the Ballards were good people but dirt poor. They moved into town when they couldn't scratch a living from the farm anymore. Mr. Ballard got a job as a janitor at school, and Mrs. Ballard worked as a maid. Grammy says she knew Mr. Israel and his sister in school, but she doesn't remember him ever having a serious girlfriend. He went away to fight in the war, and when he came back, he married and moved away. After his parents died, he and his second wife moved back to town. They basically tore down the old house and remodeled it into what it is today."

"So, who was Rosa?"

"I didn't get a chance to ask Grammy about her."

"And Granny Bert doesn't know," Bethani explained. "She remembers there was an eccentric family who lived outside of town in a great big house that looked like a Spanish castle. Their name sounded Spanish, too, but I don't remember what it was. Maybe Zapata. Or Davila." She frowned, unable to recall the name she had heard. "But if Granny Bert called them eccentric, you know they had to be different!"

"What was so different about them?" Blake wondered aloud.

"They claimed to be Spanish royalty, and they only lived here for a few years. They were rich and mostly kept to themselves. In the summertime, their grandchildren came to live with them. Granny Bert thinks there was a teenage girl, but she can't be sure. She said they seldom came into town."

"Where is this house? I don't remember ever seeing something like that."

"She says it stood empty for a long time after they left, until the state bought the land and put in the new highway. They tore the house down."

"Do you think that's who Mrs. Ballard worked for?" Blake asked.

Bethani raised her shoulders in a shrug.

"Makes sense," Megan reasoned. "The maid's son doesn't usually marry the master's daughter. Or granddaughter, as the case may be."

"We didn't press too much," Bethani added, "but maybe we should."

Blake didn't look convinced. "I don't know about that... Last week, he sounded heartbroken. This week, he just sounds bitter."

"Mr. Ballard thinks she didn't want anything to do with him, but what if that wasn't the truth? What if she had truly been in love with him, but her grandfather made her turn him away? He may be bitter for no reason."

"He has like fifty-something years' worth of reasons. She never came back."

"Does he know that for sure?" Bethani challenged. "Maybe she did, but he was already gone."

"We could do some more looking," Megan said. "With the internet, finding people is a lot easier than it used to be."

"I'm not sure our parents think that's such a good idea."

"They didn't say *not* to do it," Bethani pointed out. "Mom even agreed to help us, if she had time."

"Which, obviously, she doesn't."

"But they didn't forbid it," Bethani stressed. "They just said to give it careful thought before we did."

"It's about all I think about these days," her brother admitted. "You didn't see the look on Mr. Ballard's face when he saw the box for the first time. When he talked about her." He shook his head, trying to make sense of it all. "It's hard to believe he's so different this week. So distant."

"Maybe it's the only way he can deal with all the pain."

"I have an idea." Bethani's voice was tentative.

"Let's hear it."

"Why don't we read the letters? We can see for ourselves what she said to him. Maybe he's remembering it differently from how it really happened." She shrugged her shoulders again. "Or, maybe not. If we think there's more to the story, we can look for this woman, see if she's still out there. But if she really did brush him off, maybe he's been better off without her all these years. The letters will give us a better clue of what to do.”

“I don't know. It feels kind of wrong, reading letters meant for someone else.” His protest was weak.

“He gave them to you, so apparently, he doesn't care if you read them.”

“True.” After thinking about it for a moment, Blake came to a decision. “I'll tell you what. You two start dinner, and I'll get the box.”

“How about we start a frozen pizza, so we have more time to read?” Megan countered with a charming smile.

“If that's faster, fine. I'm starving.”

With the pizza devoured and the kitchen cleaned, the three teens sat at the kitchen table, the strongbox between them.

“Here goes,” Blake said, spinning the combination lock. With his knack for numbers, he remembered the digits without trouble.

The lock clicked open, and he gingerly pulled it free of the clasp. Like before, when he lifted the lid, the letters inside rallied for freedom.

“Wow. Look at that fancy writing,” Bethani murmured.

“And the stationary. That's the real thing.”

Blake pulled out the letters and set them aside so they could see what was beneath. There wasn't much.

A battered rose, most of its petals now scattered at the bottom of the box, with a frayed yellow ribbon tied around its stem.

A once white linen handkerchief, now yellowed with age and smudged with traces of dirt. The fine cloth was edged in delicate lace and embroidered with the initial *R*.

A small, polished stone, shaped almost like a heart.

And a small, velvet box, its dark burgundy pile embedded with age, dirt, and crushed rose petals.

"Is that—Is that a ring box?" Bethani squeaked.

"He knew this was in there and he *gave* it to you?" Megan's voice echoed with the same squeak.

"Yeah. He says it wasn't big enough to impress her."

Bethani wiggled her fingers in a 'hand it over' gesture, encouraging him to deliver the tiny box into her hands. With an expectant breath, she eased the top open.

A tiny swoosh of air escaped her lips.

"What?" Megan demanded. "Is it super tiny? Is it tarnished? Did the stone fall out? Is it terrible?"

Bethani shook her head, discarding all guesses. Her voice came out hushed when she pronounced, "It's perfect." She turned the box around to display the ring inside.

The diamond itself was small: tiny, even, by most standards. The setting made it exquisite. Layers of yellow and white gold swirled from the gemmed center, forming into the delicate petals of a rose. The band was thin and twisted like a vine.

Megan was awestruck. "That. Is. Awesome."

Even Blake was impressed. "I don't get it. Who wouldn't like that? Biggest isn't always the best."

"I think there's more to this than we thought," Bethani said. "We need to read the letters."

"It still feels a little like we're trespassing," her twin admitted. His hand reached for the stack of letters but stilled. "Like we're eavesdropping on a private conversation."

Bethani let out a dejected breath. "I know. But how

else will we know for sure? If the girl he loved rejected him because this amazing, unique ring didn't have a big enough diamond, then he was definitely better off without her. But if there was another reason she turned him down—if she did it against her will—then I think he deserves to know that."

"That's right." Megan nodded solemnly. "He's spent all these years, thinking he wasn't good enough. That this ring wasn't good enough. Maybe it was Rosa who wasn't good enough. Or maybe he's been remembering it wrong."

"Or never knew the real story from the beginning," Blake pointed out. He riffled the papers just enough that they released a soft whisper from the past. It smelt of dirt, lavender, and roses. He hesitated for only a moment before saying, "Let's do this."

There were eight letters tucked neatly inside their envelopes, properly stamped and canceled by the US Postal Service, ranging from the fall of '67 to the spring of '68. They were addressed to Mr. Israel Ballard in Juliet, Texas, with a simple return address of Suite 26, Wellmont Women's Academy in Boston, Massachusetts. Two additional letters were in unmarked envelopes, most likely delivered by hand. The loose pages, presumably the last correspondence from Rosa, were on top of the stack.

The teens passed the postmarked envelopes between them, reading the letters in no particular order. They saved the others for last, not speaking until the last person had read the final letter.

"So?" Blake asked, waiting for his sisters' reactions.

"I think she truly loved him." Bethani wiped away the tears welling in her big blue eyes. "I think her grandfather forced her to break up with him."

"Her grandparents were such snobs," Megan

agreed. "I didn't know people were really like that. They judged him by his status in life and the fact his mother was their maid, not the fact he was a smart, polite young man who loved their granddaughter."

"Her grandparents were definitely prejudiced," Bethani agreed. "They were rich and powerful, and wanted her to marry a Spaniard with a similar background. A poor white boy just wouldn't do for their pure bloodline."

Blake felt bound to defend the older man. "But Mr. Ballard ended up doing well for himself. He was some sort of engineer with the Space program. He has all sorts of gold plaques on his wall, and he owns like ten cars. He even has two garages, one of them for some really cool vintage cars. He promised to show them to me one day."

"I guess the grandparents didn't want to take a chance that he couldn't provide for their granddaughter. Did you notice," Bethani continued, "that none of these letters have her full name on it? We don't even know for sure who her grandparents were."

Megan glanced down at her arm. Her skin had a faint olive glow that spoke to her Spanish roots. "I hope their name wasn't deCordova. My family hates racism. Of any kind."

"You know what Granny Bert always says," Blake told her. "There are two things you can never change: your family and the past. You can learn from both, or learn to overcome them both, but there's no use in pretending they don't exist."

"Still," Megan insisted, "her grandparents don't sound anything like mine. I can't imagine mine ever looking down on someone because of the color of their skin, or the size of their bank account. That's just wrong."

"Obviously, Rosa didn't feel that way. I think she really loved him," Blake said.

"Did you read that one letter about how her parents were killed in a car accident, and her grandparents took her in?" Bethani motioned to the pile of papers between them. "I guess she felt obligated to them for raising her and her younger brothers. She didn't want to disappoint them. Or, as she put it, to dishonor them."

Megan wrinkled her nose in distaste. "It sounds like they even had a husband picked out for her. One with fine Spanish blood, of course."

Blake's face was long. "No wonder Mr. Ballard is bitter. In their eyes, he wasn't good enough for the girl he loved."

"So, do we just drop it? Or do we see if we can find this Rosa person? Times and attitudes have changed. And unless they're like a thousand years old, her grandparents must be dead by now. If Rosa's still around, and if she's not married, maybe she and Mr. Ballard can finally have their happily ever after."

"That doesn't sound very promising," her brother pointed out. "Or easy."

She tossed him a saucy look. "I'm up to the challenge."

"Me, too!" Megan chimed in, the sparkle in her eyes amplified by her glasses.

Blake looked back at the letters, and to the ring that was crafted and chosen with such obvious love and care. There was no other choice.

"Me, three."

12

"That's not the only thing we discovered," Madison reported to her husband as they rode the elevator to their fifth-floor suite. After a nice dinner out, they were returning to their hotel room.

She referred to her presence there in Waco simply as a 'mid-week visit.'

"The blue car had definitely been at the house before that day," she continued. "Whoever the man was, he knew Rose and visited her house several times in the days preceding his death. Has Perry learned anything more?"

"Not yet. The prints aren't in any of the criminal databases, and no one has reported a man missing, at least not in River or the surrounding counties."

"So how do we identify him?"

"*We* wait." He put emphasis on the word as he unlocked their door, clearly referring to law enforcement. "Eventually, someone's bound to report him missing. The autopsy may also give us some insight, but there's no telling how long that will take."

Madison ignored the implied exclusion. "It would help if we could find his car," she said.

"I've got my officers and the county deputies scouring the area, but there's a lot of dirt roads to go down. It could be literally anywhere."

"Granny's neighbors remember hearing dogs barking around midnight on Tuesday night. Eloy Palacios says the smaller van returned sometime before dark and stopped near the trees beside Granny's to fix a flat tire."

"Sounds convenient enough," Brash considered. "While one man distracts attention with a flat, the others pull the body into the woods. They could easily return at midnight and transfer it to the garage."

"Speaking of flats, did I tell you I had one yesterday? I went by to visit Granny Bert, and when I came back out, my front driver's side tire was almost flat. I guess the heat got to it." She shrugged before changing back to the original subject.

"I'm pretty sure you're right," she continued. "They stashed the body in the woods and came back later to move it. Two people thought they had seen unusual lights among the trees that evening. Which reminds me. Arlene Kopetsky says she had seen lights in the house at night before Rose moved in."

"Maybe Rose forgot to turn them off when she visited earlier in the day."

"Not those kinds of lights. Flashlights, or even candles, she said."

"Probably a reflection," Brash guessed. "Empty houses have a lot of odd angles and see-through spaces."

"Probably," she agreed. "We didn't get to venture into the rest of the house when we visited. Genny hinted at getting a tour, but Rose never offered. Maybe we'll have better luck next time."

"You plan on going back? Do you think she'll let you in?"

"I don't know. But I agree with you. Something is definitely off with her and that house."

"Just be careful. If we're right, this woman is dangerous."

When Brash's phone rang, Madison slipped into the bathroom to start her bedtime routine. She was taking off her makeup when he stuck his head inside the door.

"I hate to do this to you, but I have to check on something really quick. There's a glitch that needs to be taken care of before tomorrow's last session."

"No problem. I'll catch the ten o'clock news and get ready for bed. Just don't be too long, or I may fall asleep."

Brash leaned in for a kiss. "Don't worry," he assured her. There was a deliciously wicked gleam in his dark eyes. "I'll wake you up."

Madison laughed and reminded him to take his key. Finding the remote, she turned on the television and went back to her routine. She hoped to catch mention of the football camp during the sports segment.

"Before we turn to Sports," the announcer said, "we have an update on a story we brought you earlier this year. Police are still looking for Vino and Ruby Shiraz, not believed to be their real names, who were operating an unlicensed business out of a home on South Adams Street in Waco. This is not the only law the couple is accused of breaking. While staying in the home of a relative, they purportedly stole items of value, personal identification, and used the home as collateral to obtain a sizable loan. After defaulting on the loan, the couple was last seen in the Bryan-College Station area in a black '98 Ford Crown Victoria with Texas license plates beginning with KPJ. According to the homeowner's lawyer, foreclosure proceedings have since been halted, and the case is now being handled as identity fraud. If you have any information about the vehicle or the couple, you're asked to contact the Waco Police, or the TIPS line shown at the bottom of your screen."

Hearing the description of the black car unnerved Madison. The car had been seen in both Waco and Bryan-College Station. If it continued toward Houston, it would pass through River County and come near The Sisters. Was that the same black car they had seen in the spring? The one still on everyone's minds and lips?

Caught up in the previous story, Madison almost missed the segment on the youth football camp taking place on the Baylor campus this week. Brash returned to the room as the news segued into a late-night talk show. As neither of them were fans of the program, he switched the television off.

"You won't believe what I just saw on the news," Madison told him.

"Was it the reporter?" he asked, pulling his shirt free from his belt with a sigh. "Because she was just doing her job. She came on a little strong, but she was an intern trying to make a name for herself. It was just harmless flirting."

"Wait. Flirting?" Madison glanced at the blank television with a frown. In all honestly, she had been too distracted to notice.

"Never mind." Her husband wisely changed the subject. "Why are you still dressed?" he wanted to know. "I was hoping to see the little black gown when I returned."

The hour-plus drive home the next morning gave Madison time to mull things over in her mind.

Like Brash, she felt sure it was no coincidence that

Rose Belvedere and an unidentified dead body appeared in The Sisters within days of each other. Something about the town's newest denizen didn't ring true.

At best, the woman was hiding something.

At worst, she was involved in the man's death.

As for the unidentified man, Madison tried to recall as many details about him as she could. Something other than the feel of his cold, lifeless body falling against her foot; that, she would never forget! He had been relatively young, probably in his mid-thirties. He was clean shaven with neat, short hair. She knew she had seen him at an awkward time (in death, as it were), but he seemed to be physically toned and well-conditioned. He probably went to the gym or was a jogger, she mused. With no calluses on his hands and no excessive sun on his face, he had the look of a white-collar worker. She scrolled through a mental list of possible careers for the man, trying to imagine why he would visit the Sycamore house on numerous occasions.

Real estate was the obvious choice. Brash had left a message at the number Rose gave him, but to her knowledge, no one from the agency had returned his call. Then again, if Rose had obtained the key directly from Nelda, even if nefariously, there was no need for a real estate agent.

The man had to be connected to her in another way. Lawyer? Banker? Madison nibbled on her lip worriedly. There was something she was missing. Something that involved both Rose and the dead man. Whatever it was, it most likely had cost the man his life. Would there be other victims? Without knowing what she was up to, it was difficult to know who was at risk.

One person Madison hadn't spoken to yet was

Sadie Bealls. She remembered Granny Bert saying the part-time librarian and Nelda had been the best of friends while living on Sycamore. In fact, her husband Henry had been one of the 'eyewitnesses' to the infamous body in the rug. Maybe she should stop by and have a word with both.

Unlike their new neighbor, the older couple was delighted to have Madison drop by uninvited. They insisted she come in for tea and a piece of fresh zucchini bread. Uncle Jubal had delivered a mess of yellow and green squash to half the town, it seemed, particularly his oldest friends.

"I don't keep up a garden no more," Henry explained. "Hard on the back. Mine is stooped enough, without adding insult to injury."

Eventually, after discussing the heat and how Granny Bert and her globe-trotting parents were, Madison worked the conversation around to the new occupant in Nelda's house.

"I'm in no hurry to meet her," Henry admitted. "Just in case she has another rug in the house, you see."

"That's no way to talk about the woman," Sadie admonished her husband of fifty-some-odd years. "We don't know for sure and certain that she killed that man."

"What *did* you see, Mr. Bealls?" Madison asked, leaning forward.

"I saw the moving vans pull up. The dark two-door car was already there, you see. The men started unloading the vans. Box after box, chair after chair. A great big old desk and some poster boards and such. After they had unloaded both vans, suddenly, they came *out* with the rug. It was so heavy and stiff in the middle, they almost dropped it. That's what got me to thinking. There had to be a body inside there." He leaned back with a satisfied expression on his face. "And I was right, now wasn't I?"

"That's still not determined for a fact," Madison noted.

"Of course, it is! Where else did that body come from? Your grandmother ain't no murderer, and as far as I know, she ain't taken to picklin' men, neither! Of course, that man was in the rug."

Because she didn't know how to answer him, Madison turned, instead, to his wife. "Have you met your new neighbor, Miss Sadie?"

"Yes. I'm ashamed to say that I wasn't the one to initiate the contact. I kept meaning to take her a jar of last summer's bread and butter pickles, but before I could get over there, she came to the library." Sadie's smile looked pleased. "It's so nice to see how anxious she is to fit in. She wanted to learn all she could about The Sisters' history. She had plenty of questions about Randolph Blakely and how the towns were created. It's nice to see young people interested in history. So many have no idea about how things came to be."

Madison wasn't as impressed as her hostess. She couldn't imagine what it would be, but she suspected Rose Belvedere had an ulterior motive by researching the past.

"Do you know if she's related to Nelda Goldberg?" she asked, keeping her voice innocent enough. "I heard she was her niece or something."

"Oh, no. No, not at all. Nelda doesn't have but one nephew, and he's quite a bit older."

"Is she his daughter, maybe?" It was doubtful, but there was always the possibility that her grandmother was wrong.

"No, he never had children. There was an incident at the plant where he worked..." Sadie shot her husband a sharp look before he could embellish her explanation. "That boy is the only relative poor Nelda has."

Madison knew better than to doubt her grandmother's genealogy prowess, but she had felt compelled to ask. With that cleared up, it was doubly obvious that Rose Belvedere had lied and was up to no good.

After a nice visit, Madison said her goodbyes. She still had two stops to make before she went home, and one was out at the deCordova Ranch. Her mother-in-law had picked the girls up this morning and taken them to the ranch to help with one of her many projects. Madison was to pick them up when she returned.

As she drove over the railroad tracks to tend to her other errand, her car shimmied and shook its way across. She found it odd; it had never happened before. She made her stop, jumped back in the car, and noticed it pulled badly to the right. It practically dragged itself over the tracks on the return trip.

Taking no chances, Madison turned toward *Dewberry's Gas Station*. By the time she got there, her tire was almost flat. Again.

"I'd best change that for you, Miz D," the old man said. "I'll put your spare on and get this other one fixed right up. You probably picked up a nail and have a slow leak."

"Thanks, Mr. Jolly," she said. "Can I wait inside?"

"You help yo'self, missy. Go right on in there and have a Coke. Jiggle the handle a little, and any kind you like will pop right out."

The old-style 'filling station' looked like it came straight out of Mayberry. There was nothing fancy about the simple glassed-in space attached to dual garage bays. It smelled of oil and engine grease, and a faint hint of the peppermint candies the old man favored and kept in ready supply for his customers. But the air conditioning was cranked up high and the old-fashioned soda dispenser—still outfitted for glass bottles and a single quarter—would loosen its grip with just the right persuasion. A jiggle here, a fist bump there, and the bottles slid right out. The brand distinction only mattered when making a selection; in the South, often all soft drinks were referred to as 'a Coke.'

As Madison took a seat in the straight-back chair, a familiar whir told her Mr. Jolly was already replacing her flat tire. She was just thankful the tire hadn't gone flat between here and Waco. She had already had one wild ride on that stretch of highway and didn't want a repeat performance.

Soon, the old man stuck his head inside the cool building. "All done," he reported. "Your other tires are fine, and your windows are clean. You want to wait on the repair, or pick it up later?"

"I've got to run out to the ranch. I'll stop back in an hour or so if that's okay."

"It'll be ready. Say hello to the mister for me."

"Will do. Thanks, Mr. Jolly."

The entrance to the ranch never failed in impressing her. A sprawling metal sign welcomed one and all to the *deCordova Ranch, est. 1918*. The icons prancing across the metal arch—cattle, cotton, horses, and oil derricks—were a preview to what lie ahead.

The white rock road left a trail of dust behind her as Madison proceeded through fields of grazing cattle and prancing horses. Summer was a busy time on a ranch. Many of the fields she passed buzzed with activity, as a team of green cab tractors worked to cut, rake, and bail the thick grasses into hay for the winter. Other fields were planted in cotton, the plants still young and tender and sparse. By fall harvest, she knew the entire field would be carpeted by the snowy white tufts. Off in the distance, a pumpjack worked to pump crude oil from deep beneath the earth's surface. Her favorite parts of the ranch—the large stock tank where they fished, and hers and Brash's special spot along the banks of the Brazos River—weren't visible from here, but she loved it all.

Arriving at the ranch house, she found the girls helping her mother-in-law make blackberry jelly.

"Hey, Mom!" Bethani grinned. Her blonde ponytail was askew, her hands were stained from the berries, and her old t-shirt would probably never come clean, but her blue eyes sparkled with merriment, and her smile was dazzling. Beside her, Megan looked slightly less thrilled. She had obviously done this before.

"We picked all these berries ourselves!" Bethani boasted. "My arms and legs are scratched from all the berry vines, and Grammy killed a snake with a long stick, but it was a blast! You should have come with us."

"Sounds like I missed the fun," Madison agreed.

If she had ever doubted her decision to move her teenagers from the city to the small rural community she once called home, times like these reassured her. Seeing her daughter find happiness in the simple pleasures of life was a balm to her soul. How many times had Madison accompanied Grandpa Joe on forays for wild blackberries or muscadine grapes? Nothing was better than the sweet, tart tang of a wild-grown harvest.

"Grammy showed me how to make a berry cobbler, and now we're making jelly! She says I can bring some home for us."

Madison couldn't imagine Gray's mother dirtying her designer kitchen with the delightful mess now strewn about Lydia deCordova's domain. Every available surface had bowls, colanders, jars, and berries scattered among the canning paraphernalia. Somewhere among the mounds of sugar and packets of gelling magic, Madison spotted a golden berry cobbler, set aside to cool.

"It looks like y'all have a system."

"Sure do," Megan said, popping a plump berry into her mouth. "Eat all we can and cook what we can't."

"I tried to talk them into aprons, but they wouldn't have it," Lydia said with an apologetic smile. "I hope those are old jeans Beth is wearing."

"They are now."

"Can I stay longer, Mom?" Bethani wanted to know. "We're not done yet."

She shot her mother-in-law a questioning look. "Are you sure?" She couldn't tell if the girls were helping or hindering. She knew Lydia was perfectly capable of manning the entire operation by herself.

"Absolutely! Why don't you just let them spend the night? This will take most of the afternoon, and they still need to sample the rewards."

"Can we make homemade ice cream to go with the cobbler?" Megan asked her grandmother. "You know how much Grampy loves it."

"I think I have all the makings. If you girls promise to help, I think we can manage a batch for supper." The older woman smiled. It was hard for her to deny her grandchildren of anything they wanted, especially if it came from her kitchen. "Maddy, why don't you and Blake join us for supper? With my son away, there's no reason for you to cook for just the two of you. Join us. Somewhere over there, I have a pot roast in the slow cooker."

"Are you sure? You're bound to be exhausted by the time you get this all cleaned up."

Lydia winked and said, "That's what these energetic girls are for. Besides, Andy will be starved after a hard day in the field. I have to cook for him, regardless."

Madison nodded in empathy. In his early seventies, her father-in-law still worked as hard as any of his ranch hands. "But you know Blake," she warned. "He'll be starved, too. You may not have enough to fill his hollow legs."

"You forget. I raised three boys of my own and have a half-dozen grandsons. I know how to feed a teenage boy."

Madison dropped a kiss onto her mother-in-law's cheek. She truly loved this woman! She treated the twins like they were her own blood. Even better, she treated Madison the same way.

"In that case," Madison grinned, "what can I bring?"

13

Leaving the girls at the ranch, Madison sent Blake a quick text telling him of their dinner plans. He was thrilled with the prospect of Lydia's home cooking.

The road back to town was a bit of a maze. Right out of the ranch, onto a dirt and gravel county road. Follow the dips and curves, and one particularly sharp bend. Left onto the paved county road. Another left onto the farm-to-market road, which ran into First Street.

As Madison pulled out of the ranch entrance, she tucked her phone beneath her leg. Experience had taught her that the jiggle of a dirt road could rattle the device right out of the console. She cut the wheels to the right, noticing the steering wheel felt stiff in her hands. She made a mental note to mention it to Mr. Jolly. Maybe something wasn't quite right with the tire.

Picking up speed, she hit a pothole, and the car shimmied across the road. She had difficulty getting the vehicle under control, so she slowed down. She kept her speed low, knowing the big bend was coming up.

Approaching the bend, Madison eased the steering wheel to the right, but nothing happened. She used more pressure, directing the wheels to go with the curve of the road.

Still, nothing happened.

With a muttered complaint, Madison willed the steering wheel to do her bidding. She yanked harder. It was as stiff and unresponsive as if she turned it with a feather. Had her power steering gone out? She knew to brake, but she was on the downside of a hill. Momentum carried the heavy vehicle forward, no matter how hard she stomped on the pedals. Controlled by an unseen demon, the steering wheel spun on its own accord. The tires skidded atop the gravel, going into a slide. Madison braced herself for a crash.

The angels were with her that day, saving her from serious harm. The car slid off the road, backside first, bouncing and dragging down a steep embankment until it wedged itself against a thick stand of saplings and the hard, sandy bank of a deep ravine. The nose of the car shot skyward.

As the dust settled and the car's engine sputtered to a stop, Madison used the extra moments to steady her frantic breathing and collect her thoughts. Her heart still raced within her chest.

She saw her purse, thrown haphazardly against the passenger door. Most of the contents had spilled out and rolled to the backseat. After straining around to see where her cell phone had gone, she remembered tucking it beneath her leg after texting Blake. With unsteady hands, she dialed her mother-in-law's number and was met with silence. No cell service.

Out the passenger window, Madison could see the gaping hole of a deep gully. During the wet season, the hole held water, but during the summer months, it was overrun with thorny bushes, vines, brush, and bramble. If her car had landed ten feet over, she would be at the bottom of the ravine.

Thankful for small blessings, Madison unfastened her seatbelt and struggled with the weight of the door. She managed to open it enough to slide out into the brutal heat of midday, magnified now by the heat from her overtaxed engine. She recognized the hiss and alkaline stench of a busted radiator.

"Well, Maddy girl." Stuffing her phone into her pocket, she gave herself a pep talk. "There's only one way to go, and that's up."

She took in a deep breath and started climbing. Her foot slipped several times, slick against the limp grass and dry, sandy soil. She stopped to take a breather, looking around to see if there was an easier path. The gully was to the right, trees to the left. This was her clearest path, even if the steepest.

Something caught her eye in the grass. She jumped, recalling Bethani's mention of the snake Lydia had killed that morning. Then she laughed at her own foolishness, realizing the small black ribbon wasn't a snake at all, but a watch band. Moving over to investigate, she saw that it was one of those fitness watches that kept track of physical activity and the like. It looked to be in excellent shape, so she bent to retrieve it.

Wondering if it worked, she touched a button to bring it to life. The screen remained blank. Most likely, the battery was dead. If she wasn't mistaken, Blake had this same model at home. She stuffed the watch into her pocket, thinking his charger might work on it. If it didn't, she would chuck it when she got home.

Steeling herself to continue her climb, Maddy lifted her hair off her neck to catch the meager breeze. Her hair was relatively short, but she could sometimes manage to put it up. She glanced around, looking for a long stem or flexible vine she could fasten into a holder. Hardly a fashion statement, but in this heat, who cared?

Something glittered in the sunlight. From this vantage, she had a different angle of the gully behind her. She also had a more direct path to tumble *into* said gully. That knowledge urged her to return to her previous course. She turned to pick her way back, then turned around again in curiosity.

Had that been glass the sun reflected off? As in a windshield?

Instead of forging upward, Madison cautiously navigated a few steps down the incline to get a better view. From there, she saw the undercarriage of a car, up ended and half-hidden beneath a canopy of leaves. Instead of a window, the overhead sun glinted off a once-shiny fender, now crumpled and detached, and perched precariously upon a twist of vines and bramble. With time, the whole mess would sink to the bottom of the ravine, suggesting the car hadn't been there long.

She couldn't tell much about the car, but she knew it was dark blue. When she saw the bumper sticker, she knew this was the two-door coupe seen as Rose Belvedere's house. More than likely, it also belonged to the dead body found inside her grandmother's refrigerator.

With renewed determination, Madison scrambled up the steep incline and onto the dirt road. Relieved to find a signal, she called the ranch and asked for someone to come pick her up. Then she called the police department.

"Vina, this is Madison. Would you please tell Officer Perry I just found the blue car? He'll need a wrecker to get it out." She glanced back toward the ravine, where neither car was visible from the road.

"Actually, we're going to need two wreckers."

Instead of sending a ranch hand, Andy deCordova came to his daughter-in-law's aid. Together, they waited in the air-conditioned comfort of his truck until the police arrived. Officer Perry came with his same blustering sense of self-importance, demanding answers and ordering the wrecker to retrieve the blue coupe before pulling Madison's car free.

"Hold on there a minute, Buddy Ray," the rancher told the tow truck driver. "Don't you think it would make more sense to move the front vehicle, before going in for the second?"

Otis Perry jabbed a pudgy finger toward his boss' father. "*You* hold on, deCordova! I'm the one running this rodeo. Not. You." The last two words were tapped into his arm.

Madison had never seen her father-in-law angry before. To his credit, he remained calm even now, but she recognized that look on his face. It was the same cool, logical, lethal expression that often crossed his son's face. She knew Officer Perry would be wise to heed the warning that flashed in his eyes.

Without a word, Andy placed two fingers on Perry's lingering one and deftly plucked it away. His touch looked effortless enough, but she saw the flinch on Perry's face. No doubt, there was steel in the rancher's grip.

"We wouldn't want to contaminate any possible evidence, now would we?" He sounded amicable enough, but there was an edge in his voice. All but ignoring the red-faced officer, he addressed the driver as if he hadn't been interrupted. "Buddy Ray, pull the Ford up first. We'll collect our belongings and be on our way. No need to have us in the middle of official police business." He emphasized the last three words, making it difficult for Perry to challenge his rationale.

Not ready to concede, Perry tugged on his belt as a precursor to puffing out his chest. "Buddy Ray, pull the Ford out," he ordered. Suddenly, it seemed to be his idea. To Madison, he said, "While we're waiting, you can explain how you came to find the car. Seems like quite a coincidence to me."

"You can't possibly make an issue of this, too!" Madison sputtered.

"You found the dead body," Perry pointed out. "Now you find what is most likely his car. Explain that."

Andy's voice had a calm, steely resolve when he defended her. He sounded exactly like his son. "Instead of making veiled accusations against my daughter-in-law, you should be thanking her. She'd done what you and your officers haven't been able to do in a week's time. She found the vehicle," he ground out.

"Not hard to do," Perry said with swagger, "when you have inside information."

The air stilled. Andy deCordova's tall, muscular frame dwarfed Otis Perry's short, round one as he took one small step forward. His clipped, icy voice was as intimidating as his size.

"You must be referring to information she obtained from her husband. Your boss," he added, in case the man needed the reminder. "Because *I know* you aren't accusing Madison of any wrong-doing."

Otis Perry couldn't hold the other man's penetrating gaze. Suddenly interested in the process of retrieving the car, he turned away and busied himself with the wrecker service.

"That man has a lot of nerve," Andy growled. "I

don't know why my son puts up with him."

"Brash chooses to see the good in other people. I think he learned that from his father." She stood on tiptoe and brushed a kiss onto Andy's cheek. "Thanks for sticking up for me. And thanks for coming to get me."

"Anytime, Maddy. You're part of our family now, and family sticks together. You can count on me anytime you have a problem." When he hugged her, he felt the tremble in her shoulders. He looked down at her in concern. "Are you okay, hon?"

"I guess I'm still a little shaken," she admitted. "That was scary, going down the embankment backward. I don't even know how it happened. My steering wheel just wouldn't work!"

"Sounds like you lost your power steering."

"Yeah, well, now I think I may have lost my car. I think I heard a few parts fall off on the way down."

When the wrecker pulled the car up the bank and onto flat ground, it didn't look as bad as Madison feared. Three of the four tires were flat, the back fender was crumpled and hanging askew, the trunk's clasp no longer worked, and there was a mysterious dent in the back door. Yet all in all, it was better than expected.

Andy helped Madison gather her personal belongings from the car. Her suitcase had tumbled out of the trunk on the way up, so her father-in-law scrambled down the hill and retrieved it. Perry rushed them through the process, anxious to get to the blue coupe.

Madison was tempted to hang around and see what he found inside, but she realized how exhausted she suddenly was. Between the heat and the excitement, her energy was zapped. When Andy asked if she wanted to go back to the ranch or to her house, she opted for home.

It wasn't until she was changing out of her sweaty clothes and preparing to sink into a steaming tub of scented salt that she remembered the watch. She dug it from her pocket and went in search of Blake's charger. While she soaked away her stress, the watch powered up.

After the events of the day, there was a change in dinner plans. Instead of her and Blake going to the ranch for dinner, Lydia and Andy brought dinner to them, along with a vehicle for Madison to borrow. With her car out of commission, she needed a way to get around, and Brash had taken his personal truck to camp. The ranch truck wasn't as fancy or as new as her car, but it had four good tires and a steering wheel that actually worked. In Madison's opinion, that gave it five-star status.

The ice cream churned while they enjoyed the meal. The teens provided most of the conversation, with animated replays of their day. As the conversation bounced from making jelly to planting shrubs, Andy's phone rang. When he returned from taking the call, Madison read the concern in his eyes.

While Lydia directed the kids in clearing the table and doing dishes until the ice cream was done, Madison slipped into the utility room to find her father-in-law.

"What's wrong?" she asked him.

"Just adding more ice and rock salt," he said, sounding overly cheerful. "I tell you what. These electric makers are so much better than the hand crank version we used to use. This should be ready before long."

"You're as terrible a liar as your son," Madison informed him. "Was that call earlier about my car?"

Andy had instructed the wrecker to take the car to

the mechanic shop he used. With all the vehicles and equipment in constant use on the ranch, he kept the mechanics on speed dial. They were more than happy to take her car at the last minute, promising to have a look at it that very afternoon.

"Yes," her father-in-law admitted. He covered the ice cream bucket with a towel to keep the cold contained, making certain it didn't get caught in the electric motor. After giving it more care than it necessitated, he turned to face her. "I'm afraid it's not good."

"I knew I heard parts falling off!" she wailed. She had really liked that car, too. Since her marriage to Brash, it wasn't always comfortable for the five of them to ride in, but it was perfect for just her, or for carting the kids around town. She dreaded the idea of shopping for a new vehicle. She dreaded taking on a new car payment even more. Without fail, the price tag always went up.

"It's not that," Andy told her. "But there is a definite problem."

"I know the radiator was busted. What else? Is it going to cost a fortune to fix?"

"I don't know about all that. I do know that the mechanic found a serious issue with the power steering pump. It wasn't just leaking fluid, Maddy," he told her. "It had been deliberately sabotaged."

Madison stared at him in disbelief. Surely, she had misheard him! "What? What does that even mean? Who—Who would do that? And why?"

"It means, Maddy, that someone intended to do you harm. They knew how difficult the car would be to manage without power steering. You mentioned you had a low tire, too. Between the two, it was the perfect recipe for disaster."

She was still stunned. "But... who would..."

She didn't bother finishing the question. She already knew the answer.

Earlier today, she had stopped by Henry and Sadie Bealls'. While she was inside enjoying fresh zucchini bread, her car had been left unattended.

Next door to Rose Belvedere's house.

"I'm coming home." His voice was gruff.

"You'll do no such thing!" He couldn't see her through the phone, but Madison shook her head adamantly. "Brash, you cannot walk away from that camp. Those boys are depending on you."

"*You're* depending on me. I vowed to love and protect you, and that's what I plan to do."

"You can't love me from afar?" she teased.

"This is no joking matter, Maddy," Brash admonished her. "Someone tampered with your car. They intended to cause you bodily harm."

"Unless you plan to give my car a bumper-to-bumper inspection each and every time I get behind the wheel, whether you're there or here in The Sisters won't make a difference."

"It would at least make me feel better," he insisted.

"But knowing you disappointed those kids would make me feel terrible. It's only a few more days. I miss you, but I don't want you coming home. This is something you need to do."

A touch of despair moved into his voice. "What if something had happened to you today, Maddy? Something serious. I'm not sure I could bear losing you."

"Nothing serious happened, sweetheart. I'm fine. And on the bright side, at least I found the elusive blue car. Have you found out who it belonged to yet?

What's Perry saying about it?"

His sigh was loud, but he went with the change of subject. "It's registered to a Ronald Alexander from Brenham."

"What's his connection to Rose Belvedere?"

"We don't know yet."

"What do you know about him? Has he been reported missing?"

She heard him chuckle on the other end of the line. "What's so funny?" she demanded.

"You! You sound like a detective. One question after another."

"That's because you're not volunteering nearly enough information," she snipped in defense. "I feel like I'm prying it out of you."

"That's because I don't have much to tell. I spoke to Officer Abraham this evening. She reached out to Alexander's wife, but so far, hasn't had a call back. There was little evidence left in the car. It had been wiped clean of prints, and the license plate was missing. Even the back bumper sticker was rendered illegible. We only know what we know because of the VIN number. This may not be the same car."

"It is. The bumper sticker proves it." She told him Granny Bert's neighbor reported seeing a bumper sticker on the rear driver side bumper. In her mind, scraping off any identifying logo equated to proof it was one and the same car. "There was also something hanging from the rearview mirror."

"Not anymore."

"Okay, but having no prints is further proof," she added. "Why else would the car be clean?"

"Still, until we talk to the wife, we don't know this is our dead guy."

"Yes, we do."

"No, we don't," he insisted firmly.

"I just pulled up his social media account," Madison informed him. "It's the same guy. Blond hair, athletic build, nice looking. Much better looking alive than dead, by the way. According to this, he works for *Tellina*, whatever that is. He's been married to Shaylee Eddings Alexander for four years. No kids. The last time he posted was about a month ago, and that was pictures of his dog." She scrolled through his account. "In fact, he posts more about his dog than he does his wife. Let's see why... Hmm."

"Hmm? What does that mean? What do you see? What's it say?" Now it was Brash with the rapid-fire questions.

"According to his wife's page, Ron travels a lot. While he's out of town, she spends most of her time in and out. As in *out* in public, *in* the bar, *in* the hot tub, hanging *out* at the pool... You get the picture. Apparently, she's not one of those wives who minds her husband being gone all the time."

"Let's find out what *Tellina* is. Maybe that will explain his connection to Rose."

"Or, maybe he doesn't mind being away from home, either. He may be one of those husbands with a girlfriend in every town. Rose may be one of them."

"I can't relate to those kinds of guys, but I know they're out there."

"I'll see what I can dig up on social media."

Brash chuckled. "I'm sure you will. Perry won't think to check out that avenue. Misty may, but not Perry."

"Why is it that you refer to Officer Abraham by her first name, but Officer Perry by his surname? Should I be jealous?" she teased.

"'Misty' is a lot easier and faster to say than 'Officer Abraham,'" he pointed out. "She's also a lot easier to look at and much more pleasant to deal with than Perry, but you know you have no reason to ever be jealous. Long before you and I got reacquainted, she and I realized we weren't couple material." His deep voice dropped to a decadent growl. "Like it or not, Madison deCordova, you are the only woman in the world for me."

"Believe me, I like it. I thank my lucky stars every day that I'm your wife."

14

Spending time at the ranch with Grammy Lydia, the girls learned more than just cooking skills. They also learned more about the mysterious Rosa.

Lydia recalled the family from the big Spanish-style castle and knew more about them than even Granny Bert. Perhaps, she said, it was because the family lived closer to the ranch than they did to town. Perhaps it was because the name Davila implied a kinship with the deCordova clan. Or perhaps because the deCordovas, with their distant ties to a Spanish heritage and their revered standing in the community, seemed to be the closest thing the 'royal family' had as a contemporary.

Immaculada Davila tried on several occasions to reach out to Lydia and her mother-in-law, Rebecca deCordova. Try as they might, neither could warm up to the pompous other woman. Rebecca had little patience for people who put on airs, and she found Immaculada to be one of the worst. For all her talk of being related to the royal family of Spain, she failed to mention the minute detail that she and her husband had been disenfranchised from the kingdom and banished to America. Her single goal in life was to see that her granddaughter married well, so they might return to their home country.

To that end, she tried forcing a friendship between

Lydia and Rosa, hoping Lydia would be a good influence on the girl.

In truth, the friendship came easily enough. Rosa was a sweet girl, but Lydia reported that they simply had little in common. Rosa was away at her academy most of the year, learning the proper etiquette for attending a cotillion, or how to plan for a formal dinner party at a table that seated twenty-four. Lydia was newly married and learning how to manage life on a working ranch, a husband, residing in the same house as her in-laws, and feeding a hungry crew of eight ranch hands each day. When Rosa came home for summer break, she spun girlish dreams of romance and a future with her mysterious 'someone special.' Not only had Lydia already found her someone special, but she was living out her romantic fantasies with him and would soon bear his child.

There simply wasn't enough common ground between the two young women to form a true and lasting bond, she said. Lydia never did know the identity of Rosa's secret love interest, but she knew the girl's grandparents didn't approve. Immaculada and Esteban had big plans for the young beauty, and those plans didn't include a future in the Brazos Valley. Soon after Brash's oldest brother was born—so around 1969, she surmised—the Davilas moved away from the area, and she never heard from them again. In fact, she admitted, she had forgotten all about them until the girls stirred up the old, dusty memories.

Lydia also remembered that Israel Ballard's mother worked for the Davila family. If she wasn't mistaken, Israel sometimes did yard work for them, keeping their expansive lawns neatly mowed and trimmed.

Armed with the name Rosa Davila, the girls launched into an online search for the woman. By now, they estimated she would be close to seventy years old. No doubt she had married and changed her name, making searching for her after all these years even more difficult.

Grammy Lydia thought she might know someone who could help, but until they heard back from her, their efforts were stymied. Knowing Maddy had enough to deal with now, they didn't want to bother her, so they didn't ask for her help.

"We know who Rosa *was*," Bethani surmised. "Now we just need to find out who she *is*."

"Remember in Spanish class, Mr. Palacios made us learn about Spain? He had us look up all that stuff on how Spain differs from Mexico, even though they share the same language. Maybe he would have a clue on how to go about finding someone with ties to the Spanish royal family," Megan suggested.

"Maybe."

"It's worth a shot, isn't it?"

Bethani shrugged. "Sure. What do we have to lose?"

Armed with a plan, the girls worked out a scheme to visit their Spanish teacher.

With the day's high temperature flirting with the one-hundred-degree mark, and without a car of their own to drive, they were at the mercy of an adult to drive them. Granny Bert became their accomplice of choice. Claiming she needed their help programming a new satellite receiver for her television, she picked them up at the Big House and brought them home with her. There, they baked cookies and divided them onto three plates at Granny Bert's direction. One was to take home with them, one was for Mr. Palacios, and one was for another recipient. They giggled at her elusive answer, assuming she meant for her on-again/off-again 'beau,' Sticker Pierce. She had been stringing the poor man along for over sixty years.

The plate of warm cookies in tow, they walked the short distance to the teacher's house. His yard was neat and planted with an array of rose bushes, the different colors and varieties adding visual interest to the boxy space.

Reaching to ring the bell a second time, Megan jumped

in surprise when the door swung open.

"Yes?" His greeting was cool but professional, until he recognized the teens on his doorstep. Surprise took over. "Miss deCordova and Miss Reynolds. What a surprise. I rarely see students during the summertime."

"I know!" Megan said, her smile buoyant. "We were just talking about that. For nine months, we see our teachers day in, day out, and then, poof! Summer comes along, and we don't see them for almost three months. It's a shame, really."

Behind her, Bethani nodded in complete agreement.

Mr. Palacios looked amused. His dark eyes glittered as he peered over a pair of half-lens reading glasses. Taking the glasses off and pocketing them in his ever-present cardigan, he remarked in a dry voice, "So, you'd have me believe you actually missed me over the course of the last three weeks. School's not been out long," he reminded the teens.

"That, and we wanted to ask you something," Megan freely admitted.

"I make it a custom not to favor one student over another. If you're selling something, I'm afraid—"

"We're not selling anything," Bethani broke in. "You might say we came for a summer tutorial."

Intrigued, the man stood back and invited them inside. "In that case, ladies, do come in."

"We brought you cookies," Bethani said, handing them over as she passed.

"*Gracias por las galletas*," he said, wearing a rare smile.

"*De nada*."

"*¡No hay de qué!*" Megan replied, proud she remembered the proper response.

He invited them to have a seat on the formal-style sofa. The girls sat with care, afraid they might leave a mark on the heavy brocade. The sofa looked awfully expensive and quite possibly antique.

The entire room reminded Bethani of the formal living room at the Big House, the one they seldom used because it was so stuffy and uncomfortable. Their family much preferred the casual style of the family room. Their second choice was the ladies' parlor just off the entry, or, better yet, the kitchen table.

"Your house is lovely." Megan's polite compliment was ruined by her natural curiosity. "Is it just you here?"

She couldn't help herself. The decor was more suited for an older woman than it was for a man. Unless, she decided, the man was filthy rich. And if he was, why did he teach high school Spanish? Some of this stuff looked like it came out of a museum.

"Yes," he confirmed.

"Nice digs," she murmured. "I like the floral carpet."

"My mother will be moving in soon," he volunteered. "I brought in some of her things to make her feel more comfortable."

"Ah, that explains it," Bethani said, and Megan agreed.

"Now that we have the pleasantries out of the way," Eloy Palacios said, his voice hinging between amusement and annoyance, "what may I do for you ladies?"

"We were having a discussion earlier," Megan explained, "and thought you would be the perfect person to settle our debate. We're curious about the Spanish monarchy."

Stiffening, he arched his brows in a way that reminded Megan of her father. "And you thought of me?" He sounded skeptical, if not cool.

"Sure. You told us about it in class. Remember?" Bethani said.

He seemed to relax somewhat at her response. He answered most of their questions, but only after forcing them to phrase them in the proper way. With Mr. Palacios, the girls knew it was like a game, trying to coax an answer from his stingy lips.

After a few nonsense questions, they worked the conversation around to where they wanted.

"There's a rumor on the internet," Bethani fabricated, "that there's a Spanish princess living somewhere here in Texas. Is that true?"

"Do you believe everything you see on the internet?" he challenged.

"No, sir. But this story seemed plausible."

"And what made it seem that way?"

Megan decided to mix in a few legitimate details with the embellishments. "My grandmother remembers knowing a family that lived here a long time ago. They always claimed they were related to the royal family of Spain. The rumor was that they were disowned by the king and had to move to America in disgrace. We thought maybe the princess could be their granddaughter."

"If her family were disowned, she would hardly be a princess," their teacher pointed out, his eyes sharp with displeasure. He didn't seem at all impressed with their deductive reasoning skills.

"How would we know if the first part was true?" Bethani asked. "Did anyone from the royal family ever live around here?"

"Would this have been before I moved here?"

"It was probably before you were even born," Megan agreed. She took a second look at him, noting the sweater in the hundred-degree weather. "Maybe," she added.

"Then I'm hardly the person to ask."

"So, how would we know?" Bethani pushed. "How would we find out if these people really were related to the royal family? Is there a database of some kind that keeps track of them?"

"That is a great question, Miss Reynolds. However, I'm afraid I can't help you." He stood, signaling the end of their meeting. "But I do appreciate the cookies."

Bethani reluctantly rose to her feet. "If your mom's coming soon, you can share with her," she mumbled.

"Perhaps I will."

Disappointed they hadn't learned more, the girls contemplated their next plan of action as they retraced their steps. When they saw Granny Bert's Buick idling at the curb, they thought she was there to save them from walking in the heat. They thanked her as they crawled into the air-conditioned comfort.

"That, too," the older woman said. "First, we have another plate of cookies to deliver."

"To Cutter's grandpa?" Bethani asked with a smirk.

"Why would I take that old coot a plate of fresh cookies?"

Bethani shot her stepsister a knowing smile. "Uh-oh. Trouble in paradise again. But, if the cookies aren't for Sticker, who are they for?"

"We're going to pay a little visit to our town's newest resident," Granny Bert informed the girls.

"I thought she killed that guy. Why do we want to take her cookies?" Megan asked.

"Because we're helping your daddy out. We're collecting information, so I want you girls to keep your eyes peeled. I have a plan on how we're going to do it, too."

"My, my," Rose Belvedere said, her voice just short of irate. Her steadily tapping toe wasn't as disciplined. "Isn't this a surprise."

"Just one of the many pleasures you'll find living here in The Sisters," Granny Bert beamed. "We're a friendly bunch."

She didn't wait to be invited in. She barged right in, carrying the plate of cookies with her, and leaving the girls to trail behind.

Too stunned to stop them, Rose stood aside with her mouth agape.

Granny Bert stopped just inside the living room, looking around at the generic room with a huge smile on her face. "Now, would you look at this," she crooned. "This is just as cute as a button. Not a thing like the house I remember growing up in."

Snapping to attention, Rose blinked her wide-spaced gray eyes in true surprise. "*You* grew up here?"

"I most certainly did!" the older woman claimed. Nothing could be further from the truth, but the newcomer didn't know that. "It was a tight fit, but all six of us young 'uns, Momma and Daddy, and my grand-mammy and grand-pappy on my momma's side all lived in this house, just as happy as clams!"

"*Ten* of you lived here?" Rose squeaked. "In this little house?"

"Oh, and plus my cousin Roy Earl," she added for good measure. Her voice took on an extra layer of country twang. "Yes, ma'am. It was a packed house, but we had some fine times here."

"How did all of y'all fit in here, Granny?" Bethani wanted to know. "It looks kind of small, to me." As if remembering her manners, she turned to Rose with a bright smile and a handshake. "I'm Beth. Welcome to Juliet."

"And I'm Meg. We brought cookies!" She said the last as if cookies were the solution to every problem.

"Here you go." Granny Bert shoved the plate into Rose's hands.

Bombarded by the bright and smiling faces surrounding her, Rose was overwhelmed by the fast, animated greetings. Caught unawares, she was slow reacting to the old woman's trick.

Granny Bert launched into a long spiel meant to confound the still-stunned homeowner. "I know it looks small, but looks can fool you. I'm sure this nice little lady won't mind if I show you how we did it. She might need to know, too, if she ever decides to have a girl's weekend or a houseful of young 'uns. You don't have kids, do you, hon? No, I didn't think so. Too tiny of a waist. Nice belt, by the way. That alligator print is all the rage."

The old woman kept up a steady babble as she stepped backward from the room, drawing the others along with her as if she led a tour. Even Rose Belvedere trailed behind, the plate of cookies still in her hands and a dazed expression imprinted on her face.

"This front room was where we kids slept." Granny Bert used a sweeping arm motion as she walked into what Maddy reported was the office, her actions bold as a sunrise. She slyly pointed out the areas her cohorts should focus on.

"Over yonder, where those whiteboards and such are, was the boys' side of the room. Three beds, stacked from floor to ceiling. Not much head room, and they had to slide in from the side, but it was the only way to get all six kids in the room. See that screen with the pretty red and pink logo? That's where our bed was. All three of us girls slept in it, until Lucy Jane got too fat. After that, she slept on the floor yonder, where all those computers are. Back then, we didn't have those fancy phones with all the different lines. Why, that one there must have four or five numbers attached to it. When we finally did get a phone, our number was nice and simple. BR-549. None of these complicated strings of numbers we have to dial nowadays."

Rose Belvedere was slowly coming out of her daze. With a distinct thud, she deposited the plate of cookies next to the multi-line phone in question. "Now, see here—" she began.

Granny Bert went on as if she hadn't spoken. "The walls bring back warm memories of ours back then. These have maps and calendars and newspaper clippings tacked up on them. Ours had the Sears and Roebucks catalog glued right to the wood. We couldn't afford paint or fancy wallpaper, and the catalogs were a heap more entertaining. Come on out in the hall and I'll show you where Billy Earl threw down his pallet."

"Roy Earl," Bethani reminded on a murmur.

"Oh, that's right. Billy Earl was his twin brother." Leading the way out of the office, she told some inane story about how to tell the two boys apart. Bethani followed close behind, asking questions to fuel her great grandmother's wild imagination. Rose hovered hot on their heels, trying to assert some authority. No one seemed to notice that Megan lagged behind, slow to leave the office.

As they completed the tour, Granny Bert kept up her line of subterfuge. It was nothing but senseless chatter, meant to distract and dumbfound.

From the dazed look in Rose's eyes, it had worked.

"My, oh, my!" the sly old woman gushed, clapping her hands together and beaming at her hostess. The sublime-looking smile on her face almost passed for the real thing. "That was just delightful. You have no idea how happy you've made this old gal, inviting me into your lovely home and showing me around. You've brought back such warm, happy memories."

Having had little or no say in the matter, Rose didn't know quite what to say. She settled on a muttered, "I'm glad one of us enjoyed it."

"Oh, I certainly did," she assured her. "Does the old ticker good, reliving good times. Makes me forget all about the ugliness that happened here." She studied the other woman from beneath her lashes. Rose looked curious, but she failed to take the bait.

Not to be discouraged, the older woman huffed out a sigh and went on, "Finding the dead body that way. And with all that blood…"

That got a reaction. Rose Belvedere not only blanched,

but she sucked in a gasp. Curiously, her eyes flew to a spot in the kitchen, behind where Granny Bert stood.

She collected herself quickly enough. A cool mask of indifference settled on her face, and she pulled in a much slower, measured breath. "I have no idea what you're talking about," she said, her voice stiff.

"Of course, you don't, dear." Fascinated by the woman's reaction, Granny Bert pretended to believe her. "Naturally, we didn't talk about it much. We moved out the very next day."

Aloofness gave way to confusion, and confusion to curiosity. "What *are* you talking about?" The question seemed pulled from her.

"I don't want to give you the willy-nillies," Granny Bert claimed, even while she thought up a gruesome and haunting tale to tell. The woman didn't deserve any peace, after what she had done. One man was dead, and Madison very well could have been. "You have to take a bath at some point," she reasoned, "but they say the pipes still rattle from all the blood that was clogged inside. That's where we found him, you know, after he had been shot. No one knows why he chose our house, but there he was, bled out in that old bathtub. A body just can't feel clean after that, bathing in a tub stained with blood." She gave a tsk of regret before brightening. "Girls," she said with a sudden smile, "next time we come, we'll bring a stick of blood sausage for our new friend."

Looking pale once more, Rose swallowed hard and stammered, "Th—That won't be necessary."

"Are you sure? It seems the least we can do."

Her voice stiffened with resolve. "I'm quite positive."

Seeming to rethink her offer, Granny Bert nodded her gray head. "Maybe that is best," she crooned. "Are you feeling all right? You look a bit peaked, dear. Maybe you should lie down. A nice, hot bath might help." She shot the teenagers a sharp look, seeing the smiles they tried hard to contain. To draw Rose's attention away from them, she added, "And pay no attention to those stains in the tub, dearie. Just relax and put that dead body right out of your mind. We'll let ourselves out."

The girls managed to hold their laughter only until they reached the Buick.

Once inside, they howled at the old woman's antics, and at the horrified expression on Rose Belvedere's face.

15

Home early from work that day, Blake showered before coming down to fix a pre-dinner snack. He found his mother moving slowly about the kitchen, her actions stiff.

"Are you okay?" he asked in concern.

"Just sore," she assured him. "I guess I was jostled around in the car yesterday more than I realized. Plus, that embankment was steep. I used muscles I haven't used in a while."

"We can make supper tonight, if you don't feel like it."

"To be honest," she admitted, "I was thinking of ordering from *New Beginnings* and getting it to go."

"You know that's fine with me. I miss Aunt Genny's cooking." He hastily added, "No offense to yours."

"None taken." She knew her best friend was a better cook than she.

He finished making a sandwich before asking, "Hey, Mom. Who's Alex?"

"Alex?" she asked, trying to place the name. Coming up blank, she shook her head. "I don't think I know anyone named Alex. Why do you ask?"

"I found a sports watch charging on my bathroom

counter."

"Oh, that! I completely forgot. I found that yesterday in the grass. I brought it home to see if it still worked."

"When I pressed the button, it had a greeting for some dude named Alex. Wonder what he was doing in our yard?"

"Not our grass," Madison clarified. "I found it when I was climbing my way up the embankment. I thought it was a snake at first."

Her son looked amused. "A lot of people get those two mixed up."

"Don't get fresh with me, young man," she pretended to scold.

The back door opened, and the girls came in, a noisy commotion of laughter and excited voices. Granny Bert wasn't far behind, chuckling with amusement.

Their laughter was infectious. "What have you three been up to?" Madison asked with a laugh of her own. "I suspect you did more than program a television."

"We made cookies," Bethani confirmed, "and took some over to Rose Belvedere's."

Madison's smile evaporated. "You went *where*?" She balled her fists onto her hips and glared at her grandmother. "Have you truly lost your mind this time? You took my girls to that woman's house, knowing she could be a cold-blooded killer?"

"Don't worry. The only thing in danger today were the flies. With her mouth hanging open like that, she could have swallowed a whole swarm of them. That woman didn't know what hit her!" Granny Bert boasted.

"It's true," Bethani said, giggling. "You should have seen Granny Bert. She was in rare form today. She convinced the woman she grew up in the house, and that six kids slept in one bedroom! And she told this one story about not being able to tell her twin cousins apart, until a mule kicked—"

"Never mind," Madison broke in, unamused. "I've heard plenty of your great-grandmother's convoluted tales, thank you very much."

"Not these, you haven't!" Megan tipped her auburn head to Bethani's, and the girls dissolved into more giggles.

"She still had no right dragging you two over there. Rose Belvedere may be dangerous."

Her grandmother scoffed. "I'm telling you; the woman never knew what hit her. The girls did an excellent job as my supporting cast."

"This isn't a play, Granny Bert!" Madison reminded her grandmother in exasperation. "This is a real-life murder mystery. And I have every reason to believe she was responsible for my so-called 'accident' yesterday."

The girls sobered. Blake looked up from his second sandwich.

"Why do you say that?" Bethani asked. "How could she have been involved?"

Regretting her outburst, Madison realized she had said too much. Granny Bert knew the truth, but she hadn't wanted to worry the kids. Now that she had opened her big mouth, there was no backing out.

"The mechanic said that someone had tampered with my power steering," she admitted. "It was right after I had been to visit the Bealls."

"That's next door to Rose Belvedere," Megan noted.

"Exactly."

"No wonder you added that story about the bathtub, Granny Bert. Serves that horrible woman right!" Bethani fumed.

Blake always enjoyed his great-grandmother's flair for drama. His mother often worried that he followed in her footsteps. "What story about the bathtub?" he wanted to know.

"Some crazy tale that's sure to creep her out, every time she goes to take a bath. Something about a man bleeding out in the bathtub, and the stains still being there. It was hilarious, seeing her face!"

Megan piped in with a cheery voice. "I have it on video."

"How did you do that, girl?" Impressed, Granny Bert wanted to know the details.

"Easy. Cross your arms like you're bored, tuck your phone in like so, face the camera outward, and remember to move slowly." She gave a demonstration of her technique. "I recorded almost the whole visit."

"Good job, Meggie!" Granny Bert bragged on the girl. "Can you send that to our phones?"

"Sure."

Granny Bert took a seat at the kitchen table as she handed her cell phone to the teens. They could take care of the technical details better than she. "There's definitely something going on in that house," she told Madison.

"I agree, but I hope you saw more than Genny and I did."

"I pointed out things for the girls to pay attention to. For instance, why does that woman need a multi-line phone? Same thing with computers. Why two? You mark my words. She's up to something more than just calling to collect money."

Bethani nodded in agreement. "The phone had four lines. There were two routers on the desk, one for each computer, and two printers."

In spite of herself, Madison was impressed.

"Sounds like a serious setup."

"That's not all," her grandmother continued. "When I first mentioned finding a dead body, her eyes immediately went to the kitchen. I think that's where it happened. I think that's where she killed that man and wrapped him up in a rug."

Madison pulled in a deep breath that was less than steady. "Okay, this is getting too serious for my liking. Granny, under no circumstances can you take the girls back to the house. I'm serious. This woman is clearly dangerous. I don't even want you going back there."

"If it's too dangerous for us," Bethani pointed out, "it's too dangerous for you."

"That's right, Momma Maddy. You don't need to go back there, either."

"Maybe I won't have to," she said, trying to sound optimistic. "With any luck, I'll find what I need through other sources."

Her phone buzzed with an incoming call. Derron's name scrolled across the screen. "Yes?"

"Hey, dollface. I have a question for you."

"I'll see if I have an answer for you."

"I'm in the office," her employee said, clearly hinting for her to come to him.

"I'm in the kitchen. Come on over and have a glass of tea with us."

His voice took on a definite whine. "But that's *all* the way over on the other side of the house. It's like a four-mile hike," he exaggerated.

She knew she could entice him to change his tune. "Granny Bert is here."

"On my way."

Derron loved her grandmother and never missed a chance for a witty exchange with the older woman. A few minutes later, the petite young man appeared in the kitchen, arms outstretched as he blew air kisses into the room. "Ah. Some of my very favorite people in the world, all in one room!"

As usual, he was better dressed than any of the females in the room. His chino pants were crisp and pleated, his bold print, Cuban-collar shirt tucked neatly into a thin brown belt that matched his shiny loafers. With every blond hair in place, he looked cool and refreshed, despite the summer heat. Everyone knew Derron Mullins was a handsome man. Including Derron Mullins.

He sidled up to Granny Bert and said in a conspiratorial tone, "Word is on the street that some younger man did you wrong, and you gave him the cold shoulder." After a pregnant pause, he added, "And foot. And all parts in between." He wiggled his perfectly groomed eyebrows. "Say it ain't so, GB."

Falling into the spirit of his wordplay, the older woman's faded eyes twinkled. "You might say, I put that fella on ice," she cracked.

After a few more truly awful puns, Madison called a halt to their shenanigans. "Okay, you two. Enough. Remember, a man died. Derron, I'm surprised you're still here. I thought you had left for the day."

"I tried, but the phone kept ringing. Honestly, don't these people know I have a life?"

"'These people,' meaning our clients? The ones that make your paycheck possible?"

"Yes! Those! All they expect is work, work, work. How's a guy supposed to have some fun, if all he ever does is slave behind a desk all day?"

"You came in after noon," Madison reminded him dryly. "It's not even five yet."

"I know. A long day, right?" He held his hand up for a high-five from Granny Bert.

Madison shook her head in defeat. When the two of them were together, they were impossible. "You said you had a question for me?"

"Besides the obvious one of *why are you wearing those clothes*?" He trailed his eyes over her body, lips curled in derision. He had taken her shopping for her wedding trousseau, but still she dressed like her grandmother.

"Besides that."

"Oh. Well, Mabel Crowder wants to hire us to write a letter for her."

Madison waited for him to say more. When he dipped his blond head to Granny Bert's gray one and said something that made her laugh, Madison prodded, "What *kind* of letter? A *j*? An *o*? I do a great *k*, with cute little curlicues and squiggles."

"Good one, girl!" he approved with a snicker. He beamed over at her grandmother. "There's hope for our girl yet."

"I don't know about that," the older woman harrumphed. "She found no humor in the trick I played on Rose Belvedere this afternoon."

"Ooh, Rose Belvedere. I hear she's a sharp dresser."

Before the conversation got derailed even further, Madison snapped her fingers, hoping to gain his attention. "Derron. Over here, boy." She then whistled, as if calling a puppy.

"You're cruel." His voice was dry, but his eyes danced with humor. That was a good one, too. "Very well. Mrs. Crowder wants to know if we can write a letter on her behalf, requesting to represent her in small claims court."

"Are you insane? We aren't lawyers! We can't represent her in court."

"She only wants us to speak on her behalf and explain her side of the situation. You know the poor dear has a lisp."

"Lisp? Her tongue is tied tighter than a chastity belt on a nun!" Granny Bert hooted. While Derron and the teens snickered, Madison chastised her grandmother's outburst.

"Nonetheless," Madison said sternly, speaking over the giggles, "we aren't legal counsel. You told her that, right?"

"Yes, but she said she was willing to take her chances."

"What possessed her to think *In a Pinch* could represent her in court?"

He shrugged his petite shoulders. "Miss Wanda had a similar problem with an unpaid bill. I wrote a scorching letter on her behalf, raking the company over the coals for badgering her when she had clearly settled the matter. I suppose she told Mrs. Crowder."

"What has Wanda gotten into now?" Granny Bert muttered. "I swear, that woman's head is so high up in the sky with this new beau of hers, she can't see through the clouds!"

"Beau? She's *cheating* on me?" Derron feigned a crestfallen expression.

"I'll remind myself there are children in the room," Granny Bert, almost regretfully, "and keep my mouth closed on that one."

"And please keep it that way." Madison's glare held a warning. "Derron, I don't know what letter you wrote for Miss Wanda, but I don't want to be associated with this in any way. We are *not* qualified to give legal advice."

Dinner was done, the kids were in bed, and the house was quiet. Madison tried convincing herself she was sleepy, but her mind wasn't having it. Between her restless thoughts and her achy body, she couldn't get comfortable.

She headed downstairs in defeat. A glass of wine accompanied her to her office, where she settled into her white leather chair and turned on her computer. Time to surf the web.

Last night, she had been too tired to do any serious stalking on social media. Today, she was sidetracked with business calls and mundane recordkeeping. This was her first opportunity to snoop around on the web.

A deeper dive into Ron and Shaylee Alexander's lives revealed that the couple was in their mid-thirties, lived in a comfortable house in a trendy neighborhood, and had three dogs they adored. Both had a large network of friends, but very few were designated as family members.

Determining who Ron's employer was proved more elusive. Nothing in the man's profile hinted at his profession or his workplace, other than the one reference to employment at *Tellina*.

Shaylee's employment was easier to track. She sold exercise equipment through direct sales and in-home instruction parties. According to her profile, she was one of *In Shape's* top Sculptors, as they were called.

Amused at the new twist on the age-old *Tupperware* business model, Madison scrolled through some of Shaylee's posts of past parties and hostesses. She was surprised to see two familiar faces among the photos. Apparently, Lana Kopetsky and Sheree Blackburn had attended a party in Navasota shortly after the new year. Both were decked out in sparkly exercise clothes and, with their hair and makeup 'just so,' looked more prepared for a photoshoot than an exercise class. None of the other women looked familiar.

Knee deep in stalking territory, Madison found a

loose trail connecting Shaylee and her husband Ron to other people in and around The Sisters. And while Madison herself had no social media 'friends' in common with the couple, she was surprised to find that many of her real-life friends did, including Genny, Derron, and even Miss Wanda.

Indeed, it was a small world.

Seeing Miss Wanda's profile pop up, she thought about the older woman's presence on another social media site. What had she called it? The *Silver Circle*? In a new window, Madison did a search for the dating service. An advertisement popped up, extolling the virtues of the exciting new social connection for mature adults. It looked legitimate enough, even if she questioned the integrity and authenticity of some of its users.

Going back to the first window, she typed in the name Rose Belvedere and hit enter. Four possible matches popped up, but she knew she had the right profile when she saw the picture of a vibrant pink rose. Still in stalker mode, Madison clicked on the photo.

The page loaded with more images of the flower. Most of Rose's posts were about gardening, cute cuddly animals, and fashion trends. The majority were shared from other pages or websites, with only a few carrying a personal message.

The 'intro' section about her was sparse. She was currently self-employed, with no previous employer listed. She called Houston her hometown but listed Juliet as her current residence. Most other details were missing or marked private. She only had 79 friends, suggesting her profile was relatively new.

Madison clicked through a few of her friends, noting most had profiles also marked as private. After checking six or more, Madison realized they all had one thing in common: they each had an avatar or generic image for a profile picture. Few were of an actual person.

Were any of them even real? Like Rose, most had fewer than a hundred friends.

As the wine relaxed her, Madison stifled a yawn and considered stopping where she was. Curiosity, however, won out. Just a little more snooping, and she would call it a night.

She clicked through several names, following where the trail took her. She concentrated on the few contacts featuring pictures of real people. Meredith was friends with Brandon, who was friends with Jill. Jill lived in Conroe and worked at a nursing facility called *Golden Standards*. The name sounded vaguely familiar. Wasn't that the name of the place where Nelda Goldberg lived? Seeing that one of Jill's friends was Rita Goldberg, she felt certain it was.

Madison noted that many of Jill's other friends worked at assisted living centers and nursing homes. At least two worked at *Senior Styles* in Waco, and one of them had linked a local news story to her feed. Intrigued, Madison clicked on the link. It was, in fact, the same story she had heard on television at the hotel, the one with mention of a black Crown Victoria.

Madison knew about the Six Degrees of Separation theory, based on the rationale that, in just six steps or less, everyone was connected in some way. She could even apply that theory here. Rose was connected to Meredith (1), who was connected to Brandon (2), who was connected to Jill (3), who was connected to Bev (4), who referenced a black car (5), that fit the description of the car from a few weeks ago (6). Using the infamous six-step theory, she could assert that Rose had a connection, however loosely, to the mysterious black car.

It took one fewer step to connect her to Nelda Goldberg, whom she claimed was her great-aunt.

Now even more curious, Madison retraced her virtual steps, looking for more connections. Jill was also friends with Toni, who was a Sculptor with *In Shape.*

Excited, Madison wiggled in her chair. *Those same six steps just connected Rose to Ron Alexander!*

Common sense told her it wouldn't stand up under scrutiny, but it reinforced what she and Brash believed all along. There *was* a connection between the two. If the blue car wasn't fodder enough, this offered more.

Perhaps there were other connections she could make. Someone had been photographed against a blue and silver logo. Where had she seen that before? For whatever reason, it brought to mind Miss Wanda, but she was getting too groggy to make the connection. Maybe it was time to head upstairs. She could always pick this up tomorrow when her mind was fresh and alert.

As she logged off and shut down her computer, she heard a chirp from the security system. Madison flipped open a cleverly disguised panel to reveal the state-of-the-art command center. With a few simple keystrokes, she could access all cameras, alarms, and keypads. There were similar panels in the kitchen and the master bedroom.

Seeing nothing out of the ordinary, she started closing the panel. This time, the chirp sounded twice. Like the backup camera on her car, the frequency and intensity escalated with the impending danger.

Madison peered closer at the grainy images on the screen. The system used night vision imagery, but the view was still distorted at a distance. When enabled, motion-activated lights helped chase away the shadows but couldn't differentiate between squirrels and intruders. For that reason, the lights were usually disabled. Tonight was no different.

Holding her breath, Madison waited as the alarm emitted three distinct bleeps. Whatever the threat was, it came closer. She watched the screen, detecting slight movement in the left front area of the yard, just beyond where she stood now. Was that someone moving among the trees? Or was it just a stray dog?

Four chirps.

Now five.

And that shadow was too large to be a dog.

As the threat came nearer, and the night vision camera focused, Madison could see it was definitely a person. He or she wore an over-sized sweatshirt and a cap pulled low, obscuring hair and face. *Sensing* more than seeing, Madison thought it was a woman who slipped from behind a tree and raced up to the porch, sending the alarm into a frenzy.

Heart in her throat, Madison hit the light panel. The blackness evaporated, melting against the mega wattage of a dozen flood lamps. The front yard was now as bright as day.

The woman instantly jerked away, shielding her face with her arm. All Madison saw was a pair of large, dark sunglasses and an elbow.

As quickly as she had appeared, the woman raced across the lawn. With the help of a waiting step ladder, she easily scaled the wrought-iron fence with its pointed finials atop the spires. Like a shadow, she vanished into the night.

The alarm quieted, but not Madison's heart. It clattered in fright.

Rose Belvedere was getting bolder.

16

Fridays were always busy for *Marvin Gardens*. Aside from landscaping and planting needs, people wanted their lawns cut and trimmed for the weekend. Already, patrons requested Blake by name. The youth proved to work quickly but efficiently.

He already had a packed schedule for the day when Mr. Combs called him and informed him of an added assignment. "I know it's lunchtime," his boss apologized. "I know you're hungry. But we've had a special request by one of our best customers. A semi-emergency, he called it. Can you squeeze it in before going to Allen Wynn's?"

"How big a job is it?"

"Just a small yard to cut and trim."

"Sure, Mr. Combs. I'll take care of it." What other choice did he have? He might die of starvation, but the boss called with a special request. He couldn't turn him down.

"I knew I could depend on you, Blake. The address is 724 Second Avenue. The client is expecting you."

Blake was familiar with the address. It was Mr. Palacios' house, around the corner and across the street from Granny Bert's.

When he arrived and knocked on the door, he

found his language arts teacher in frantic preparation for his mother's unexpected early arrival. His ever-present cardigan was absent as he answered the door with a broom and dustpan in one hand, a pan of burnt rolls in the other.

"Mr. Palacios? I'm here to mow your yard."

"Yes, yes. Nice and short. Be sure to trim the hedges, as well."

"Is everything okay, sir?"

"Nothing could be further from 'okay,'" he said with blunt aplomb. "My mother is arriving two days earlier than expected. Her car should be here before five this afternoon."

Blake didn't understand 'the car' part, but he was confident about the yard. "If you're worried about the lawn, don't be. I'll have it in shape before she gets here," he assured the teacher.

"If only the house were in shape." The weary tone in his voice drew the teen's attention.

Blake looked past the doorway to see an overturned end table, a vase of flowers strewn across the carpet, and a shattered ashtray nearby. In the kitchen beyond, smoke billowed from an open oven. The deafening trill of a smoke alarm pierced the thick air.

"Do you need help, Mr. Palacios?"

"You have no idea," the man said dryly.

"I can fix that."

"You worry with the yard. My mother despises a messy lawn.'"

"Yes, sir, I'll take care of the yard. I didn't mean I'd help with the house. I meant my sisters."

"Bethani and Megan?"

"Yes, sir. I can call them and get them to come right over."

Eloy Palacios looked tempted, but he shook his

head with obvious regret. Before he could speak, Blake broke in. "No offense, but it looks like you can use a hand. The girls will be happy to help."

"Thank you, but I can manage."

Blake ignored the stiff dismissal. As Mr. Palacios closed the door, Blake called his twin and explained the situation. Before he had completed the first round of the yard with the lawn mower, both girls were there to help.

Mr. Palacios answered the door again the second time an irritated growl, assuming Blake had encountered a problem. He wasn't prepared for the two teenage girls on his doorstep, pushing their way into his living room.

"This house is full of smoke!" Bethani cried, batting the air away from her sensitive nose. Not unlike her great-grandmother, she took charge. "Let's get some windows open and this place aired out!" She went around, opening windows while Megan had the sense to turn off the still-glowing oven.

At least the smoke detector had been disabled and silenced, but the air still churned with smoke.

"I've got this, Mr. Palacios," Megan assured him. "You go do something else. Bethani and I will clean the kitchen."

Too stunned to argue, the man did as instructed.

Less than two hours later, the lawn was neatly mowed and trimmed, the sidewalk swept, and the tools stashed away. Blake joined his sisters inside, even though he had other customers waiting. As Mr. Comb had said, this was a bit of an emergency.

"Smells a lot better in here," he said with approval. Instead of smoke, he smelled something delicious, with notes of vanilla and brown sugar. It made his empty stomach growl in protest.

"A trick I learned from Grammy," Megan said.

"You can't ever go wrong with fresh baked goods. It takes away the worst odors and leaves the house smelling yummy. Plus, you have something delicious to eat. Win/Win."

"Where's Mr. Palacios?"

"We sent him to get freshened up. His mother should be here in about an hour. That gives him time to shower and change before she gets here. Apparently, he has to 'dress' for her arrival." Rolling her blue eyes, Bethani used air quotes to express her thoughts on the subject. She lowered her voice to a loud whisper, leaning in so her words didn't carry. "She sounds like a real tool. Worse than Grandmother Annette. Everything has to be just so. No wonder Mr. Palacios always looks so serious. He was probably never allowed to be a kid."

"I don't think he's as old as we thought, either," Megan admitted. "He just acts and dresses old." She looked around, pleased with how the room looked. "We need to get out of here before she comes. The house is spotless, the cookies are cooling, and five's a crowd. Especially since they haven't seen each other in like three years."

Before they reached the door, the doorbell rang. Bethani looked at the others with a stricken expression. "That can't be her already! Can it?"

"Only one way to find out," Blake said, "and I still hear the shower running." He strode to the door and pulled it open.

A man in a suit and a frumpy little hat stood on the doorstep, his arms folded primly in front of him. "Is this the Palacios residence?" he asked in a formal voice.

"Yes, but—"

The man didn't wait for further explanation. His heels clipped along the sidewalk as he retraced his steps. Blake stared beyond the chauffeur to the vintage Bentley pulled up along the street. He now understood the reference to 'the car.'

The chauffeur opened the rear door and helped a tiny, well-dressed woman from within. She recoiled as a blast of heat greeted her but quickly hid her discomfort. Dressed in a fine suit of pale gray complemented with sapphire-blue accessories from head to toe—shoes, handbag, jewelry, hat, and even gloves—the woman barely came to his shoulder.

Watching the scene unfold from their collective stance at the door, Megan hissed, "What do we do? We aren't supposed to be here!"

"But we are, so it's up to us to welcome her," Blake reasoned.

"Poor Mr. Palacios," his twin sympathized. "His mother is here. Who wears gloves these days? Especially in the summer."

"But those look like real sapphires," Megan murmured.

As the woman neared, they could see she was still a beauty, despite the fine wrinkles on her face and the generous streaks of gray in her dark, upswept hair. Instinctively, the three teenagers lined up side by side, their posture straight. Megan's hand went up to tame her messy auburn hair. Blue eyes wide, Bethani soothed her wrinkled t-shirt in place.

In a most formal voice, the chauffeur announced, "I present *Senora* Palacios."

The tiny woman turned dark, expectant eyes to the trio in the doorway.

When no one immediately spoke up, Blake took the lead. "Hello, ma'am." He thought to stand back, herding the girls behind him as they made room for the woman to step inside. It was hardly his house, but he felt the need to fill the awkward silence. For lack of something better to say, he added, "Welcome."

Mrs. Palacios stepped inside her son's humble home, her eyes sweeping across the tastefully decorated room. A hint of recognition flashed across her face when she saw the sofa and rug, but her expression didn't soften.

"I'll bring your luggage, madame," the chauffeur murmured.

"I'll help!" Blake was out the door before his sisters could stab him with furious glares, fueled by what they clearly construed as his defection.

Left alone with the stiff Mrs. Palacios, neither girl was certain what to do. Not only had the tiny woman seen the frantic expressions on their faces, but she wore a look of confusion upon her own. Bethani rushed to say, "Uhm, your son will be out in a minute."

Dark eyes turned upon her, quite piercing beneath arched brows. "And you are...?"

"I'm Bethani. We're some of his students. We just dropped by to... to pick up something."

"That's right," Megan said, flashing her megawatt smile at the older woman. "I'm Megan. Your son is helping us with a special summer project." Her eyes twinkled with the private joke. After today, the man owed them. Surely after this, he would go out of his way to help them learn more about the Spanish aristocracy and one elusive Rosa Davila.

"We had no idea he was expecting company," Bethani added for good measure.

"Have a seat," Megan offered, waving toward the brocade sofa.

Mrs. Palacios perched on the edge of the cushion, her posture stiff. *Regal* came to mind. Towering above her, Bethani felt like an awkward giant.

"Sit," the woman instructed, her tone almost

impatient.

The girls did as told.

Silence stretched between them, until the older woman mercifully asked, "You are my son's students?" Although her English was impeccable, her voice had a distinct accent.

Megan rarely met a stranger, and this stiff, formal woman was no exception. The teen went into a long description of her son's teaching style. In addition to Spanish, he also taught language arts. In that class particularly, Megan claimed he practiced his 'irritating habit' of answering every question with a question. She even rolled her eyes, forgetting for a moment that this was his mother.

At the same time, doors opened on either side of the room. Just as the luggage arrived through the front door, Eloy Palacios stepped from his bedroom door. The surprise on his face was evident. He looked, for a moment, like a deer caught in the headlights.

Feeling sorry for him, Bethani jumped to her feet. "Look who came early!" she said with false enthusiasm.

The teens left as quickly as they could after that, but not before Mrs. Palacios issued a surprise statement.

"You ladies will join me for tea tomorrow." It was more of a summons than an invitation. "Three o'clock."

Madison hated it when work interfered with her snooping, but that's what happened. She spent most of the day at *Cessna Auto*, filling in for her aunt and uncle. By the time she ran her Friday errands for Miss Sybille, stopped at the bank and the post office, and attended to a few other small errands, the day had all but slipped away. When Granny Bert invited her for dinner, she knew it was hopeless to start now. Her internet stalking would have to wait.

Granny Bert treated them to dinner at *Montelongo's*. Aside from *New Beginnings*, it was one of the few restaurants in The Sisters, and the only one that served delicious, authentic Mexican food. The frozen margaritas there were especially popular.

The twins were full of stories about their day and their impromptu good Samaritan venture. Megan had gone back to her mother's for the night, but Bethani told all about her baking trick and how she had apparently charmed the stiff Mrs. Palacios.

"It was hard to tell," she admitted. "The woman reminds me a lot of Grandmother Annette. She doesn't show a lot of emotion, and you can tell appearances mean a lot to her. Maybe that's why she didn't invite Blake to tea tomorrow afternoon. After mowing the grass, he was kind of gross."

"Hey, you had the easy part!" her brother protested. "You were inside, in the air conditioning. I was sweating it out in the hundred-degree heat."

"Tea is something most men don't appreciate," Madison reminded her daughter. She gave her son an indulgent smile. "The sandwiches are too small. Everything is bite sized."

"I don't know why people like to tease us like that," the boy said, shaking his blond head in disgust. "Give me a decent-size portion, not bird bites." He scooped up a huge portion of gooey chili con queso on a tortilla chip and stuffed it into his mouth.

Across the table, Wanda Shanks laughed at the boy's voracious appetite.

"I can't wait to try out all the buffets in Vegas," she said with a glimmer in her eyes. "It's been years since

I've been back there."

"You're not actually going, are you?" Granny Bert demanded. She turned to her friend with an exasperated expression.

"Yes! I just sent my money in. I'm so excited." She wiggled in her seat, not an easy feat considering the confinements of the booth.

"What hotel are you staying at?" Madison asked.

"I don't know. Vartan is taking care of all the arrangements. He's arranging for the airline tickets, hotel, and even the drinks. It's one of those all-in-one package deals. And it's only $1,417 for a full three days!"

Madison exchanged a concerned look with her grandmother. She was certain she could find a better deal on her own, unless they were staying in one of Vegas' top hotels. The fact that she sent the money to an unknown, online 'friend' was even more concerning.

"How did you send the money? You didn't give him your credit card number, I hope?"

"Oh, no. I sent one of those new money orders. Even though I had trouble with one earlier this year, I decided to give it one more try."

"What trouble?" Granny Bert asked.

"The problem Derron helped me with."

"What new service?" Madison asked. "I'm not familiar with anything new."

"I don't remember what they call themselves. Instead of taking cash down to the bank or post office, you can give your debit card over the phone, and they sell you a money order. It's so much easier that way. They'll even mail the money order for you and send you the receipt. After Christmas, I was a little strapped for cash, so I used it for an overdue bill. Worked like a charm," Miss Wanda beamed.

"Then what was the problem Derron helped you with? Why did he write a letter for you?"

"There was some confusion on the other end. The hospital claimed they never received the money, even though I had proof of the money orders I sent." She brushed away the matter with a wave of her hand. "Derron wrote a very stern letter, and I haven't heard from them since. That's why I decided to give it another shot."

All sorts of warning bells went off in Madison's head. "Miss Wanda, you do know the purpose of a money order is to make a secure cash transaction, right? With cash?"

"Of course. And a debit card is the same as cash. The woman on the phone assured me it was every bit as safe as a traditional service, simply more convenient. These days, you have to think outside the box, you know." She tapped her head, disturbing the unnaturally black hair. "I don't blame the money order people. It's not their fault the hospital isn't keeping up with the times. The hospital didn't initially accept the money order, but after Derron's sharp dressing down, I'm sure they're feeling rather foolish."

The arrival of their meal interrupted further discussion.

"These shrimp stuffed chili rellenos are good," Granny Bert said, giving the new dish her full approval.

Having ordered the same thing, her friend agreed. "They remind me of those divine ones we had at that restaurant in Waco."

Granny Bert's brow puckered as she tried to place the meal in question.

"You remember. That's the day we went to Wal-Mart and ran into Arlene Kopetsky. She was in a snit because that daughter of hers had left her there to fend for herself, while she was off running other errands. Arlene was having trouble with that little go-cart they gave her to drive."

Granny Bert nodded. "I remember now. She darned near ran over that whole display of paper towels."

"That's right. And then we went to the restaurant right around the corner from the Super Center."

"I know the one. That's where that man almost knocked me over. Remember? We were coming out of the little girl's room, and he and his date were making a dash for the door. I wondered if they were sneakin' out on the bill, they were in such a hurry."

Wanda's chubby cheeks wobbled as she nodded vigorously in recollection. "Yes, yes. His date had on that big floppy hat and those huge sunglasses. Kept her face down, like she didn't want to be seen."

"In that get-up she was wearing, who could blame her?" Granny Bert snorted. "Her heels were about as long as her shorts. That floppy hat covered more skin than those skimpy shorts did!" She snorted again, for good measure. "The things some people wear out in public."

"They were both so rude. The man barely even apologized."

Granny Bert's fork froze in midair, loaded with a cheesy shrimp en route to her mouth. "That man," she mumbled, sounding somewhat dumbstruck. "That's where I saw him."

"Granny? Are you okay?" Madison asked in concern.

"That was him!" Warming to the thought, she set her fork down, straightened her shoulders, and said with conviction, "That's it! That's where I saw him. At the restaurant in Waco."

"Who?"

"That Ronald Alexander man. The dead man from my refrigerator!"

The waitress had returned with drink refills. Hearing Granny Bert's outburst, she gasped and jerked away, sending a glass of tea sailing through the air. It landed on the table behind them, in the middle of a sizzling plate of fajitas. The man at the table came up in an outrage, the front of his pants soaked through.

Oblivious to the commotion all around them, Miss Wanda kept eating. "Yes, I'd say these taste almost as good as those from that day, rude man and all." She waved her fork in the air. "Oh, and Madison, I remember the name of that company now. *PhoneGrams*. They're the ones that sold me the money order."

"Where did you hear about them?" Something about the whole set-up still didn't sound right to her.

"They called me, as I recall." She nibbled on a tortilla chip as she talked. "No, I take that back. I called them. That sweet little girl from the billing department gave me their number and suggested I use them." She shook her head in disgust. "That's one reason I got so upset when the hospital didn't want to accept money from there. I only used *PhoneGrams* because one of their own told me about it."

"Why did you say they didn't want to accept the money order?" That part didn't sound right, either.

"I have no clue. Something about it could be fraudulent. But the money came out of my checking account, clear as day. Derron sent a photocopy of my statement."

"At least you got it cleared up," Granny Bert comforted her friend. "I hear poor Mabel Crowder has a similar problem with an unpaid bill. They're threatening to take her to a small claim court to collect."

"I told her she should have Derron write a letter. It's to *Texas General,* too, the same hospital my bill was from. Like me, she had already paid the bill, and they're still hounding her."

"That's rather odd, don't you think?" Madison murmured.

"Not really. Last year, when I fell and had my ankle X-rayed, I went to that new *Texas General Hospital* in College Station. Mabel was in the ER with some sort of stomach distress. With Christmas and all, neither of us were able to pay right away."

"I meant that you would both have billing issues from the same hospital."

"Did she pay the same way you did?" Granny Bert asked. "That PhoneOGram place?"

"*PhoneGrams.* No 'o,'" she corrected. "And, yes, but Mabel also used some 'alternate solution' that was supposed to save her money." Miss Wanda rolled her eyes. "No one offered me a way to save money. *PhoneGrams* even charged a $12 service fee for expediting my order. Not that it did Mabel any good, mind you. Now the hospital claims they never got her payment, either."

Madison frowned. This story sounded worse by the minute. "What kind of alternate solution? Who told her about it?"

"That sweet little girl in billing. The same one who told me about the money order place." Wanda dropped her voice to a conspiratorial level. "Technically, she wasn't supposed to tell either one of us what she did, but, like I say, she was really sweet. Their card system was down the day she called me, or else I would have paid direct. She suggested I call PhoneGrams so the payment would process the next day and stop the pesky calls from collections."

"What was her suggestion for Mabel?"

"Her bill was a lot more than mine, what with all the tests and all. The girl said they didn't like to advertise it, but they offered reduced billing for people who met certain guidelines. Mabel called the number, and she must have qualified, because she only had to pay half the original amount. She sent the payment through *PhoneGrams*, just like me."

"Except the hospital never received it." Madison twisted her mouth in thought. "Do you know the name of the company she went through?"

"Mabel said it was something that brought wine to mind. Then again, she does like her drink." Miss Wanda drained her margarita and looked around for their waitress to order another. The girl was still at the table behind them, apologizing profusely for her clumsiness. "Dearie! I'll have another one of these, please."

Madison wasn't ready to end the conversation. "One more thing. Do you happen to remember the name of the girl from the hospital billing department?"

"Pearl, maybe? Or Opal? I'm sure I have it written down at home. She was a real sweetheart."

"Except that you and Mabel still kept getting bills."

"That was clearly the hospital's error," she stated adamantly, "and a different department than the one she worked in. And when I sent the money to Vartan this morning, it went through without a hitch."

17

Because of her late-night visitor, Madison wasn't comfortable leaving the kids alone to visit Brash in College Station. They were both disappointed with the change of plans but agreed it was the safest course of action.

When she told Brash about the incident, he once again threatened to come home.

"It's only three more days," she had told him. "We'll be fine. I doubt she'll be stupid enough to make a return visit. Rose Belvedere doesn't strike me as stupid."

"No, but she's obviously dangerous."

"I found a loose connection between her and Ron Alexander. And between her and the black car." She proceeded to tell him about her sleuthing and her theory of six degrees of separation.

"Entertaining concept," her husband agreed, "but it won't hold water."

"I know. But at least it's something. What else have you learned about Ronald Alexander?"

"Very little. We finally reached his wife, and she confirmed the last known contact with him was on Monday evening. As far as she knew, he was in Waco handling a business matter for *Tellina*. She wasn't exactly sure what her husband did for a living." His voice dripped with ridicule as he explained, "She didn't want to pry in his personal business."

"But he's her husband!" Madison protested the absurdity of such a statement.

"As long as he brought home a paycheck, she didn't bother with the details. And before you ask, no, we still can't reach the company. I suspect it's bogus. As for Ron's background, I suspect the same."

"He certainly kept a low profile on social media," Madison agreed. "But I'm still digging."

"I've changed my mind. I don't want you doing this any longer. It's gotten too dangerous."

Even though he couldn't see her, she swung her head in disagreement. "I can't just walk away now!"

"If Ron Alexander was an alias, it's because the man had something to hide. We already know Rose Belvedere has lied on multiple fronts. Her background is about as clean as Alexander's. In my experience, background checks that read like a book are usually fiction. Obviously, she feels threatened by you, afraid you'll expose her for the fraud she is. She's already tampered with your car. She's getting even more aggressive, coming to the house. You need to walk away while you still can. If it means I come home tonight, so be it."

In the end, she convinced Brash to stay at camp, and he convinced her to practice extra vigilance.

Unwilling to give up just yet, Madison dedicated the morning to online sleuthing. She started with social media.

This time, she clicked through Rose Belvedere's friends who had generic or avatar profile pictures, seeing where that trail led. Surprisingly, she kept seeing many of the same people. In several instances, if she followed the trail long enough, she landed on

Keondra Hill's page, a healthcare worker from Waco. The same Keondra who worked at *Senior Styles* and posted the newsfeed about the couple last seen in a black Crown Victoria.

Curious, Madison went to the news site and backtracked to when the story first broke. When she saw that the scam victim was a resident at the Senior Styles facility, she knew she could be on to something.

It was Saturday, so she knew it was a long shot. The detectives on the case might not be working today.

She called anyway, identifying herself as a consultant for The Sisters Police Department. After being placed on hold twice, a woman's voice came on the line. "This is Detective Audra Cao. I understand you're seeking information on one of our active cases?"

"Yes. I should tell you up front, I'm only a consultant with the department. But the chief of police—"

"Your husband, Brash deCordova. Correct?"

A note of caution moved into Madison's voice. "Yes. That's correct."

"I've known Brash for years." The detective's warm assurance chased the caution away. "Good coach. Even better cop. And, of course, I followed your television show and all the hype with your recent wedding. How can I help you?"

"This may be nothing, but I'm finding a few too many coincidences to feel comfortable about a case I'm involved with. I haven't connected the dots yet, but I think one of your cases earlier this year could be loosely, if not directly, related to a suspicious death here in The Sisters. What can you tell me about Vino and Ruby Shiraz?"

There was a long sigh on the other end of the

phone. "Not nearly enough. I can't even tell you if those are their real names. What I can tell you is that Hilda Becker is a longtime Waco resident who now resides at a local assisted living center. Like most of the people there, she's lonely and hungry for visitors. Several months ago, a couple came to the center, befriended her, and convinced her that one of them— Vino, she thinks—was related to her late husband. They produced an old Bible, some fuzzy photographs, and a few old-looking letters that supposedly established a connection to the late Stan Becker. They visited several times, bringing small gifts and remembrances, before announcing that they liked the area so well, they were moving there. They also convinced Mrs. Becker they would be nearby to help care for her, as she had no children of her own.

"When the house they were supposedly moving into needed minor renovations, Mrs. Becker generously volunteered the use of her home. She still had her residence on South Adams and liked the thought of someone staying there again, if only for a short time. As you may have guessed, that short stay lingered into a long one. When the couple brought a paper for her to sign, Mrs. Becker thought it was a work order to have a plumbing issue fixed. Soon after, their visits dwindled to a brief hello now and then. It wasn't until her longtime banker called that Mrs. Becker became suspicious. By that time, it was too late."

"I understand they used her house as collateral for a loan?" The disgust was clear in Madison's voice.

"After a nasty fall, Mrs. Becker left the house suddenly. When they moved in, the so-called relatives had access to all her sensitive information, including her social security number, banking information, and a valuable collection of jewels and artwork. After selling everything of value, they used the deed on the house to secure a sizable loan. They defaulted on the loan and left town, leaving her good credit in shambles."

Madison was outraged. "They preyed on a vulnerable old woman and used her generosity against her! How utterly horrid."

"I couldn't agree more," Detective Cao said.

"What about their credentials? Didn't the bank check them out? Or did they rely solely on Mrs. Becker's credit?"

"They gave references, but none were legit." Over a rustle of papers, she seemed to read from a report. "Vino claimed to work for *Chianti Enterprises* and listed a Barbera Amrita as his direct supervisor. After the initial phone call confirming employment, the number no longer worked. There's no official record of the business or the supervisor. The entire thing was a setup."

"I think the news mentioned that the couple was conducting an unlicensed business from the home. Let me guess. Meth lab?"

"Nothing so sinister. But it was a residential neighborhood, and they claimed to have a business. Mostly online, but neighbors complained about the excess of vehicular traffic. With Mrs. Becker's signature on the paperwork, it was the only thing we could throw at them that would stick, at least until we launched a thorough investigation. They skipped town the next day."

"Does the name Rose Belvedere mean anything to you?"

"No. Should it?"

"Just a hunch I'm working on. What about the name Ronald Alexander?"

"Alexander. Alexander... I may have seen a BOLO

with that name earlier in the week..." Another rustle of paper and a few taps on a keyboard, before she reported in a deflated voice, "I don't see it now. Sorry."

"That's because we found his body. He's the suspicious death I mentioned."

"I'll run the name through our databanks, but don't hold your breath. If he's connected to the Shiraz couple, he's likely as slippery as they are."

"One last thing. Do you have a description of the couple?" Madison asked.

"Verbal, but no photos. Even the surveillance cameras at the bank couldn't get a good shot of their faces. Witnesses say Ruby Shiraz is tall and slender. Very attractive, with long red hair. Vino was small and wiry, with dark hair and a little mustache. Mrs. Becker said her Stan was the same way; claimed it was the Italian in him. She also said they were both 'snappy dressers.'"

Thanking the detective for her help and saying goodbye, Madison jotted down what little information she had gleaned. It wasn't much, but it was a start.

She typed *Chianti* into the search engine, knowing the futility of it before hitting the enter key. If the Waco PD couldn't find anything concrete, neither could she.

Over thirty-one million results popped up, most of them connected to the wine produced in central Tuscany. Madison wrinkled her nose at the prospect of searching through them all. The detective had used another word with the name. *Industry*? Or, was it *Enterprises*?

That narrowed the search down somewhat. Just under a hundred thousand hits for enterprises by that name. *Piece of cake*, she smirked to herself.

For curiosity sake, she typed in *Barbera Amrita*

with Chianti Enterprises. A litany of wine choices flooded her screen. Well over five hundred thousand results popped up, some with images.

Wine bottles.

Wine lists.

Liquor stores.

Vineyards.

Restaurants that served the vines' finest.

Reviews by wine enthusiasts.

They were all there. All three words—Barbera, Amrita, and Chianti—had hits tied to the wine industry.

Coincidence? Madison thought not.

Madison thought it reeked of a scam. Even *vino* was another word for wine. Ruby was the color of red wine. And shiraz? If she weren't mistaken... She typed the word into the search engine. *Yes!* Shiraz was a wine made from dark-skinned grapes and identified with the historical Persian city of the same name.

Madison realized that their entire persona had been a hoax. A devilish and elaborate scam to trick a vulnerable old woman out of her property and her credit. *How low could a person stoop?* Madison fumed at the thought of their evil-spirited treachery.

She suspected Rose Belvedere worked a similar scam. Who knew? She and Ruby Shiraz could even be one and the same. The hair color was wrong, but that was easily rectified with a bottle of dye. Otherwise, the description fit. Tall, slim, and a 'snappy' dresser.

Even the MO was the same. Like Ruby, Rose had convinced a vulnerable old woman that she was family. Like Ruby, she had finagled her way into Nelda Goldberg's house. And like Ruby, she worked from home. The similarities were chilling.

But, who, she wondered, *had played the part of Vino?* Ron Alexander was the first to come to mind, but the description didn't fit. He wasn't small and dark. The mustache and dark hair could be changed—even a fake tan could make him seem darker than his natural skin color—but there was no mistaking Ron's athletic build as 'small and wiry.'

Perhaps it had been the decorator. The man witnesses described as dressing like Derron could also be petite like him; perhaps that was why her employee's name sprang freely into their descriptions. She made a note to ask them about the man's coloring.

Even if Rose proved to be Ruby Shiraz—even if they proved her guilty of embezzlement and fraud—it still didn't tie her to Ronald Alexander. What was Madison missing? There had to be a link somewhere.

"Mom?"

Madison looked up to see Bethani standing at the office door. "Sorry to bother you when you're working."

"No problem, sweetie. What can I help you with?"

"Megan and I are supposed to visit Mrs. Palacios today, but I have no idea what to wear."

"A cute sundress should be appropriate," Madison replied. "But wear something on top, like a shrug. You don't want excess skin showing."

The teen rolled her blue eyes. "You sound like Grandmother Annette. 'It's not proper for young ladies to reveal too much skin.'"

The imitation was so spot-on, her mother laughed. "She's right, you know."

"I think Grandmother and Mrs. Palacios would get along famously. Both are obsessed with good manners and proper etiquette and dressing the part."

"There's nothing wrong with learning the proper rules of society."

"*High* society," Bethani reminded her. "We come

in more at mid-range."

Laughing, Madison agreed with her daughter. "Wear the dress you wore to church last week. It brings out your beautiful blue eyes."

"What about shoes?"

"Not flip-flops. How about your white sandals with the flat heel?"

"Hair? Up—" she demonstrated a casual upsweep, "or down?"

"You'll look gorgeous, either way."

"You're prejudiced," the teen accused.

Madison flashed a smile. "Sorry. Part of the job description."

The phone rang, and she grabbed it as she blew her daughter a kiss.

"Madison, dear? This is Clovis Bishop. Last week, you asked about the internet service my nephew works for. He's here now if you'd like to speak with him?"

"Yes, ma'am, that would be great."

A man's voice came across the line, identifying himself as George. He worked for a semi-local internet company and was happy to answer any questions she might have. Madison pretended interest in speeds and capabilities, inquiring about different options.

"What if I wanted something like you gave my friend Rose, over on Sycamore Street?" she finally asked.

George seemed surprised at the request. "You mean the separate routers, or the other?"

"Let's start with the routers. What will that do for me?"

"Well, in her case, she wanted a different router for each computer. That gives each one their own IP address and their own identity. One can't see what the other is doing, so to speak. If one were a work computer, for instance, and the other was personal, it could keep your boss from seeing what you did on your own time."

Interesting, Madison thought. Aloud, she asked, "And the other things she requested?" She only hoped he didn't ask for specifics. She had no idea what 'the other' entailed.

"In my opinion some of it was overkill, but if she's processing a lot of credit cards and wants speed and security, that was the way to go. Especially when she'll be accessing other people's sensitive data, such as their bank accounts and such. She didn't want to leave a trail for hackers to follow. We installed top of the line security measures for her, which didn't come cheap. The other stuff was easy. A few extra power strips and remotes for her background screens, that sort of thing. I guess she didn't know you can do virtual backgrounds on the internet these days, but whatever. We aim to make the customer happy."

"Of—Of course." Madison thanked him and stumbled through a good-bye, trying to absorb this latest information.

Why did Rose Belvedere need separate modems?

It could be exactly as the technician said. Perhaps her boss was a stickler for details, and separating the two was just easier.

Perhaps she did need added speeds and security measures when completing transactions for the collection agency.

But *why*, her mind screamed, did she need to access people's bank accounts? That went well beyond the scope of how legitimate debt collection agencies operated.

Which left just one option. She didn't work for a legitimate debt collector.

Or maybe she did but had another on the side.

Madison thought back to the day she had asked if Rose worked for one or more companies. Rose's reply— "I'm not sure working for more than one agency at a time would be ethical"—hadn't really been an answer.

Perhaps, Madison considered, the extra security measures were on her *personal* computer, the one she used for illegitimate projects. Projects like tricking old ladies out of their homes and accessing their personal information. Maybe that explained the second router.

"That didn't even require six degrees," she muttered aloud. "Use second computer for evil (1), access sensitive matter (2), get away scot-free (3)." Her mood was dark. "Well, I have news for you, Miss Rose Belvedere. Or Ruby Shiraz. Or whoever you really are. You didn't count right." Madison squared her shoulders and added the final degree, determination moving into her voice.

"Get shut down by a hick town (4). In the words of Barney Fife and our own Granny Bert, we need to nip this in the bud. Nip. It. Now."

18

"Genny, this looks delicious!" Madison told her friend. When Genny had called and invited them to dinner, Madison abandoned her online research in favor of a meal she didn't have to cook.

"And it smells even better," Blake added, taking in a deep, appreciative whiff. "Aunt Genny, I sure miss the days when you lived with us and did all the cooking."

He belatedly shot his mother a guilty look, but Madison merely laughed. Secretly, she agreed with him.

"She's married to me now," Cutter reminded the teen. He snagged his wife by the waist as she set the last platter onto the table. With a playful wink, he said, "She's my cook." There was nothing playful about the hint of possessive pride in his voice. He clearly adored his wife.

Across the table at the Montgomery household, Bethani's face was animated. "Did I tell you about the food Mrs. Palacios served today?"

"Yes, but tell me again," Genny insisted, taking a seat beside her husband. "I want to know all about a formal Spanish *La Merienda*."

"Can I at least say the blessing first? That way,

Blake and I can actually eat the food, while you two just blab about it," Cutter teased.

"Make it fast," his wife quipped. "We have an important conversation waiting."

The firefighter wouldn't be rushed through his prayer. He thanked the Lord for their day, the family gathered in their home, the surprising shower that moistened the ground that afternoon, the freedoms of their country, and the plentiful food upon their table. After Blake echoed his 'amen,' it was time to eat.

As platters and bowls passed around the table, Bethani described the elaborate *tapas* served at the tea party. She still couldn't believe that Mrs. Palacios had gone to such effort and expense for two teenage girls. There had been a wide assortment of extravagant foods, all decadent and delicious.

"And the table!" she raved. "It had a white linen tablecloth. I knew it was expensive by the way it draped, even before I saw all the cut lace. There was a gold oval tray in the center, with the most elegant tea set I've ever seen in my life. It had tiny little flowers on a creamy background, and everything was edged in gold. The feet, the handle, the lid. Even the forks and spoons were gold. There were long, tapered candles in fancy crystal candle holders, and Mrs. Palacios lit them with a long, fancy match holder, and later put them out with a gold candle snuffer. There were crystal chargers under the plates, and everything was simply perfect!"

"It sounds it," Madison said, still amused by her daughter's enchantment. The teen had raved about the tea party since Madison picked her up from the Aikmans, on her way to the Montgomery ranch.

Cutter looked slightly confused. "Why, again, did a woman you don't know invite you and Megan over for a tea party?"

Bethani shrugged. "I guess to thank us for helping her son the day before."

"I did all the heavy lifting," Blake grumbled. "I'm the one who worked up the sweat. You didn't see me at that fancy table."

His sister giggled. "Probably because you *were* sweaty!" She picked up her glass, holding her little finger aloft. "This wasn't a redneck event," she assured her brother, using her best haute voice. "This was strictly blue *blood*, my good man."

"What's the story on those two, anyway?" Genny asked. "Mr. Palacios has always struck me as odd. He comes in the restaurant occasionally, but he's always so reserved. And he has the craziest way of answering questions."

"Tell us about it," Blake groaned, rolling his eyes. "Next year, I'll have him *twice*. Language arts *and* Spanish. I won't get a straight answer out of him in any language!"

"I can't place the guy," Cutter said with a frown. "What's he look like?"

"Dark hair with little gray, dark eyes. Kind of nice looking, but a bit dainty for a man. Always wears a sweater."

"Ah. I know the one." The sweater resonated with him. "Yeah. Strange guy. We had a call about a gas leak at his house one time. He literally knew nothing about how a water heater worked. Didn't even know how to light a pilot. I doubt he's done any strenuous labor in his life. Probably never even gotten his hands dirty."

"After meeting his mom, you're probably right," Blake agreed. "She had a 'car' bring her from the airport. Not an Uber. A chauffeur. And get this. He was in a Bentley."

While Cutter whistled in appreciation, Bethani

couldn't help but giggle. "He had on a silly-looking uniform and everything. He treated her like she was royalty, even *presenting* her to us." She imitated his stiff, formal voice. "I present to you *Senora* Palacios." She laughed again. "He may as well have said Queen Elizabeth. She really does have a regal air about her, especially wearing those jewels and gloves."

"She actually had gloves on?" Genny asked in surprise.

"Gloves, hat, suit. The whole shebang. Yesterday, she wore her 'traveling' suit. It looked itchy, like wool or something heavy. Today, at least, she had on a linen suit that looked a lot better for the Texas heat. But I swear the jewels she wears are real. She had on sapphires yesterday. Today it was a pink stone to match her suit, but they looked real enough. I *know* the diamonds are real." She wiggled her fingers, indicating all the rings the older woman wore.

"Obviously, they come from money," Madison said.

"She reminds me of Grandmother Annette," Bethani went on. "On the outside, she looks all stiff and formal. But, once you get to know her better, she's actually very nice. I think she's lonely. I'm not sure she had a happy marriage, either."

"Why do you say that, sweetie?"

"It was something in her eyes. She told us about all the places she had lived. Mostly Madrid, but also in Europe, and even northern California. Megan asked why they moved so much, and she said it was her husband's wish. But if you ask me, it sounded more like it was his command."

"Where is her husband now? Did he come, as well?"

The teen shook her head. "He died about a year ago."

"Mr. Palacios never mentioned that to any of us," Blake commented.

"I know. She said they were never close. The thing is, when we said we were sorry for her loss, she didn't even look all that sad. She looked sort of... relieved." A frown tugged at her expressive mouth. "I think he may have been mean to her. I think he was rich and powerful, and she had to learn all the fancy manners and wear all the jewels and fancy clothes to suit him. She hinted that wasn't who she really was."

Blake was already learning his stepfather's smirked brow. "You got all that from having tea with the woman?"

His twin shrugged. "You know Megan. She can get anyone to talk. We found out she had lived here in The Sisters a long time ago, when she was young. She said of all the places she had lived, this was the only place she was ever happy. The only place that ever held her heart."

"I have to agree," Genny said. "I lived in France when I was studying to become a chef, and in many places around the US once I became one. But this has to be the best place of all," she turned to her husband and smiled, dimples showing, "because this is where I found my true love. This is where my heart is."

Blake was unusually quiet as they passed the bowls for a second time. He ate more than his fair share, but when the conversation turned to another topic, he didn't follow along. His mind was somewhere else.

His twin noticed after a while. She poked his leg with her foot, throwing him a frown. "What's with you?"

"Just thinking."

"Don't strain your brain. It's not used to a strenuous workout."

"You think you're so cute. If only you knew."

"Okay, you two," Madison broke in. "Knock off the loving compliments."

"He's acting all weird," Bethani accused. "He just passed the potatoes without getting a third helping. That's not like Mr. Walking Stomach. And you know how much he likes Aunt Genny's ranch potatoes."

"You feeling okay, honey? You aren't getting too hot at work, are you?" Madison asked her son in concern.

"I'm fine. I was just thinking about some of the stuff Bethani said."

"I know what will make you feel better," Genny said with a smile. "Dessert! I made one of your favorites. Lemon meringue pie."

"All of your desserts are my favorite," Blake confessed, his smile charming.

"I'll help," Madison offered. She gathered empty plates on her way, leaving Blake to his last-minute helping of ranch potatoes.

"So?" Bethani prodded. "What are you thinking about so hard?"

He was slow to answer. "Hear me out. It's a far-fetched notion, but a lot of what you said makes sense, in a weird kind of way."

"Stop talking in riddles and tell me!"

"Mrs. Palacios obviously has money. According to Cutter," he gestured to the man at the end of the table, finishing off his own plate, "Mr. Palacios never had to do much on his own, which could mean he had servants to do it for him. Rich boy, and all that. We both saw the woman's jewels. We both saw the car. She's lived in Spain and all those other places, even though she's originally from here. She has a gold-plated tea set and fancy crystal dishes, for crying out loud. You said yourself that she acts all regal. Who else does that remind you of?"

"Grandmother Annette."

"Besides her."

Bethani thought for only a moment. Eyes wide, she sucked in a surprised breath. "Are you thinking what I think you're thinking?"

"You didn't happen to catch her first name, did you?" Blake asked.

She shook her head no.

"It makes sense, though," he insisted. "She was in an unhappy marriage because she loved someone else. Like Aunt Genny, she's lived in a lot of places, but this was where her true love was, so this is where her heart stayed. The only place she was ever happy, and the place she came back to."

"You truly think Mrs. Palacios is Rosa? Mr. Ballard's Rosa?" Bethani's blue eyes twinkled with the intriguing thought.

"Yes," Blake said, his voice strong with conviction. "I truly do."

Back at home that evening, with her belly full and her own kitchen unscathed, Madison picked up the online search where she had left off.

"Who says the internet isn't watching?" she mumbled aloud. Ads for wines and vineyards popped up on her screen, inspired by previous searches. "Look up a couple of random things, and they hound you for days."

But when one ad in particular popped up, followed by a podcast, she knew it was time to make another visit to Rose Belvedere's.

19

"She's never going to let us in," Genny predicted.

"I admit, Granny Bert and the girls made it more challenging for our second visit, but have faith. She'll let us in."

Once again, they stood on Rose Belvedere's front porch, pretending to be the Sisters, Forever welcome committee. Madison held a huge potted plant in her arms. It was a mixed variety pot, but the clincher, she was certain, was the knock-out rose bush with its profusion of hot-pink petals. She had a feeling the recipient wouldn't be able to resist.

"Maybe she's not home. We've already knocked twice."

"She's home," Madison said with confidence. "That fancy little black car is in the driveway, and I saw her curtain move in the office. She knows it's us and is trying to wait us out."

"It's working, too." Genny fanned her flushed face. "It's like a hundred degrees here in the shade."

"Try holding this ginormous plant!" her friend huffed. She shifted on her feet, her back already aching. "Just remember that fainting routine, if I chicken out of my plan."

"You never did tell me... Well, hello!" She broke off

mid-sentence to offer Rose a huge, overly bright smile. The homeowner had finally come to the door. "For a minute there, we were worried you weren't home."

"One could only wish," the other woman muttered, not even trying to utter the words beneath her breath. "Can I help you?"

"As you can see, we come bearing gifts." Genny motioned to the plant behind her.

Madison poked her head around the side of the roses and smiled. "Hello."

"Hello."

When Rose made no move to invite them inside, Madison stepped forward. "This is getting mighty heavy. Can we please come in now?"

Abandoning all pretense of hospitable charm, Rose turned away as she flung the door against the wall. If they insisted on coming in, she wouldn't stop them, but she clearly didn't welcome their visit.

Madison pretended not to notice. "Compliments of Sisters, Forever!" she said cheerily, setting the pot down in what she knew was an ill-advised location. Her arms and back ached, and she was eager to be relieved of the heavy load, but she had an ulterior motive for placing it where she did. "If you haven't been to *Posey's Petals and Plants* yet, you really must go. This is one of their creations," she rattled on.

"It's lovely," Rose replied, somewhat grudgingly.

"And did you notice the knock-out roses?" Genny pointed out. "We requested them, knowing how much you favored the flower."

"It's hard to see, with it all the way over there. It's almost in the hallway." She shot Madison a reproachful glare.

"Sorry, but that thing was heavy!" Madison shook her arms as if to work the kinks out of her muscles.

Unfortunately, it wasn't too much of an exaggeration. Without being invited, she plopped down in the nearest chair. "Whew! That was rough. I need to catch my breath."

"That reminds me," Rose said, her expression dry. "Your grandmother stopped by one day. Like you, she made herself right at home."

"Oh? You've met my grandmother?" Madison attempted an innocent look.

"And your daughters. Of course, they didn't use their full names. I don't believe you did, either, the first time we met." Her eyes were sharp, attesting to the fact that little slipped past her. "I suppose it should be refreshing, having a reality television star assuming the public doesn't recognize them. Most of them milk that sort of tacky stardom for all it's worth."

It was a back-handed compliment if ever she heard one. Madison simply smiled sweetly, not letting the other woman get to her. Even if she was dressed to impress—today, she wore a summer sweater combo and capri pants in mint green—Madison refused to be intimidated by a lowly criminal. *This woman scams helpless old people*, she reminded herself. *Pretty-is is not pretty-does.*

"Have you had a chance yet to meet your neighbors?" Genny asked.

When she took a seat on the sofa, Rose gawked at the audacity of her unwanted guests. Clearly exasperated, she threw her hands upward in defeat. Grumbling beneath her breath, she reluctantly took a seat on the opposite end.

"Not really," she answered. "Most aren't as persistent as you two. However, I did meet one girl who lives behind me. Lana, I think it is?"

"Yes, that's right. Lana Kopetsky. Her mother lives

just across the street."

"Yes. Apparently, she has a habit of cutting through other people's lawns as a shortcut." Her puckered frown said she wasn't impressed.

"Have you had a chance to use any of the coupons we gave you?" Madison asked. She tried to 'hide' the pained expression crossing her face when Rose looked in her direction.

"Not yet."

A small gasp escaped Madison's lips, and her arm came up to cradle her stomach.

"Are you okay?" Genny asked her friend in concern.

Rose frowned.

Madison bit her lip, using enough force to make the pain real. She shook her head in an 'ignore me' gesture.

"You really should use the coupons. They're a great way to sample all we have to offer," Genny went on.

"I've been quite busy. I do work from home, you remember." It was a none too subtle barb at being disturbed in the middle of the workday.

"About that..." Genny said, looking almost embarrassed to go on. She pushed forward. "I know you said you don't take outside clients, but I have a problem I was hoping you could help me with. I normally don't allow customers to charge, but occasionally, I allow business accounts. I have—"

Madison gasped again, this time louder. Genuinely concerned, Genny frowned. "Madison? Are you sure you're all right?"

"You know the trouble I have with my stomach," she said, bending slightly at the waist. "You go on. I'm fine." She rocked slightly in the chair, trying to appear as if she writhed in pain.

Genny knew this must be part of the plan because,

to her knowledge, her best friend of over twenty years had no such problem. "If we need to go..."

"No, no. You need her help," Madison insisted. "She's the expert."

"She's right," Genny seemed to confess. "I do need your help. I broke my own cardinal rule of—"

This time moaning, Madison jumped from the chair and made a dash toward the hallway. "Please excuse me! I have to go!" She scrambled past the potted plant and raced toward the bathroom. As she slammed the door, she heard Genny's attempt to diffuse the situation.

"I, uh, apologize for my friend. She, uh, has an issue with... dairy..." She clearly grasped for a plausible excuse to explain Madison's sudden dash to the bathroom.

"She should have enough common sense to avoid it!" Rose snapped.

When she started up, Genny grabbed her arm. "Please. It's terribly embarrassing for her, as you might imagine. The stories I could tell you from over the years..." What looked like a shudder of horror was an attempt not to laugh aloud. "She won't be long, and I really do need your help. I need to collect a debt from a customer."

"I told you. I don't take outside clients."

"Please? Just this once? I'm willing to pay you handsomely for your help."

Madison didn't hear the rest of the conversation. She imagined Rose asked why she was so worried about recouping the charge if money weren't an issue. She was tempted to hang around in the hall and hear what excuse Genny came up with, but she really needed in that office. She tiptoed past the living room entrance, satisfied that Rose's attention was on the papers Genny insisted she look at.

Quietly as a mouse, Madison slipped into Rose Belvedere's office. At first glance, nothing was amiss. It looked like any functional office, well organized but slightly messy from use. She hurried behind the desk so she could see the computer screens. One monitor displayed an accounts page with the *Timely Collections* logo clearly visible in the address bar. It appeared to be a perfectly legitimate request for an overdue bill, now handled by the collection agency.

The other screen was blank, but one swipe of the mouse brought it back to life.

This monitor was opened to a different site. Three sites, to be exact. Madison moved the mouse over the different tabs, taking pictures with her phone as each page opened. She didn't dare dawdle; she didn't know how long she had before Rose came looking for her. She only took time to pull up the computer's history log and snap another photo of the screen, before moving away from the desk altogether.

There were two remote controls on the desk. Madison picked up the first one and pressed a button. A speaker came to life, the sound low enough not to alert the women in the next room. The recording sounded oddly like the background of a busy office, with keyboards clacking, phones ringing, and people talking. Pressing another button, she heard standard elevator music. A third button played a muted stock market report, underscored with more office noise. She clicked it off and reached for the second remote.

With a slight whir, the background screen behind Rose's desk began to wind upward. With *Timely Collections'* logo out of the way, another was visible. *What*, she wondered, *was PG Solutions?*

The second button on the remote brought down a muted floral screen, the one she had seen in Megan's video. Over a field of white and cream-colored roses,

Blush Investments was particularly visible in red and pink.

Button three brought down a familiar blue and silver screen. In spite of herself, Madison gasped aloud. Rose Belvedere's treachery reached further than she suspected! Not only had Madison seen this screen the first day she snooped, but she had also seen it on Miss Wanda's computer. It was the background for *Silver Circle*.

Biting her lip in disgust, Madison pressed the last button. Down came a sophisticated screen that elegantly touted *The Castellina Agency* logo.

With pictures of the different screens documented on her phone, Madison pressed the buttons in reverse, hoping that the action would rewind each one. It worked, but she had forgotten which screens had been down to begin with. Was it *Timely Collections*, or *PG Solutions*? When she accidentally pushed two buttons at once, something jammed. One screen was stuck halfway up, halfway down. She jabbed another button, but nothing happened.

She heard Rose say her name. From the sounds of it, she wanted to check on her indisposed 'guest,' while Genny tried valiantly to keep her attention. Knowing her time was up, Madison pushed one more button and hoped for the best. The motor whirred and stopped. A puff of smoke expelled from the ends.

"Oops," she said, feeling a bit panicked. Her hands moved in a frenzy until she came up with an idea. She placed the remote upside down on the floor, next to the chair leg. With any luck, Rose would surmise she dropped it when getting up to answer the door and somehow rolled over it with her chair.

Tiptoeing out of the office, Madison hurried back to the bathroom, where she flushed the empty toilet, ran water in the sink, and found a can of air freshener to clog the air with. While searching for the air freshener, she found something of a surprise, but there was no time to wonder why Rose had such vastly different wigs. One touted long blonde strands, while the other was a riot of short, black curls. Madison splashed water on her face, patted it only half dry, and staggered from the room. She rounded the corner, just as Rose escaped Genny's clutches and stormed toward the hall.

"I'm *so* sorry about that." Madison did her best to look contrite. "I'm horribly embarrassed."

"You should be," Rose snapped, batting at the heavily rose-scented air. "The odor is atrocious. We could smell you all the way into the living room," she lied.

Madison was on the verge of making a smart remark—something about imagining how awful it must smell in prison—but she wisely thought better of it. No need antagonizing the woman. With any luck, Rose Belvedere/Ruby Shiraz would soon have firsthand knowledge of the prison system and its many unpleasant odors.

"I do apologize. Genny, I think we'd better hurry before the next round hits. Rose, enjoy your plant."

Madison skittered around the potted plant, 'accidentally' wedging it into the doorway. Rose would have to move it before she could access the hall and find the mess in her office.

If they hurried, she and Genny could be long gone by then.

"Ohmygosh!" Genny cried, the minute they had crawled into the ranch truck. "*What* was that?"

"That was me, pulling a Granny Bert. I'm getting rather good at it, too." Hearing the words fall from her mouth, Madison frowned. "I don't know whether to be proud of myself, or horrified." She gunned the motor and peeled out of the driveway, afraid she might see Rose chasing after her in the rearview mirror.

"Granny Bert will definitely be proud!" her friend assured her. "She should be proud of me, too. I had to do some fast talking to keep Rose on that couch with me."

When Genny started to laugh, Madison joined in with her. They were still laughing when they reached the Big House.

"*Now* are you going to tell me what was so important you had to drag me away from my couch? I don't get many afternoons off. I had big plans for myself, a bottle of wine, and my newest book. You wouldn't even tell me what we were looking for."

"That's what makes you a great friend. You don't ask questions, you just come when I call."

"You're still not going to tell me, are you?" Genny realized with a groan. Madison opened the door and led the way through the kitchen.

"Granny Bert should be here any minute. I'll show you both when we get to the office," she promised. "It's easier that way."

20

"I know you had plans for a good book, but in this case, truth may be stranger than fiction."

Madison commented on Genny's earlier statement as they trekked into the office. She would never admit it to Derron, but sometimes, it did feel like a four-mile hike.

"It's about time you two got here." Granny Bert greeted them as they stepped into the office. The older woman was already settled into one of the wingback chairs in front of her granddaughter's desk.

"You should have seen this one, Granny Bert," Genny announced, beaming with pride at her best friend. "She's definitely been learning some of your tricks."

While Genny retold the story, Madison tuned out their laughter and uploaded the new photos to her computer. She opened additional windows to the links she wanted.

"Genny's right, girl," her grandmother crooned. "You make me proud, following in my footsteps."

"Heaven forbid," she muttered. "Whenever you two are ready, I'll fill you in on what I've learned so far."

"We're ready."

"Are you two familiar with the theory of Six Degrees of Separation?"

Genny's blonde hair danced with her animated nod. "Sure. We all have enough in common that we can connect the dots, however faintly, in just six steps."

"Use it all the time," Granny Bert assured her. Her grandmother's gray hair didn't dance as attractively as Genny's, but her head moved the same. "Take the number twelve. Twelve o'clock last night, Wanda calls me all hysterical, says she can't reach lover boy. She's supposed to leave in twelve days, the money's gone from her account, and she has no proof of anything she purchased. It cost her twelve dollars to lose track of well over a thousand. Sticker Pierce has been married twelve times, which is roughly the number of times I ignored his calls this weekend. I stopped at *Ngo's Donuts* and brought a dozen over. Clearly, the number twelve is connected to both heaven and hell."

"Sticker has *not* been married twelve times," Madison protested.

"Close enough. Besides, he's been flirting with his new rep for the Western wear line, who's at least twelve years younger than him." She sniffed determinedly. "I'm still not taking his calls."

"Whatever." Waving their rocky relationship aside—*they were worse than teenagers!* —Madison continued with her theory. "I, too, have been using the six degrees theory to prove a connection between Rose Belvedere and Ron Alexander. The thing is, I found more than I ever imagined. This woman is like a rose with a dozen thorns. She has her hook into all kinds of scams!"

"Like what?" Genny wanted to know.

"You remember that black car we kept seeing a few months ago?"

"Sure. What about it?"

"I think that was Rose, scouting out her next victims. We already know she's pretending to be Miss Nelda's niece, even though nothing could be further from the truth. When I was in Waco with Brash last week, there was a story on the news that had an eerily familiar ring to it. A couple named Vino and Ruby Shiraz convinced an elderly woman, also living in an assisted living facility, that they were related to her. They moved into her house, used it as collateral for a loan, and left town in a black Crown Victoria, last seen in the Bryan-College Station area."

"That's directly between here and Waco," Genny noted.

"Yep. And get this. The description of this couple sounds a lot like Rose and her well-but-oddly dressed 'decorator.' The hair color was wrong—"

"Dye," Granny Bert threw in.

Madison nodded in agreement without breaking stride, "—but everything else fits. Including one of the references the couple gave for prior employment. They gave the name of Barbera Amrita with *Chianti Enterprises*. The—"

"*Chianti?*" Genny cried. "Chianti is the most famous wine region in Tuscany. And all of those—shiraz, barbera, amrita, even *vino* and ruby—have to do with wines."

"I see a pattern evolving." Granny Bert voiced the observation made by all.

Genny nodded. "Inventive names with one central theme."

"Yes, but the plot thickens," Madison said with a cryptic smile. She turned her computer monitor so that the other two could see. "I noticed something on Megan's video, and then on a web search, that compelled me to go back to Rose Belvedere's office.

Granny, remember when we had dinner with Miss Wanda Friday night? She mentioned that the debt collector referred Mabel Crowder to a company that could reduce the amount she owed. She said the name reminded her of wine. As in *blush* wine." Madison tapped the screen, indicating the red and pink *Blush Investments* logo.

Granny Bert narrowed her eyes. "Isn't a blush wine another name for a rosé?"

"It certainly is. And not only that," Genny said, "there's a wine called Belvedere Rose. The Chianti wine trail leads from Florence to Sienna, and winds through some of the most beautiful vineyards you've ever seen. Some date back to the ninth century. It's a gorgeous drive, taking you through Greve, Radda, Panzano, Castellina, Forte di Belve—"

"Castellina!" The gasp came from Madison. She had never visited Italy. It was one of the things she and Gray had talked of doing 'one day.' Sadly, one day had never come for them. Even before his unexpected death in an automobile accident, Italy lost its romantic appeal for the estranged couple. They may have continued living in the same house, but they no longer lived in the same life.

"Castellina," Madison went on, "is one of the names of her so-called businesses. See? *The Castellina Agency.*" She pointed to the picture on her screen.

Genny's voice was thoughtful. "Forte di Belvedere is in Florence. Hmm. Rose Belvedere. If I'm not mistaken..." She punched something into the search engine of her phone. She gave a pleased nod when she saw the results. "Belvedere also refers to a building with a view, such as a turret, pavilion, or arbor." She looked up with a wry smirk. "Rose Belvedere. Or, in other words, rose arbor."

Granny Bert harrumphed. "She certainly likes her

play on words."

"You know what Shakespeare said," Genny murmured. *"A rose by any other name would smell as sweet,"* she quoted.

"The trouble is, I smell something rotten!"

Madison nodded in agreement. "I'm sure she never thought we country bumpkins would figure it out. But unless I'm sorely mistaken, Rose Belvedere and Ruby Shiraz are one and the same. There's no telling what her real name is. She's created this elaborate network of aliases and shell corporations to hide behind, and to weave her web of deceit."

"Didn't Wanda also mention the woman in collections had a name like Pearl, or Opal?" Granny Bert asked. "I imagine it was another jewel. As in Ruby. Aka Rose."

"Unfortunately, this isn't all that I discovered. There were just too many coincidences. In the video Megan shot, I saw some curious looking charts tacked on the wall. After doing a little digging, it gave me a good idea of what she was up to. I went back today to confirm my suspicions. I feel confident about many of her scams, but there could very well be others."

"So, what's her game?" her grandmother asked. "What's this woman up to?"

"I found several fake social media accounts. Each persona has very few friends, but one thing they all have in common is a connection to the health facilities where Nelda Goldberg and Hilda Becker live. I think she has someone on the inside who acts as a scout, finding her a likely target. The ideal target is someone in a nursing facility who owns a home but has little or no family. That way, there's no one to question a new relative who suddenly appears and tries to make nice. Once Rose, aka Ruby, gains their confidence and the keys to their house, she has a new office to work from.

Rent free. I think she truly does work for a legitimate collection agency, *Timely Collections*. I saw a billing page on her computer that looked legit. The thing is, that computer has its own modem, own printer, own IP address, everything. Her *other* computer has the same things, but it's set up for the lucrative business she runs on the side.

"My theory is that she uses the legitimate job to aid and abet her scams. I think she targets some of her legitimate clients to scam, mostly the elderly who are more prone to trust and don't always question things, particularly modern technology. As in Mabel Crowder's case, she pretends to take mercy on them and suggests an alternate way of paying their bill. She recommends *Blush Investments*, or maybe this *Chianti Enterprises* or *The Castellina Agency*."

She tapped her computer screen.

"See this? This is her browsing history, and it shows she visited all these sites on a regular basis. I think when Joe Blow says he can't pay his five-hundred-dollar bill, she sends him to one of these other shell companies, who offers to settle the bill for about half the cost. Then, to squeeze even a few more pennies out of her hapless victims, the helpful rep suggests they use *PhoneGrams*, another room in her little house of horrors. She charges an additional twelve dollars to send fake money orders, all which deposits into her account. There was a ledger for it on the wall."

"If it weren't so disgusting," Genny murmured, her mouth hinged open, "it would be brilliant."

"Again," Madison warned, "there's more."

Granny Bert looked at her sharply. "That's not enough? Is there no end to this woman's evil?"

"Apparently not. I spent most of yesterday afternoon on the computer. I looked through so many sites and profiles, I thought my eyes would cross. But I found a couple of random videos that gave a whole new dimension to her scheming ways."

While she moved the mouse to pull up a new window, Genny asked, "Do they explain why she has all the background screens?"

"I think so. Look at this video of the supposed 'founder' of *Silver Circle*."

An attractive blonde with a lilting Irish accent explained the concept behind a social organization designed for people sixty and over to meet and mingle. She claimed to have developed the site after seeing how lonely her own mother was after her father's death.

"That woman looks suspiciously like Rose Belvedere," Granny Bert accused. "The hair and the voice are wrong, but she was wearing that same outfit the day I dropped by. You can't see it, but she's wearing a belt with alligator print that matches her shoes."

"*Silver Circle*? Is that Miss Wanda's *Silver Circle*?" Genny asked.

"I'm afraid so. Rose's search history shows multiple visits to the site. I don't know for certain, but I suspect it links directly to a user by the handle of Silver Fox. He's Miss Wanda's supposed friend. The one she just sent over fourteen hundred dollars to, via *PhoneGrams*. I think that's what *PG Solutions* stands for." She displayed the picture of the background screen discovered in Rose's office.

"Silver Fox?" Granny Bert scoffed. "I'd say weasel is more the word."

"He claims his name is Vartan Roosevelt, and he supposedly works with an investment firm in New York. His profile picture is an avatar, a pattern I recognize for most of Rose Belvedere's personas."

Genny narrowed her eyes in thought. "Vartan. I saw that in a book of baby names recently." She turned her attention back to her phone before announcing, "Yep. Right here. It's Armenian for 'giver of roses.' And Roosevelt means field of roses. Again, a play on names."

"At least she's consistent," noted Granny Bert.

"Poor Miss Wanda." Madison's voice was sympathetic. "She just lost fourteen hundred dollars *and* a boyfriend!"

"I tried telling her not to stake her hopes on something as flimsy as an online romance, but she wouldn't listen. She was certain he was the best thing since sliced bread."

Genny tsked in compassion.

"I also found this brief video recorded by a cell phone. The person was praising the helpful rep at *PG Solutions* for going 'above and beyond' during a difficult time. They managed to record at least part of their conversation. The lighting is bad, but tell me that doesn't look like Rose Belvedere," Madison challenged.

Both companions peered at the hazy image on the computer. "Her hair still looks blonde," Genny observed, "but this time, it's up in a bun. But it definitely looks like her."

"I found two wigs in her bathroom. Which would explain this next video."

Madison pulled up what appeared to be an interview between a slender, well-dressed man and a woman who, without the black curls, could pass as Rose Belvedere.

"The decorator, you think?" Granny Bert asked.

"More than likely. In the video, he pretends to be with a local television station, even though he never specifies where he's located. She says her name is

Sherry Madeira—"

"Also wine," Genny noted.

"—and she works with *Blush Investments*, helping people consolidate their loans. I imagine they use this link on potential new victims to 'prove' their legitimacy. With a change of hair styles and accents, she suddenly has yet another persona."

"Absolutely amazing." Genny made the reluctant admission, and Granny Bert murmured her agreement. For once, even the older woman seemed at a loss for words.

"Brash comes home tonight, and I'll run all this by him, but I'm sure we can expect an arrest very soon," Madison said with confidence.

"That's all fine and good," her grandmother nodded, finding her voice, "but it still doesn't prove that this woman killed Ronald Alexander."

She had hoped they wouldn't notice. Rubbing her forehead, Madison huffed out a defeated sigh. "I know. There's something we're missing."

"What if *Tellina* is short for *The Castellina Agency?*" Genny asked. "Isn't that where this Ron supposedly worked?"

"Yes. And that could be it, but I'm not sure what it proves. I still can't prove that Rose Belvedere did whatever it is that killed the man."

"What *did* kill him?"

"Honestly? I have no idea." She huffed out another breath. "I'm not sure the coroner even knows."

Home from his football camp, Brash settled onto the settee in their bedroom turret, his wife tucked in beside him. He arrived home in time to have dinner with the family, but Blake had monopolized most of the conversation. The teen was eager to hear every detail of camp, especially the ones involving former and current football legends. Now, it was time to unwind and relax, with a cold beer in one hand, and his wife in the other.

When Maddy filled him in on the details of the case, he smiled at her with pride. "It sounds like you've done a great job, sweetheart. You've put together a case for some impressive circumstantial evidence. I've known people convicted on less."

"So, will you arrest her first thing tomorrow morning?" Even she could hear the hopeful note of anticipation in her voice. It sounded also like glee.

"I'm afraid it doesn't work like that."

Madison sat up, pulling away from the shelter of his arm. "Why not?" she demanded.

"First of all, we'll need to verify what you found. It's one thing to suspect all her scams, but another to prove them. That will probably require a court order to seize her computers and search all her records. That takes time."

"What if we don't have time? What if she finds out we're on to her, and she skips town again?"

"Is there any reason to think she might be suspicious?"

Madison squirmed a bit beneath his sharp gaze. "Not if she believes she was the one to drop the remote control and roll over it."

His dark-auburn head fell back against the cushions. "Aw, Maddy. Please tell me you didn't compromise the entire case."

She managed to sound halfway confident. "I don't think I compromised it. Complicated it? Maybe. All I did was burn up her motorized screen device. It's not like I tampered with evidence or anything."

"At least there's that."

Ignoring his sarcasm, Madison settled back against the wall of his chest, only to pull away again a few moments later.

"You seriously don't think there's enough to arrest her?"

"At this point, I'm not certain I want to."

"What!" she demanded.

"You've done a great job of revealing her scams. Nothing would make me happier than seeing her shut down and put behind bars for fraud, embezzlement, identity theft, and whatever other charges we could throw at her. But all those pale in comparison to murder charges. That's what I really want to pin her with."

"So, she just gets away with scamming all these people?" Madison cried, incredulous.

"I didn't say that. But we may have to hold off on those charges for now. We may need to see where the murder investigation leads before we charge her with a lesser crime."

"But she's taking advantage of people, Brash. She's cheated them out of their houses and their credit. She even posed as a man to trick Miss Wanda into falling for her romantically and sending her over fourteen hundred dollars. That's not right!"

"I agree. It's despicable on every level. And we'll catch her on it, but it may have to wait. First, I need to tie her to this murder."

"What do you have so far?"

"Nothing. Absolutely nothing." He ran his hand over his face in a weary gesture. "There were fibers on the body that were consistent with a synthetic rug, but we can't prove they came from Rose Belvedere's house. Eyewitnesses can't even agree on the color of the van that carried the rug away, much less the rug, itself. The time of death is inconclusive, given his body was stored inside a cooler. Autopsy results won't be in for a while, but the coroner isn't optimistic. He thinks the cause of death will be ruled inconclusive, if not natural causes. There just wasn't anything to see."

"Healthy men don't just die for no reason!"

"I agree. But without a murder weapon, and without an obvious cause of death, we simply don't have a case."

"All the more reason to at least charge her with identity theft!"

"All in good time, sweetheart. All in good time."

21

Just because she understood her husband's stance on the Rose Belvedere case, didn't mean she had to like it. Madison decided a compromise was in order.

She knew, of course, that it was Brash's call to make. He was chief of police and the reigning official in charge. She was a lowly consultant on the case, and an amateur, at that. Murder was a serious crime and carried with it a longer and stiffer punishment. If he thought it best to temporarily overlook the woman's other wrongdoings to go for the harsher charges and penalties, Madison had no choice but to comply.

That didn't mean, however, that she couldn't continue her investigation. When Rose was eventually charged with fraud and identity theft, Madison wanted the charges to stick. She intended to have irrefutable proof against her, making it impossible for her to avoid retribution for what she had done.

"You just caught me," Arlene Kopetsky told Madison when she arrived. "I'm waiting for that daughter of mine to carry me back to my leg doctor."

"I won't take but a minute of your time. I dropped by to bring you cookies." Handing her the offering, she asked, "Your surgeon is in Waco, right?"

"Yes, but I'm having second thoughts about having

Lana drive me. She can't seem to keep her wits about her these days."

Madison had to agree. "I did notice she seemed a bit stressed."

"It's gotten so bad, her boss made her take a leave of absence."

"Where does she work now?" Not that she kept up with the woman's employment, but it seemed to Madison that Lana seldom stayed in one position too long.

"For Myrna Lewis. She grows all those plants and herbs, you know, and bottles them with fancy labels that say *Myrna's Majesties*. To be honest with you," Arlene confessed, "I never thought my girl had it in her, but she's learned quite a bit working with Derron's aunt. I know none of us are fans of the woman, but Myrna Lewis does grow a mighty fine garden. Her yard is as pretty as a picture. And she sent some sort of herbal remedy over that took the ache right out of my ankle."

"That's good. And it's good that Lana has found something she enjoys. Hopefully, she'll feel better and be back to work soon." She smiled encouragingly, all the time wondering why anyone would want to work with Myrna Lewis. The woman was a thorn in her side.

The truth was, Madison often filled in at the *Dean Lewis Insurance Company*, but she mostly dealt with Myrna's husband. Now that Myrna had a greenhouse in their backyard, growing and selling her herbal remedies, she seldom came into the office any longer, which suited customers fine. One of life's biggest mysteries was how a man as nice and amicable as Dean Lewis could be saddled with a wife such as Myrna. Their personalities were like night and day.

From what Madison heard, Myrna's horticulture

venture was doing well enough that she needed more help, especially since her last helper had wound up going to prison. If Lana was happy working there, more power to her.

As if they had conjured her up, Lana's voice called out from the kitchen door. "Mom? Mom, I'm here! I brought you some of those cookies you like from—" She stopped abruptly, seeing her mother had company. "What are *you* doing here?" she demanded of Madison.

"I just came by to visit with your mom. And I brought her cookies, too." She smiled sheepishly, indicating the crumbles dusting Arlene's upper lip.

"I don't know why you keep turning up like a bad penny, but—"

"Lana Elaine! You apologize this minute. That's no way to speak to Madison. She was just being kind, bringing me some Gennydoodle cookies."

"But she's always here!" the other woman accused.

Madison noticed that today her hair was halfway combed and styled, but her clothes were still baggy and hardly her style. For the first time, it occurred to Madison to look for a baby bump. Perhaps pregnancy would explain her cranky and erratic behavior.

Stifling a bit of a gasp, Madison noticed that she did, indeed, have a rounded belly beneath the over-sized tee. *Who*, she wondered, *was the father?* She kept a man about as long as she kept a job.

"Don't worry. I'm on my way out," Madison assured her with a bright smile. "Just one last thing I wanted to ask, Miss Arlene. Do you happen to remember seeing either of these men before?"

Arlene took the phone she offered, adjusting her glasses to better see the screen. "Why, yes. This one helped that woman across the street on move-in day. He was in one of the vans. He helped with the decorating."

Madison had tracked down the man from the video interview and found a profile with his supposed name and picture. He may have told Hilda Becker his name was Vino, but on social media, he called himself Cristo. No last name, just Cristo.

"If you happen to see him again, please let me know." Madison swiped over to Ronald Alexander's photo and presented it to the older woman. "And this man?"

"Why, that's the man from the rug!" Arlene gasped. "He came to the house that morning in the blue car. The next I knew, he was in Bertha's refrigerator!"

Her outburst startled Lana so badly she let out a stifled cry and threw the box of cookies into the air. The top came open and bits of Gennydoodles rained down, the pieces scattering across the floor.

This time, Madison left Lana to clean up her own mess.

"Hey, Blake." Danni Jo Combs curled her hair around her finger as she called out a flirtatious greeting to the lanky youth.

"Hey, Danni Jo." He grinned in return. Getting to see the pretty girl every day was one of the best parts of his summer job.

"My grandfather said to tell you there's been a change in your schedule. Instead of the Muehlers, you need to go back to Mr. Palacios' house."

"Why?" he asked in concern. "Was he not happy with the job I did on Friday?"

"Just the opposite, apparently. He says you did such a good job, he has another project in mind. He insists on you coming.”

“Cool.”

Danni Jo brought him two bottles of cold water, brushing closer to him than necessary. “Stay cool out there today. It’s awfully hot.”

Grinning down at the perky brunette in her cute summer outfit, he nodded. She had a way of wearing ordinary clothes—a t-shirt with a watermelon design and white jean shorts—and making them look anything but ordinary. “That’s exactly what I was thinking,” he told her with a wink. “Hot.”

Blake pulled up at the Second Avenue house five minutes before schedule. Mr. Palacios met him and led him around to the backyard.

“This is really cool, Mr. Palacios. I like what you did back here.”

The backyard, fenced and not visible from the street, was an oasis of lush greenery and abundant blooms. A path made of red brick wound through an impressive variety of plants and flowers. Many were grouped in colorful clay pots. There were two fountains in the garden and several seating options. Blake’s favorite touch was the brick archway and wrought-iron accents. They lent an old-world Spanish vibe to the space.

The language arts teacher showed him the simple task he wanted done. In Blake’s mind, it didn’t make sense to hire the job out, but the customer was the boss. If that’s what he wanted, that’s what Blake would do. It took less than forty-five minutes to complete.

When he knocked at the back door to announce he was done, Mrs. Palacios answered the door.

She looked different today, the teen noticed. She still wore a dress, but this one was much less formal and almost looked comfortable. The biggest change was in her face. Today, she wore a smile.

"Yes, come in. *Sí, sí.*" She handed him a towel, ignoring the confused look on his face. "You may wash up just through there. Hands, arm, neck, and face."

Assuming he must be a sight, Blake peered into the bathroom mirror with a sense of trepidation. He was surprised to find very few smudges of dirt staring back at him. Regardless, he washed as best he could and dried off with the provided towel before rejoining her in the kitchen.

"Come, come," she instructed, leading him into the adjacent dining room.

The set table wasn't nearly as formal as the one his sister had described. Today, it had a dark-blue cloth and ordinary dishes, if, he amended, gold-trimmed china was considered 'ordinary.' Instead of a fancy tea set, there was a semi-fancy tall glass pitcher, filled with wedges of fresh fruit floating in an ocean of tea. A tiered tray held a variety of tiny cookies and cakes, but his attention was drawn to the platters on the table. Just seeing the savory tidbits made his stomach rumble in greeting.

"You can eat, yes?" the petite woman asked.

"I can always eat," he assured her.

"Sit. I will feed you."

He made a half-hearted attempt to protest. "You really don't have to, ma'am."

"I insist."

Remembering his manners, Blake offered, "Let me help you with your chair."

Once they were seated, Mrs. Palacios passed ramekins filled with olives, cherry tomatoes, and cubed cheeses. Next, she passed a platter with fried peppers and some sort of fritter. Curious, Blake took two of each.

"*Patatas bravas,*" she said, pointing to the fried

fingerling potatoes on the next platter. "Calamari and *datiles*. Dates wrapped in bacon."

"You shouldn't have gone to so much trouble," the boy murmured as he piled everything she offered onto his plate.

"What are *tapas*, if not a celebration of food?"

"I love celebrating food!"

The woman chuckled, a sound he hadn't thought possible the first time he met her. She had undergone a dramatic transformation in a very few days.

"Where's Mr. Palacios?" he thought to ask.

"He had errands to run. You can keep an old woman company, *sí*?"

With his mouth full, Blake simply nodded.

"I know how quickly a stomach empties, working in the garden," she said. A tiny smile teased the corner of her lips, put there, perhaps, by a memory that teased her heart. "I knew a young man much like you. He worked hard and ate well. I served him *tapas*, as well, but he preferred American food. Sandwiches suited him fine."

Blake thought of the ham and turkey sandwiches Mr. Ballard had served. Apparently, his tastes were still the same.

"It makes me happy, seeing a young man eat so. My Eloy, he doesn't eat so well. He says the foods are too rich and remind him of a life he did not like. I share his sentiment, but I do not hold it against the food. Other than my son, the cuisine is the best thing to come from my years away."

It was the perfect opening. "My sisters said you used to live here?"

"Very many years ago when I was just a girl. About your age, I would expect."

"Did you go to The Sisters High?"

"I'm afraid not. I lived here only in the summers."

Trying to keep the excitement from his voice—this *had* to be Rosa! —Blake attempted to sound casual. "So, you must still have friends here."

Her face tightened, and he thought for a moment that she would slip into the reserved coolness from Friday. "I did not keep in touch, I am afraid. I lost track of the few friends I had."

"That's too bad. Did you know my great-grandmother? Bertha Cessna?"

Wrinkles puckered across her forehead. "The name sounds familiar, but it's been so many years. I do remember a girl a few years older than I. Her name was Lydia. Lydia deCordova. She was a good friend to me."

"Hey! She's my grandma!" Blake said with a bright smile. This definitely was Rosa. "Well," he clarified, "my step-grandmother, and Megan's true one. But Grammy treats me and Bethani as good as she does all the other grandkids."

Mrs. Palacios looked stunned. "Lydia deCordova is your grandmother?" she echoed.

"Step-grandmother." He felt the need to stress the fact, even though it mattered little. Funny, how the heart didn't bother with titles and distinctions. "Her son Brash married our mom a few months ago. I guess you'd say they're still newlyweds."

"I did not realize *Senorita* Megan's surname was deCordova. Is Lydia still of good health?"

"If her cooking is any indication, yes, ma'am! After making jelly all day, she brought a huge dinner to our house the other night. She never slows down. Next to Granny Bert, she's the busiest person I know."

"If God had blessed me with grandsons, I would cook for them the same way she cooks for you." There was a sadness in her words.

Blake made his inquiry carefully, sprinkling the

questions in among conversations about the food and the garden, and the places she had lived. It turned out that she had, indeed, lived in the house that looked like a Spanish castle. She didn't even look sad when he told her it had been torn down.

From what he pieced together, she married young and moved to California, where her only child was born. The family then moved to Spain, where the lifestyle was 'not to their liking.' Further comments about their massive home, the cooks and chefs who insisted on preparing meals for them, and the private schools her son attended, hinted at a life of wealth, extravagance, and privilege. There was no mention of happiness. In fact, Blake had the impression of the exact opposite; he thought she and her son both sounded miserable.

He wondered if that was why Mr. Palacios was always so solemn. As a child, had he never learned to laugh? He seemed far older than the fifty his mother confirmed him to be. Was that how people with money and royal bloodlines acted? Like Granny Bert always said, a smile didn't cost a dime, but it was a great investment. It wouldn't endanger the family fortune if he spent more time smiling and less time frowning.

The gold-trimmed china and golden trays had been handed down from generations before her. Some pieces came from her family, some from her late husband's. Both had traces of royalty in their bloodlines, but Blake could tell that it meant little to Mrs. Palacios. She went so far as to reveal that she came back to The Sisters because it was the only place she had ever been allowed to be her 'real self.' Her son had taken the job here because she always spoke fondly of the area.

By the time Blake left, he was convinced that this

woman was Rosa Davila from Mr. Ballard's past, and that she hadn't married Esteban Palacios out of love but out of duty.

In his opinion, fate had dealt the young lovers of long ago a losing hand, but it wasn't too late to draw new cards.

Now, he just had to convince Mr. Ballard to give her another chance.

The opportunity came sooner than expected.

Mr. Ballard wanted some new ideas for expanding his backyard oasis. He came into *Marvin Gardens* to get a quote on adding a fountain and perhaps an arbor. An outdoor kitchen might be nice, as well, with a brick oven. Even though light-colored stone was all the rage these days, he preferred traditional red brick.

Marvin Combs was the one to mention the work they had done at Eloy Palacios'. He didn't call a name, but he described the work his crews had done to create the archway and elaborate brick pathways.

"Excuse me, sirs," Blake said, respectfully butting into their conversation. "If the homeowner wouldn't mind us touring his backyard, I'd be happy to take Mr. Ballard over for a look."

His boss wasn't sold on the idea. "I'm not sure..."

"That might be helpful," Israel Ballard countered. "I could see the quality of your bricklayers and get a feel for what I do and don't want."

"Very well. I'll contact the homeowner. If he has no objections, we'll let Blake take you by for a look and go from there."

"Perfect." Mr. Ballard smiled at Blake. "Good idea, son. I'll want you on the project, if possible."

"That's up to Mr. Combs and the timing, sir.

School starts back mid-August, and football practice before that. I'm not sure what my schedule will look like then."

"We'll work something out," his boss assured him. "You've been a hard worker. I don't want to lose you."

"Thanks, Mr. Combs. I appreciate that." Blake's smile was wide and proud.

Two days later, Blake and Israel Ballard arrived at the house on Second Avenue.

Eloy Palacios met them outside and led them around back, via an ornate iron gate at the side of the house. When Mr. Ballard admired the workmanship, their host promised to give him the name of the supplier.

Touring the impressive backyard, Blake jotted down notes on what Mr. Ballard liked and hoped to replicate. He snapped a few pictures while the men discussed gardening tools and favorite plants and shrubs.

"Can I say hello to your mom?" Blake asked. He wasn't certain what he would say, exactly, but he had to convince her to come out into the garden.

Mr. Palacios returned the inquiry in his unique—and often infuriating—manner. "I don't know. Can you?"

The teen rephrased the question. "Do you object if I say hello to your mom?"

"Be my guest."

Working out different speeches in his head, he soon learned they weren't necessary. Mrs. Palacios answered the door the moment he knocked. She had a tray in her hands, seemingly waiting for him to hold the door open for her.

"I have *refrescos*," she announced.

Now that she was allowed back in a kitchen, she spent her days stirring up delicious experiments. For so many years, her husband would not hear of such a thing. They had servants for that, he insisted. With only her son to cook for, she was eager to share her talented exercises with others.

"I'll get that for you," the teen offered.

"*Gracias*, but there's another tray there on the counter."

Together, they carried the offerings out to a wrought-iron table. While Mrs. Palacios fussed with the arrangement, Blake wondered if he should alert her to the identity of her other guest. He discarded the notion when he realized Mr. Ballard would be as blindsided as she. He decided it best if they made the discovery on their own.

No one needed to know he suspected they shared a past. No one needed to know he helped facilitate today's reunion. After all, he reasoned, it could happen in town, or it could happen here. The chance meeting could go well, or it could be a disaster. At least this way, they had some privacy when dealing with the outcome.

Hearing their footsteps approaching, Blake offered to take the tall glass pitcher from Mrs. Palacios' hands; he didn't want her dropping it in surprise and chance anyone getting cut.

"I see my mother has refreshments set up for us," he heard the language teacher say. "It's rather warm out today, but at least there's shade and a nice breeze."

"I've never minded a little heat." Mr. Ballard's voice had a nice, rich ring to it. He seemed to have recovered from last week's melancholy.

Still fussing over today's lighter version of *tapas*—chilled shrimp, fresh guacamole, chunks of cured ham, pickled peppers and fresh tomatoes on skewers, and a variety of sweets—Mrs. Palacios didn't immediately turn.

"Allow me to introduce my mother, Rosita Palacios. Mother, this is—"

The petite woman turned in her elegant manner, a polite smile of greeting already in place. The color drained from her face, right along with the smile. She stared at the man being introduced.

"Israel?" she whispered.

In response, his voice was hoarse. "Rosa?" He took a tentative step forward. "Is that you?"

Eloy's dark eyes darted between the two, clearly confused. "Mother? You know this man?"

Her head jerked, in what served as a nod. "I did," she murmured. "A very long time ago."

"A lifetime ago," Israel echoed. A sharp edge had slipped into his voice.

"This is the man, isn't it?" Eloy's question sounded more like an accusation.

"Now is not the time for this discussion, Eloy."

Eloy's reply was cold. "I think this discussion is long overdue, Mother."

"We have company, Eloy!" she cautioned. She turned anxious eyes back toward the silent man between them. "Please, excuse my son," Rosita Palacios begged. She motioned for Israel to come forward. "What you must think of me as a hostess! Please, sit. I have refreshments for you."

"This is the man from your past," her son continued. "The man you couldn't let go."

"Oh, believe me. She let go," Mr. Ballard charged.

No one remembered the teenage boy in the background. No one knew how heavy his heart felt. This wasn't going at all like he had anticipated. Mr. Palacios and Mr. Ballard both sounded angry. Mrs. Palacios sounded sad.

"No." The younger of the two men wouldn't be

quieted. "She never loved my father. Our life with him was miserable because her heart wasn't in her marriage."

"Our life was miserable," Mrs. Palacios spoke up, her voice gaining courage, "because your father was a harsh, demanding man. He cared for wealth and appearances, more than he cared for his family. You know this to be true, Eloy."

"Perhaps, if you had loved him more—"

"No, Eloy. If *he* had loved us more. We carry no blame for his shortcomings."

Feeling like an outsider, Blake shrank back as much as the small space would allow.

"But you were in love with someone else! I heard Father accuse you often enough." Sounding more like a sulking child than the brilliant teacher Blake knew him to be, Eloy Palacios threw an accusatory glare at Mr. Ballard. An arm flung in his direction followed. "*This* man, from the look on your face!"

Rosita Palacios, known as Rosa in her youth, lifted her chin and looked into Israel's eyes. Time had touched her face, but it was still beautiful. It softened now, as she stared at the man she hadn't seen in over fifty years. "Yes," she said in a strong voice. It held not an ounce of shame. "This is the man I loved. This is the man my grandparents forced me to turn my back on, so that I might marry well and have the life they had chosen for me. It was never my choice."

She shifted her dark eyes to her son, and her voice softened. "But I cannot regret my marriage because it gave me a son. You were the one good thing that came of my grandparents' interference. The one true accomplishment of your father's pompous, inflated life. And the only joy and happiness he ever gave me."

Blake pushed further into the edges of the airy space, wishing he could disappear altogether. *He should have never interfered!*

Then he heard Mr. Ballard's voice. It held a note of wonder. A note of hope.

"Is that true, Rosa?"

Her dark eyes glistened with unshed tears. "Yes."

Israel cleared his throat, pushing through the emotions gathered there. He nodded to the carefully set table before them. "You've gone to such trouble with refreshments. It would be a shame to let such a delicious feast go to waste."

She smiled at the extended olive branch. It lifted years off her face, hinting at the youthful beauty who had first stolen his heart. Eloy watched them with a wary expression, but there was no denying the look of happiness on his mother's face. It was a look he seldom saw. Before he could help with her chair, Israel Ballard stepped forward and did the honors.

It was then that Rosa remembered her other guest. "Blake? Where are you, *niño*? Come. Sit. Eat."

He stepped forward nervously. "I—I need to get back. I have another appointment." He looked at Mr. Ballard expectantly, uncertain of what to do. "Should I come back for you, sir?"

"That won't be necessary, son. At the most, it's a few blocks' walk." Israel's expression was hopeful as he looked down at his beloved Rosa. "And we have much to catch up on. Fifty years' worth."

Exchanging goodbyes with the others, Blake turned to go. Israel's voice stopped him before he reached the side of the house.

"Oh, and Blake?"

"Yes, sir?"

The older man's eyes twinkled. "I may need that box back."

22

Brash was no closer to finding a connection between Rose Belvedere and Ronald Alexander than he had been before. To say the least, he was frustrated with the lack of evidence his team had produced.

Making matters worse, Shaylee Alexander couldn't be reached for additional questioning. Her phone number no longer worked, and she had moved, leaving no forwarding address. Even the Brenham Police Department lost track of her.

In no time flat, the case had officially stalled.

His old friend Detective Audra Cao called him with a tip that brought with it a fleeting sense of progress. *Senior Styles Assisted Living* was saddened to announce the death of one of their contracted staff members, Ron "Alex" Alexander. According to the facility's staff, Alexander was an independent health and exercise instructor. Quite popular with the residents, his weekly classes were always well-attended and had a waiting list for new enrollees.

Brash called *Golden Standards* in Conroe and heard a similar story.

The glimmer of hope came when Alexander's contracts named *The Castellina Agency* as his official employer, establishing a viable link between the dead man and their prime suspect. The link weakened with each failed attempt to connect with the agency. Phone calls and emails went unanswered, paper trails vanished into thin air, and online searches—even through official sources and tax filings—bogged down amid alternate spellings, broken links, missing files, and a mishmash of conflicting information.

"What now?" Madison asked. It was a surprisingly pleasant evening, so they enjoyed a few minutes in the backyard swing. "Does that mean you'll pursue the identity theft angle?"

"Not yet. I want to give Rose Belvedere a little more time. Given a big enough garden to roam, I imagine she'll get tangled in her own thorns before this is all done."

"But Ron Alexander is obviously her connection inside the facilities," she insisted. "He had to have been the one who targeted likely victims and helped her to scam them out of their homes and their life savings."

"And so far," Brash pointed out, "it's been a very lucrative partnership. Why would she kill him off now? There's tons of other facilities and defenseless victims out there, just waiting to be scammed. Why kill her ace in the hole?"

"I didn't say I knew all the particulars," his wife grumbled. "But it makes perfect sense."

"That's the thing, sweetheart. Murder doesn't make sense. Why and how one human being can kill another is one of those things in life I'll never understand."

Brash's phone rang, displaying Officer Perry's name across the screen. He excused himself to take the call inside, saying he needed to consult his laptop. Madison waited alone for a while, but when he didn't soon return, she decided it was time to go in.

Thinking she heard the murmur of voices, she ducked around the side of the house to see if the twins had returned. They had convinced their parents they were in dire need of soft serve ice cream from the Dairy Queen in Riverton.

Expecting to see two blond teenagers, she was unprepared for the sight of her grandmother and Sticker Pierce locked in a tight embrace outside the kitchen door.

"You know I'm just an old fool when it comes to you, Belle," the cowboy crooned.

"To any woman," Granny Bert said, but her voice lacked its usual bite.

"No, Belle. Just you. None of the others have ever mattered. It's always been you."

Granny Bert was taller than the grizzled old cowboy who held her in his arms. In her youth, her advantage of height and age had bothered her. She admitted now that she had made a mistake, allowing a yardstick and a calendar to rule her relationship with her first love, but she had never regretted her life with Joe Cessna. She loved him more than she had ever loved the smooth-talking cowboy, even if his flowery words did still stir a fire in her heart. She didn't plan to ever marry again—no man deserved to live in Joe's shadow—but she didn't mind keeping regular company with her flame from the past.

It didn't hurt that he was still a looker. All the ladies were jealous of her and the hold she had on the legendary rodeo star. Sticker Pierce was quite the catch, by any account. He had his own Western wear company and numerous ranches and rodeo companies scattered out around the western states, along with a string of ex-wives and offspring. He claimed they had only been a distraction from his one true love, but Bertha knew the truth. Sticker loved women. He might love her best, but he was a sucker for anyone in a skirt.

He dipped his white head to the side, so that his handlebar mustache wouldn't get in the way of kissing her. In Bertha's opinion, that was another of his better attributes. He was still a mighty fine kisser.

Just before his lips covered hers, he noticed they weren't alone. His hand, which had been scandalously low on the older woman's backside, slid back to her waist. Unabashed, he brushed his lips against hers lightly before whispering they had an audience.

"Maddy! We were just about to knock," Granny Bert claimed. "What are you doing outside?"

"It was a pleasant evening, so we were sitting outside until Brash got a call. I was just heading back in." She eyed the arm still loose around her grandmother's waist. "What are you two doing? Or, need I ask?" she teased.

"This old fool brought me a whole hoop of red rind cheese," her grandmother said, but the words were softened with a note of pleasure. "He went all the way to that butcher shop in Burton to get it for me, knowing how I lost mine to the dead body. There's no way I can use a full hoop before it ruins, so I thought I'd share with you. I know Brash and Blake are both partial to this kind."

"Aww. How sweet of you, Sticker." Madison smiled. It really was a thoughtful gesture, and so much more personalized than flowers. "Come on in. Brash should be off the phone soon."

Two hours later, the kids had returned, and the older couple was gone. Madison and Brash locked the doors and climbed the stairs to the second floor, ready to call it a night.

"I hate to admit it," Madison said, "but Granny Bert had a valid idea."

"Maybe. But hearing those words fall from her lips just puts fear in my heart."

Knowing his solemn expression was greatly exaggerated, Madison placed a hand to her heart. "Men less brave than you have been known to run away, screaming and wailing, when they hear that phrase."

"It's the last thing anyone wants to hear from your grandmother. *I have an idea.*" His broad shoulders shimmied. "It's enough to make a grown man cry."

"But in this case," she dared to point out, "it makes sense."

"Maybe."

"Rose seemed unusually interested when we told her the background of The Sisters. She latched on the part about Randolph Blakely being one of the richest men in the state and deeding the town sites to his daughters. If she's been researching it at the library, you know she's working an angle. I think Granny is right. She's trying to find a loophole. Something she can bilk for all its worth, whether it be an obscure clause she can collect on, or some hoax she can pull on the good citizens of our community."

"I wouldn't doubt it," Brash agreed as they reached their bedroom. He continued into the huge ensuite bath, where he pulled a towel and washcloth from the shelf in anticipation of a hot shower.

Madison trailed in behind him, still considering her grandmother's suggestion. "So why not pull a scam on *her*, for a change? All we have to do is convince her there's a little-known clause in the town charter that promises a piece of the town's wealth and prosperity to anyone who owns a stake in a certain venture. We'd have to make it sound convincing, but I believe she's just greedy enough to fall for it."

"I'm not saying she doesn't deserve it, but what

would it prove? Unless she's willing to kill to get a piece of the stake, it still won't prove she's a murderess. Even that won't prove she killed Ron Alexander."

"Can we at least lay the groundwork? What would it hurt if we set it in motion, just to see how she reacted?"

She knew he wavered when he didn't immediately shut down her suggestion.

"You understand that absolutely no money can exchange hands." His voice was as unyielding as stone, but it wasn't a no. "If she actually invested in the project, you could be charged with embezzlement."

"Of course!"

He still didn't look convinced. "There's something we're missing, Maddy." He reached in to turn on the shower. "Something we're overlooking. Scamming Rose won't clear things up. It may just complicate things further."

With the sound of the water drowning out her words, Maddy grumbled, "Maybe so. But at least it would make me feel better."

"Genny will be by soon to pick me up," Madison told him the next day.

"I know it's hard being without a vehicle. We'll go shopping for one tomorrow," Brash promised. "Being out of the office for almost two weeks, I had a ton of work to catch up on, but I can finally see the light of day. I should be able to get away tomorrow to go with you."

"I'm not looking forward to it, if you must know the truth," Madison informed him as she cleaned out her purse. "I hate buying a new car."

"Said no woman ever," he teased.

"This one does. Gray always made it about the latest and the greatest, not the one I wanted or the one we could afford."

"Then you are in for a treat," Brash promised. "Car shopping with me is all about finding the car that works best for what we want and what we need. It's all about cup holders, charging ports, and safety features."

"In that case, it might not be so bad," she said, smiling. She rounded up loose change from the bottom of her purse. "For our vacation fund," she said, dropping eighty-seven cents into his hand. "Oh, and this."

"What am I supposed to do with this?" he asked in amusement, eying the fitness watch she handed him. "Hock it?"

"Do whatever you like with it. I found it on the side of the road when I went down the embankment."

"Does it work?"

"Once I juiced it up to Blake's charger, it did." When her phone chirped with a text message, she leaned over and kissed him. "Genny's here, so I'm gone. Love you."

Sliding into the front seat of her best friend's car, Madison considered the placement of the cup holders with new appreciation. "Do you like your car?" she asked, looking around the roomy cabin. "Brash says we'll go car shopping tomorrow, but I haven't the foggiest notion of what I want."

"I do, but I'm thinking of trading it off for an SUV."

"Really? I didn't know you wanted one."

"I hope that one day soon I'll need the room. Car seats are easier in SUVs, I hear."

Madison sent her friend a sharp but tentative look. She didn't want to sound as eager as she felt. "Does that mean...?"

Genny shook her head. Maddy didn't miss the fine mist that gathered in her eyes. "Not yet," she acknowledged softly.

"It will happen, Gen. Don't get frustrated."

"I'm thinking of making an appointment with a specialist. Maybe it's time I was tested for infertility. I'm not exactly a spring chicken anymore."

Madison made light of the situation. "You're all of forty years old. That's not exactly ancient."

"No, but it means my eggs are forty years old, too," she said glumly. "Things tend to dry up and wither away after years of non-use."

"Not necessarily. I know lots of women who have babies well into their forties." As much to lighten the mood as to share her new tidbit of gossip, Madison's eyes twinkled with a secret. "And I think I know someone else around our age who's about to have her first child. Her eggs aren't dried up, and I doubt yours are, either."

Genny jumped at the chance to change the subject. "Yeah? Who's that?"

"Lana Kopetsky. I swear, I think she's pregnant. It all makes sense now. Her mood swings, her baggy clothes, her sallow skin, her unkempt appearance. She's probably had morning sickness. I remember those days all too well. You don't care what you look like, as long as you're not green."

"Who's the baby daddy?"

"No clue."

"Wow. I didn't see that one coming."

"I don't know for certain," Madison admitted, "but it makes sense, don't you think?"

After a moment's consideration, Genny nodded.

"Actually, it does. That's one aspect of getting pregnant I'm not looking forward to. I hear hormones can literally make a woman crazy."

"You. Cannot. Be serious."

With just one eye visible from the other side of the door, Rose Belvedere stared at the two women who were, once again, standing on her doorstep.

In reply, Madison and Genny offered timid smiles. With a half wave of her hand, Genny tried a weak but cheery, "Hello."

"No." Rose's rejection was blunt. "Whatever the question, the answer is no." Without fanfare, she slammed the door in their faces.

Madison rang the doorbell once again.

Then, a second time.

On the third ring, the door flew open. The normally composed Rose glared at them, her face contorted in outrage. Her lipstick was smudged, the neat tuck of her blouse into a starched and pressed skirt was askew, and her hair, usually so smooth and artfully arranged, looked as if she had fallen through a wind tunnel. "*What* do you want?" she demanded.

Madison's reply was simple. "To come in."

"No."

Again, she slammed the door.

Again, Madison rang the bell.

Genny knocked.

After a steady repeat of *ring, ring! knock, knock! ring, ring! knock, knock!* the door opened. With a snarl, Rose snatched Madison's arm and dragged her inside the house. Genny made it through just before the door slammed behind them.

"Don't say I didn't warn you!" Rose snapped.

"We need to talk."

"You need to leave," she countered. "This instant."

"We can't," Madison argued. "We know you're onto us."

The sharp retort died upon Rose's lips. Startled, she did a double-take at her unwanted guest. "What did you say?"

Genny nodded. "We know you've been to the library. We know you've figured it out."

"Figured...? Look. You two must go. Now."

Ignoring her strange behavior—the unflappable Rose Belvedere almost looked *nervous*—Madison and Genny helped themselves to a seat on the sofa.

"*Not now!*" Rose all but begged, her tone urgent.

"Oh? Are you in the middle of one of your podcasts? Or a commercial, maybe?" Madison had discovered a small series of podcasts recorded by the dark-haired 'Sherry Madeira.' As it turned out, the interview was only the beginning.

"I don't know what you're talking about."

"It doesn't matter. What matters is that you've stumbled upon our secret, and now we have to deal with it."

"Surely, *you're* not threatening me, too!"

In a moment of uncertainty, Madison glanced at Genny. *Too?* What was Rose talking about?

Every bit as confused as her friend, Genny forged ahead with their plan. "We—We aren't threatening you," Genny assured her. "We've come to make you an offer."

Rose stared at them, stunned.

Madison nodded. "You obviously know about the clause in the town charter. We're prepared to cut you in on the deal."

"*If* you meet certain requirements." Genny added the stipulation with an air of importance.

"Honestly, ladies, now is not the time to have this discussion." Rose looked almost frantic. "If you could come back—"

"Why come back?"

The voice came from the hall.

Belatedly, Madison realized Rose wasn't alone. Maybe that explained her strange behavior.

"I, for one," the unseen person said, "would love to hear more about the clause in the town charter."

Curious, Madison and Genny watched as the person stepped from the shadowed doorway.

"Lana!" Genny gasped.

Madison's gasp held a question. "Lana? I—I didn't realize you and Rose were friends." Her gaze shot quickly between the two, trying to read their body language. Rose looked uncomfortable while Lana, for once, looked confident.

"Oh, we're not," Lana assured her. Her voice was deceptively light.

"Do you... work for her?" Madison guessed.

"Hardly."

An uncomfortable silence stretched across the room, the connection between the two women still unclear. Rose moved to sit in the armchair. An air of resignation weighted her movements.

"Please, do tell us more about the town charter," Lana said. "You were in such a rush to barge in here and discuss it. Don't let me stop you."

"It was just something we wanted to discuss with Rose. We didn't realize she had company," Madison said. She started up from the sofa. "We can come back."

"No," Lana said. "Sit."

Something hard and unpleasant moved into her voice, reflecting in the glint of her eyes. "I insist."

Madison reminded herself that this was Lana. Two

of the last three times she had seen her, Lana had been a total mess. Rude and antagonistic, yes, but harmless. Clumsy, even. There was no reason to be alarmed now. The edge in her voice, the keen brightness in her eyes, could be attributed to hormones. Hadn't she and Genny just said how hormones could literally make a pregnant woman crazy?

Her eyes dropped to Lana's stomach now, noting the swell beneath her baggy t-shirt. The woman was definitely pregnant. Madison should cut her some slack. There was no reason for the hairs on her neck to stand at attention. No reason to feel this ridiculous sense of fright. Lana Kopetsky was harmless.

...Wasn't she?

"Honestly, we didn't mean to intrude," Madison said. "We'll come back at a more convenient time. Right, Genny?"

"Absolutely!" Genny flashed an easy smile, but Madison sensed her wariness. She was as confused as Madison was, teetering between feeling threatened and feeling foolish. She could see the same question in her friend's eyes. *It was foolish, right, to be frightened by Lana?*

Genny pushed to her feet. When Lana stepped forward, the bleached blonde had never seemed so tall and menacing. She didn't say a word. She simply stood in Genny's path for a moment longer than necessary, before dropping onto the arm of Rose's chair.

"Why rush off?" she asked. Her long leg swung back and forth, directly in front of Genny's escape route.

That was how it suddenly felt. As the air crackled with unspoken tension, Madison felt as if she and Genny were trapped.

Madison felt a buzz on her wrist, alerting her to a text message via her smart watch. She turned her wrist so that the screen and its one-word message from Brash was visible only to her. What did *Abort* mean?

Her movements smooth, she pretended to cross her hands in her lap. While she covertly drew a question mark and hit the 'send' button, she kept her eyes on Lana and faked a friendly smile.

"I was wondering what your connection to Rose was, but then I realized. You two are neighbors. You live on the next street over, right?"

"I suppose you could call us neighbors," Lana agreed.

Rose's words were full of thorns. "Lana definitely likes to take a shortcut through my lawn."

The blonde's mouth stretched into a smile, but the sentiment didn't reach her eyes. "You might say that's how we met."

Genny threw Madison a quizzical look. There was an undercurrent between the two women in the other chair, something that snapped and swirled in the heavy silence. It almost felt as if Lana's perch on the armrest was a subtle threat of some sort to the homeowner. Her posture looked casual enough, but if they weren't friends, why would she sit so close?

Madison entertained similar thoughts. Lana claimed they weren't friends. Lovers, perhaps? She discarded the thought as quickly as it entered her mind. She knew for a fact that Lana preferred men; her swollen belly was proof enough of that. If Brash's experience with Rose meant anything, the dark-haired woman in the chair wasn't gay, either. There had to be another connection between the two, and she wasn't betting on the friendly neighbors angle.

Another buzz on her wrist, this message lengthier.

Needing a diversion so she could read it, she blurted out, "I see your plant is doing well."

The unexpected statement drew their startled gazes toward the potted plant she indicated. It was the one she and Genny delivered the last time they were here, now moved to a more suitable location.

While their eyes sought out the plant, Madison read her husband's text.

Rose didn't kill Ron Alexander, aka Alex. The watch detected no heart rhythm an hour before she arrived. Still guilty of fraud, so don't jinx case. Abort mission.

Watch? The words didn't make sense, until she remembered that Blake said the sports watch she found belonged to a man named Alex. It didn't take six degrees of separation to make the connection. She found the watch near the gully where Ron Alexander's car was ditched. Alex was short for Alexander. Since one of the functions of the watch was to track heart rate and physical activity, an abrupt stop for both could indicate the time of death. In just three degrees, she could reasonably assume the watch belonged to their victim.

Her mind raced through the details as she remembered them. Witnesses saw Ron Alexander (apparently Alex to himself and his friends) arrive around eight a.m. and go into the house. Rose, by multiple reports, didn't pull up until a good hour and a half later. If the watch indicated the time of death as eight thirty, it could absolve her of murder.

That fact didn't sit well with Madison. She knew Rose Belvedere was a criminal. She scammed and defrauded innocent people, profiting off their misguided trust. Maybe that wasn't the same as murder, but it was illegal. Rose Belvedere—aka Ruby Shiraz, aka Sherry Madeira, aka who knew what else—deserved any punishment meted out. The stiffer, the better.

A resigned sigh moved through her shoulders. No matter what Rose Belvedere deserved, it wouldn't be right to accuse and charge the woman with murder, not if she were innocent. And no matter how certain Maddy had been to the contrary, it appeared as if Rose hadn't killed the man found in Granny Bert's refrigerator, after all. Where he came from and who put him there remained a mystery, but that was another matter. The only consolation was knowing that Rose Belvedere could still be charged with embezzlement.

As usual, Brash was right. Madison didn't need to jeopardize the case by muddying the waters with some ill-fated scam of her own.

Mentally settling the matter in her mind, Madison started to stand. She wasn't certain she could bring herself to apologize to the dark-haired woman who defrauded people for a living, but she could at least leave her home. It was up to Brash and the legal system now. Her part was done.

"I don't think so."

The barked words came from Lana.

Madison looked at her in surprise, having almost forgotten the blonde was there. Madison was so shocked to learn how wrong she had been about Rose, that she somehow forgot Lana's unexplained presence here and her most recent erratic behavior. It seemed that each day, Lana displayed a different version of bizarre. Today's rendition was as confusing as all the rest, even if this one did feel more unsettling. Something about it was almost... menacing.

Yes, she decided. *Menacing was a good word for*

it. If she didn't know better (and she did, didn't she?) that looked like a threat in Lana's angry glare.

"Pardon me?" Madison asked in a frosty voice, using her stance to stare down at the other woman.

"You're not going anywhere. Not until you tell me how you knew."

Madison's confused expression was real. "How I knew what?"

"You've been following me. You keep showing up at my mother's. You keep coming here. Now here you are again, just when I happen to be here. I know it's no coincidence. Not when you insist on ignoring my warnings."

Madison shot a worried look at her friend. It was as if Lana were coming unhinged again, right before their eyes. "Warnings?"

"Do you *always* have so many flats?" Lana taunted in a snide tone.

Madison gasped. "That was you? *You* sabotaged my car?"

"Even the power steering?" Genny echoed.

In reply, Lana hooked her thumb toward her companion in the chair. "Do you really think Miss Rose Queen over here is going to dirty her hands, crawling around in a car engine? And how would she manage climbing a fence in her high heels?"

"You?" Madison repeated, completely flabbergasted. "But... why?"

"So you would mind your own business!" Lana snapped. When she jumped to her feet, Madison lost the advantage of height. They were both roughly the same five-foot, seven inches tall. "It was his wife, wasn't it? She's the one who hired you!"

"Who—Whose wife?" With each change of subject, Madison felt like a pinball inside a machine, batted from one flipper to another.

"Alex's. She found out we were having an affair and hired you to trail me, didn't she?"

The balls zipped through Madison's mind, pinging off random thoughts.

The strange lights at night, the ones Miss Arlene said looked more like candles.

The blue car, seen here at random times during the day, even before Rose moved in.

The woman Granny Bert saw at the restaurant in Waco, the one wearing sunglasses, a floppy hat, and the skimpy clothes Lana normally favored. Eating lunch with the very man in question. At the exact time Lana left her mother in Wal-Mart while she ran 'errands.'

The convenience of a vacant house, just behind the one Lana shared with a roommate. In the yard Lana often cut through, en route to her mother's.

The dropped trays and scattered cookies. The erratic behavior and frayed nerves.

The baby in Lana's womb. Fathered, perhaps, by a married man.

A man who was now dead, discovered in Granny Bert's refrigerator.

It was the last thought that struck a discord. With their rhythm disrupted, the balls inside her head spiraled into a free fall.

Distracted, Madison didn't notice her best friend covertly sending a text.

"It was an accident," Lana blurted out, unexpectedly. As she moved to pace around the room, wringing her hands one minute and torturing her hair the next, she looked like the beleaguered, distraught woman of recent days.

Along with her confidence, the menacing attitude vanished. If anything, she looked pathetic. Her shoulders curled in on themselves, so that she hunched over the swell in her abdomen, the one she now cradled with both arms.

"I didn't know," she said, her voice taking on a keening wail. "I didn't know he had a heart condition. I didn't know he already took supplements for performance. I thought the mixture of herbs would be good for him. He worked so hard, teaching exercise classes in all three towns. He was always so busy. Always on the road. I only wanted to help him." She broke into loud, heart-wrenching sobs.

The tears robbed her feet of progress. She stopped in front of Genny, appearing on the verge of collapse. Torn between compassion and confusion, Genny eventually stood and awkwardly put her arms around the sobbing woman.

Lana latched on to her as if she were a lifeline.

"I swear, I didn't mean to kill him. He—He started gasping for air. Said he couldn't breathe. Th—That was the first time I knew about—about his heart." It was difficult to make out her words, between the hiccups and the intermittent sobs. Her voice was still thick with tears. "L—Later, Myrna told me the herbs could be dangerous for some people. But I didn't know. I swear, I didn't know!"

Genny murmured empty assurances to the distraught woman.

Even Madison attempted to console her. "It sounds like his death was an accident, Lana," she said kindly. "You had no way of knowing the herbs would interfere with his other medications or supplements. He probably went into cardiac arrest."

"But—But I just left him there!" The words were wrenched from her broken heart. "How could I have done that? He was so pale, and so still. I—I panicked. I ran away. And then when I came back, there were vans in the yard, and people in the house. And—And then she put him in a *refrigerator*!" She screamed the last at Rose, as if that were the hardest of all to take.

Lana pulled away from Genny, raking the back of her hand across her smeared mascara and her snotty nose. She wiped both on the leg of her pants. "How could you have done that?" she demanded of Rose. "How could you just erase him like that?"

Rose had regained her regal attitude, no longer intimidated by the hysterical, snotty-nosed woman. Tilting her chin in the air, she claimed, "I have no idea what you're talking about."

"I saw you." Lana's voice strengthened into something hard and determined. "I saw what you did. You and those men wrapped Alex up in a rug and carried him out to the van. You mopped the floor, and they took his car away. Just like that, you erased him! Like he never existed in the first place."

Some of Rose's aloof demeanor slipped. Madison saw her swallow hard, before her eyes glittered a cold, steely gray. "You're no better than me. *You* left him to die on the kitchen floor!" she spat.

Madison understood Rose's disheveled hair and mussed clothes now. When Lana flew into her, Madison guessed it wasn't the first time. Rose put up a deflecting arm, but not before Lana made a swipe for her hair.

"Stop it!"

All four women froze at the sound of the deep and unexpected baritone. In tandem, they turned to see Brash standing in the kitchen entry, his hands propped onto his waist. Framed there in the doorway, he looked large and mighty, and more than a little intimidating.

"How did you get in?" Rose demanded.

"Side door was unlocked."

"I don't know how much you heard," Madison

informed her husband, "but I think you'll be interested in what both these ladies have to say."

Brash had his trademark smirk, but Madison had something every bit as powerful. She had her *mom voice* and her *mom look*. She used them both now as she turned to address Rose. "There was something about a rug..."

23

One week later, Sunday dinner at the deCordova house was a noisy, boisterous event.

"I'm just glad to have it behind us," Madison said. There was a note of finality in her voice.

"What a crazy, convoluted case!" Genny agreed. "Rose was guilty, just of something different from what we suspected."

Brash agreed with a nod. "It all makes sense now. One of the things that never added up for me was how she was able to settle in so quickly. An hour after the moving vans left, everything was in place. Everything but a television set." He helped himself to a serving of fresh snap green beans from Uncle Jubal's garden. "Now I know why. It was never a home. It was nothing more than a two-bedroom office, right from the beginning."

"An office at poor Nelda's expense," Granny Bert snorted. She passed the platter of corn on the cob to Sticker.

Genny giggled. "With rented furniture, straight off the showroom floor. I can't tell you how foolish I felt, carrying on about how cute and adorable everything was!"

"'Magazine ready,' I believe the term was,"

Madison reminded her.

"*Modern Warehouse*, maybe."

Madison couldn't help but laugh. "I still remember the look on her face when you asked who her decorator was. You looked so sincere, even though there was nothing original about any of it. Not even the cheap artwork."

Genny slapped a dramatic hand to her heart. "Don't tell Cristo. He'll be crushed."

"Cristo is currently sitting in the McClennan County jail," Brash informed them, "on multiple counts of identity theft, fraud, embezzlement, tax evasion, criminal trespassing, tampering with a corpse, and a long list of other crimes. His charges aren't nearly as long as Rose Belvedere's."

"Did you ever find out her real name?" Cutter wanted to know. He piled a healthy portion of King Ranch Chicken onto his plate.

Brash nodded as he reached for a roll. "I kid you not. We think it's Ima Joy Schmuck."

A round of snickers traveled the length of the table.

"No wonder she made up a new name!" Bethani giggled.

"Yes, but one would have done nicely. There was no need for a dozen or more," her mother pointed out.

"With as many scams as she was running, there was," Brash contradicted. "It's amazing she was able to keep them all straight."

"I guess that explains all the charts and graphs she had tacked up on the walls," Megan reasoned.

"And thanks to that video you made, we have proof." There was no mistaking the pride in her father's voice. "You did good, sweetie."

"It was Momma Maddy who tied it all together and made sense of it all."

"You did good, too, sweetheart." Brash leaned over to kiss his wife. "Thanks to you, we have enough solid evidence to put all of them away for a very long time."

"It wasn't just me," she reminded him. "Granny Bert and Genny did more than their fair share. It took all of us to pull this case together, especially when it splintered off in a surprising direction."

"Can you imagine what Rose must have thought," Genny mused, "when she walked in that morning and found Ron Alexander dead on her kitchen floor?"

Madison nodded. "She couldn't very well call the police because it would draw suspicion to her own criminal activity."

"I guess the next best thing to do was to stuff his body in a rug and dispose of it."

"She must have watched that *Matlock* rerun like everyone else," Granny Bert grumbled. "But why *my* refrigerator?"

"Ease of access," Blake supplied.

Brash used his trademark smirk. "Not to mention a blatant lack of security."

In reply, Granny Bert sniffed and changed the subject. "I believe we were discussing our cunning skills of reasoning and deduction."

Brash lifted his tea glass in a toast. "I admit, everyone did an exceptional job. And it served as a good reminder to me. Never be so hyper-focused on an expected outcome as to ignore other possibilities." He freely admitted his own shortcomings with a shake of his auburn head.

"I was so certain Rose was guilty of murder. When I realized the watch belonged to Ron Alexander and that Rose was innocent, I realized we were dealing with two distinct crimes. Even before I got Genny's text, I was headed to the house to run interference, hoping to salvage at least one of the cases. I was as surprised as anyone to find Lana there, confessing to murder."

"But it really wasn't *murder*, was it?" Granny Bert stressed the word. "You didn't charge her."

"I didn't see the need, but it was really up to the DA. After hearing all the evidence, she didn't think it was worth pursuing, either. Yes, Lana gave Alexander a concoction of herbs, but she didn't realize they would have an immediate and fatal effect. She didn't act with malicious intent. And there's no definitive proof the herbs killed him."

"Like I always say," Granny Bert harrumphed, "just because something is natural doesn't mean it's healthy."

"What about Miss Wanda? Will she get any of her money back?" Cutter asked. "Will any of the victims?"

"It's doubtful, but there's always hope."

"If we're through with the gloomy stuff," Blake broke in, "I have some good news to report."

"And it's about time!" Genny proclaimed, raising her glass with a cheerful smile.

"What's the good news?" Brash wanted to know.

"Remember that old strongbox I found at Israel Ballard's?" He gave a summary to the others at the table, bringing them up to speed on the story.

"I'm sorry, son," Brash apologized. "With all that was happening, I forgot to ask how that was going. Did you find out who the girl from his past was?"

"I did," the boy replied proudly. He slid his gaze to his sisters and amended the answer. "*We* did."

"Really? I have to admit, I'm a little surprised, after all these years. So? What did you decide to do about it?"

"To tell you the truth, the decision was sort of made for me." He launched into the full tale, interrupted from time to time with input from the girls. The trio was obviously proud of their detective skills and the results.

"I wouldn't be surprised," Blake told them, "if he didn't finally put that ring on her finger. I think they'll be married by fall."

"That soon?" Madison asked, surprised.

"*Soon?*" Sticker spoke up for the first time. "He's waited for fifty years! Almost as long as this one has kept me waiting." He jabbed a thumb in Granny Bert's direction, looking thoroughly disgusted. "A man can only hang on for so long, before he feels his grip startin' to slip."

"What are you complaining about, you old coot?" she shot back at him. "You've had a mighty fine support web all this time. Every time your grip *slipped*, as you call it, you fell right into the arms of another woman." She named them off, mixing in a few names like Honey Bunches and Buckle Bunny to make the list longer. "Don't be feeling sorry for this one," she warned the group at the table. "He's managed to suffer his way through just fine without me."

"But life is so much better with you by my side, Belle," he crooned, trying to put his arm around her shoulders.

Granny Bert shoved him away, but a bloom of pleasure appeared in her wrinkled cheeks. "Enough of that," she proclaimed. "Pass the squash. And speaking of that... did you ever find out what happened to that mess of squash Jubal left in the Avocado?"

"No," Brash admitted, "we didn't." In the scope of things, it had fallen completely off his radar.

"Well, there you go," Granny Bert said with a decided nod. She nodded to the three teenagers seated across the table. "These young 'uns did a fine job finding the *other* Rose by another name, aka Rosa, aka Rosita. They can help with this case, too."

Amused by the parallel—she hadn't thought about the similarity in names, until now—Madison's reply was somewhat distracted. "Wait. What? What case?"

But the girls were paying attention. Bethani and Megan answered at the same time as Granny Bert, laughter ringing in their voices, "The Case of the Missing Squash!"

Special Note from The Sisters Tourism Center

Thank you so much for reading. I hope you've enjoyed visiting with us here in The Sisters and that you'll join us here again soon.

If you'd like to support tourism (readership) in The Sisters, Texas, please leave a review on Amazon and other sites of your choice. It's makes all the difference to the success of a series and to me, personally.

Drop in for an e-visit anytime. Contact me at beckiwillis.ccp@gmail.com, or www.beckiwillis.com.

If the name *Texas General* sounds familiar, you may recognize it from my new series, *Texas General Cozy Cases*. Look for more interaction between the two series in the upcoming book, **Bye, Buy Baby.

Again, thank you for reading!

ABOUT THE AUTHOR

Becki Willis, best known for her popular The Sisters, Texas Mystery Series and Forgotten Boxes, always dreamed of being an author. In November of '13, that dream became a reality. Since that time, she has published numerous books, won first place honors for Best Mystery Series, Best Suspense Fiction and Best Audio Book, and has introduced her imaginary friends to readers around the world.

An avid history buff, Becki likes to poke around in old places and learn about the past. Other addictions include reading, writing, junking, unraveling a good mystery, and coffee. She loves to travel, but believes coming home to her family and her Texas ranch is the best part of any trip. Becki is a member of the Association of Texas Authors, the National Association of Professional Women, and the Brazos Writers organization. She attended Texas A&M University and majored in Journalism.

You can connect with her at http://www.beckiwillis.com/ and http://www.facebook.com/beckiwillis.ccp?ref=hl. Better yet, email her at beckiwillis.ccp@gmail.com. She loves to hear from readers and encourages feedback!

www.ingramcontent.com/pod-product-compliance
Lightning Source LLC
Chambersburg PA
CBHW071731190726
48292CB00003B/707